W9-BVZ-678

Murder
— on the —
MOOR

Books by Julianna Deering

From Bethany House Publishers

THE DREW FARTHERING MYSTERIES

Rules of Murder

Death by the Book

Murder at the Mikado

Dressed for Death

Murder on the Moor

A DREW
FARTHERING
MYSTERY

Murder
— on the —
MOOR

JULIANNA
DEERING

BETHANYHOUSE

a division of Baker Publishing Group
Minneapolis, Minnesota

Gloucester Library
P.O. Box 2380
Gloucester, VA 23061

© 2017 by DeAnna Julie Dodson

Published by Bethany House Publishers
11400 Hampshire Avenue South
Bloomington, Minnesota 55438
www.bethanyhouse.com

Bethany House Publishers is a division of
Baker Publishing Group, Grand Rapids, Michigan

Printed in the United States of America

All rights reserved. No part of this publication may be reproduced, stored in a retrieval system, or transmitted in any form or by any means—for example, electronic, photocopy, recording—without the prior written permission of the publisher. The only exception is brief quotations in printed reviews.

Library of Congress Cataloging-in-Publication Data
Names: Deering, Julianna, author.
Title: Murder on the Moor / Julianna Deering.
Description: Minneapolis, Minnesota : Bethany House, a division of Baker
    Publishing Group, [2017] | Series: A Drew Farthering mystery
Identifiers: LCCN 2016035446| ISBN 9780764230059 (cloth : alk. paper) | ISBN
    9780764218286 (trade paper)
Subjects: LCSH: Murder—Investigation—Fiction. | England—Fiction. | GSAFD:
    Mystery fiction.
Classification: LCC PS3554.O3414 M88 2017 | DDC 813/.54—dc23
LC record available at https://lccn.loc.gov/2016035446

Scripture quotations are from the King James Version of the Bible.

This is a work of fiction. Names, characters, incidents, and dialogues are products of the author's imagination and are not to be construed as real. Any resemblance to actual events or persons, living or dead, is entirely coincidental.

Cover design by Faceout Studio
Cover illustration by John Mattos

Author is represented by Books & Such Literary Agency

17 18 19 20 21 22 23   7 6 5 4 3 2 1

To the One who restores my soul

— One —

A nd I sank down where I stood, and hid my face against the ground. I lay still a while: the night swept over the hill and over me and died moaning in the distance; the rain fell fast, wetting me afresh to the skin.'"

At Farthering Place, nestled in the Hampshire countryside, the rain also fell fast, drumming against the windowpanes, joining the wind and the thunder to make the cold October night even more forbidding. Eyes closed, Drew Farthering lay on the sofa before the library fireplace, his head in his wife's lap, listening as she read from *Jane Eyre*.

"Poor Jane. I'm glad we're in here and not out there."

"Don't interrupt," Madeline said, but there was a smile playing at her lips and in her periwinkle-blue eyes. She was never very good at scolding. "'Could I but have stiffened to the still frost—the friendly numbness of death—it might have pelted on; I should not have felt it; but my yet living flesh shuddered at its chilling influence.'"

"I beg your pardon, madam, but there is a telephone call for you, sir."

"My yet living flesh shudders." Drew opened one baleful eye at the butler's interruption. "Is it critical, Denny?"

Dennison merely looked appropriately grave. "I couldn't say, sir. The gentleman claims it is urgent."

Drew sighed and sat up, disturbing the black-and-white cat sleeping on his chest and the pure white one nestled at his side.

"Sorry, Eddie girl," he said as, unperturbed, the tuxedo cat stretched and settled herself next to Madeline. The white one glared at him and sat down near the fire to groom himself. "Sorry, Chambers, old man."

Drew stretched as well and then smoothed down the back of his hair. He couldn't imagine who'd ring up this time of the evening. True, he'd been taking a bit more interest in Farlinford Processing these days, but surely any matter of urgency would be directed to Landis, who managed the company for him. And it seemed likely that if there were a difficulty concerning Madeline's family in Chicago, the caller would have asked to speak to her directly.

"Did the gentleman give his name?"

"A Mr. Hubert Bloodworth, sir, of Bloodworth Park Lodge, Bunting's Nest, Yorkshire."

"Hubert . . ." Drew frowned and looked at Madeline. "Do we know any Bloodworths, darling?"

"Well, I certainly don't. Why don't you just go see what he wants?" She snickered at him. "And don't pout."

"I do not pout," he said, standing with all the dignity he could muster. "I was merely thinking it sounded familiar."

Dennison cleared his throat. "The gentleman, sir?"

"Right. Right." Drew followed the butler out of the library and down the corridor to the study. "He's not selling anything, is he, Denny?"

"He assures me he is not, sir. Shall I inquire again?"

"No, that's all right. You toddle off to whatever it is you do this time of night, and I'll see to our Mr. Bloodworth."

Drew frowned again as he picked up the telephone. Bloodworth. Bloodworth of Bunting's Nest, Yorkshire. Not exactly Smith or Jones of Southampton. Could he have heard it before?

"Drew Farthering here. What can I do for you?"

"Ah, Drew," said an unfamiliar voice. "Thank God."

Drew's frown deepened. "I beg your pardon. Do I know you?"

"Do forgive me. I know it's been ages. I shouldn't have expected you to remember." The man made an apologetic sound somewhere between a chuckle and a cough. "Hubert Bloodworth. We were at Eton together."

"Hubert Bloodworth," Drew mused half under his breath, and then a startled laugh escaped him as he pictured a gawky boy of fourteen with carrot-colored hair and jelly-jar spectacles and bony wrists that poked out of always-too-short coat sleeves. "Not Beaky Bloodworth from Holland House. Good heavens, it *has* been ages. Beaky, old man, how are you?"

"In a bit of a pickle, I'm afraid. That's why I called you. I've read about you in the papers, you know, about you solving those murders. I thought you might be able to help me, too."

"I haven't made headlines for months now, and I'm not an actual detective or constable or anything, no matter what the papers say."

"The police haven't done us any good so far. We thought perhaps . . ."

"We?" Drew asked.

"Oh, dear, I've made a muddle of it already. I say, Drew, would it be too much of a bother if I came over to Farthering Place and told you all about it? It's rather a long story."

9

Drew chuckled. "Certainly. If you'd like. I can't promise I'll have a clue about what to do, but I'd be happy to listen. How about you come down next week sometime?"

"No!" Beaky drew an audible breath, obviously struggling to compose himself. "I'm sorry, but I was hoping I might come round tonight. I'll try to keep it brief, I promise."

"Tonight? All the way from Yorkshire? That's two hundred fifty miles."

"Actually, I'm here at your inn. I've driven most of the day, and now—"

"In this storm? Are you mad?"

"It was raining a bit when I left the Lodge, but the drive down wasn't so bad. Cold, of course, but that was all till I got into Hampshire. It's a devil of a storm, isn't it?"

"Monstrous," Drew agreed. "Are you sure you hadn't rather take cover at the Queen Bess and come up in the morning?"

"I know it's a wretched imposition, Drew, but if there's any way we could make it this evening, I'd be terribly grateful."

"All right, come along. We'll be waiting for you."

"Beaky Bloodworth?" Madeline pursed her lips, fighting a giggle. "Beaky?"

"He did have a rather . . . memorable nose," Drew said, "but I expect he grew into it years ago."

"Haven't you seen him since Eton?"

Drew shook his head. "He went to Cambridge and we rather lost touch. Not that we were all that close, to be honest. I haven't thought about him in years. I never thought he'd track me down."

"That's what you get for making a spectacle of yourself in the papers all the time."

"I haven't made a spectacle of myself since that mess in Beaulieu nearly a year and a half ago." He patted his lean stomach. "I'm getting fat and lazy."

"Yes, I've noticed." She pressed herself into his arms. "I don't suppose he said what he wanted to see you about."

A flash of lightning illuminated the lawn and the driveway, revealing Dennison holding an umbrella over the head of someone wrapped in a long overcoat and with his hat pulled down to shield his face from the rain.

Drew lifted one dark brow. "I suppose we'll find out now."

There was a minor commotion at the front door, and then Dennison appeared. "Mr. Bloodworth, sir."

He stepped back to reveal a young man in his mid-twenties, half a head taller than her husband and a good forty pounds lighter. His clothes were rain-soaked and no longer fresh, but they were quality goods and well-tailored. Either he had a wife or an excellent valet or both. He looked as if he could well afford at least one of each. His face was pleasant, if plain, but even under his thick glasses his nose was certainly memorable.

"Beaky, old man." Drew went to him, clasping his hand, drawing him into the room. "Come over to the fire. It's a beastly night. Tea, Denny, if you please. I think we can all do with a cup. Let me introduce you to my wife, Madeline."

Madeline smiled into the man's bewildered pale blue eyes and offered her hand. She had seen more true redheads since coming to England than she'd ever seen in America, but Beaky Bloodworth surpassed the most brilliant of them.

"Mrs. Farthering, it is very good to meet you." He clasped her hand briefly, his wide mouth touched with a shy smile. "I feel as if we've met already after all those stories in the newspaper. Drew tells me they're exaggerated, but I'm hoping

11

the two of you and Nicky Dennison are every bit as clever as they say."

She glanced at Drew and then looked again at Beaky. "You know Nick?"

"Oh, certainly. We were all at Eton together. Not that we were in the same house, but the two of them did get me out of a jam or two now and again. I've never forgotten it."

"I could never abide bullies," Drew said, looking faintly embarrassed, "but I doubt you need anyone to rescue you from the Latin room cupboard at this late date."

"And where is Nicky these days?" Beaky asked. "I understand he's your estate agent now."

Drew nodded. "He'll step in when our Mr. Padgett is ready to retire. But he won't be back here before tomorrow afternoon, like as not."

"That's rather a shame. I was hoping to see him, too."

"He telephoned a couple of hours ago," Drew said. "Seems he smashed up his car trying to get round a tree the storm brought down when he was coming back from Southampton. He's stranded in Durley until he can get it mended. But do sit down and tell us what's bothering you. Ah, here's tea."

Mrs. Devon came in with a steaming pot of tea and some apple cake fresh from the oven. Soon Drew and Madeline and their guest were huddled before the fire.

"Do forgive me barging in, Mrs. Farthering." Beaky clutched his teacup more tightly in his long, thin fingers. "Madeline, I mean. I should have telephoned from the Lodge before presuming to come all the way here, I know, but the line was down and I thought I might as well drive down as not. My wife's half distracted with worrying, and if I don't do something and soon, I'm afraid she'll go back to London, and Raphael with her."

Madeline looked at Drew, baffled. "Raphael?"

"Perhaps you ought to start at the beginning, old man," Drew suggested. "Where is the Lodge, and how'd you end up in Yorkshire? I thought your people were in Windsor."

"They were," Beaky said. "But they're all gone now. Everyone save my sister, Celia, who's married to a doctor in Bournemouth. Anyway, last Christmas my uncle Hubert passed on."

"He's the one who sent you to Cambridge, I take it," Drew said with a hint of a grin. "Well, we'll forgive him anyway."

Beaky chuckled. "He was very insistent about me following in his footsteps, and without his patronage, the only way I could have joined you and Nicky at Oxford would have been as boot boy."

"Well, never mind that. How did you end up in Yorkshire?"

"Uncle left my father the old Lodge, Bloodworth Park Lodge, up near Bunting's Nest, and not to be too vulgar about it, rather a lot of money along with it. But Father died not even a month afterward, so it all came to me. I was married in March, and it only seemed right to take the missus up to the ancestral hall to live. Start our own little dynasty, you know."

"Ah, capital! Congratulations." Drew put his arm around Madeline's waist. "Wedded bliss is something I highly recommend."

Beaky turned pink in the ears. "I've had nothing to complain of. At least not until now." He stopped, blinking as if he were startled. "No, I don't mean I have any complaints about my wife. Nothing like that. It's just that things have gotten rather unsettled the past few weeks. And then last Wednesday . . . well, last Wednesday they found our vicar dead on the steps of the church."

Madeline gasped. "How terrible."

"It was awful," Beaky said. "The police haven't any evidence. Someone bashed in his head with a stone from the walkway. No fingerprints. No motive. No suspects."

"I read about the case," Drew told him. "Just a few lines in the *Times*. I didn't realize you'd be involved."

"Involved? No. Nothing like that. It's just, well, there have been other things, several things, that have seemed odd. At the Lodge, I mean." Beaky smiled weakly and fidgeted with his teaspoon. "Sabrina tells me I tend to give all the details except the ones that matter."

"Sabrina's your wife?" Madeline asked, encouraging him to go on.

Beaky's pale eyes lit. "Yes, she's—"

"Hold on there," Drew said. "Not Sabrina Prestwick, is it? I heard she was married this spring. I had no idea you were the groom."

"Sabrina Bloodworth now, thank you. I'm still not quite sure how it happened, but she said yes. If you've met her, you know she's rather wonderful."

"Yes, I've met her."

Drew still smiled, but there was a hint of wariness behind his eyes now. Who was this girl and what did Drew know about her? But that discussion would have to wait until Madeline and Drew were alone again.

"But what's been happening at the Lodge?" Madeline pressed. "I hope no one else has died."

"No, no." Beaky took a nervous sip of tea. "Just little things mostly. I'm afraid the old place needs a bit of fixing up. Uncle wasn't much for spending his money, which is why I ended up with so much of it. But the north wing is completely uninhabitable, and there are always little creaks and groans and such in a place that size. Sabrina's got it in her head that the Lodge is haunted, or at least that wing is. And now that there's been a murder, she's sure we'll all be slaughtered in our beds."

"And what do you think?" Drew asked, and there was that slight narrowing of his eyes that meant he was adding two and two and definitely getting something other than four.

Beaky winced. "To be honest, Drew, I don't know what to make of it. There have been some rather peculiar sounds in the night, but most of those seem to be coming from the moor and not the house. Our gamekeeper says it's poachers more than likely, and I'd be surprised if there weren't any. Sabrina swears someone was following her the last time she and Raphael were out walking."

Madeline glanced at Drew and then back at Beaky. "Who is Raphael?"

"That would be her little terrier. Nothing but six pounds' worth of hair, I think." Beaky smiled. "He's not a bad little fellow, but I'm not sure he's going to be up to a Yorkshire winter. Sabrina either, for that matter."

"If she doesn't like the cold in October," Drew said, "she's not likely to think much of it in January and February."

"I think she'll grow to love the old place. In time." Beaky set his teacup down and leaned forward in his chair. "I've got to figure out what's going on before she's so frightened she won't stay anymore. The police are horridly slow and don't seem to know what to do with a real murder investigation. They've been utterly useless on the other things, too. Haven't got time for our nonsense, I expect, but that doesn't let my wife sleep any better at night, I can tell you that."

"I dunno. Sometimes the police are doing more than they let on. It's been only a few days. Perhaps you'd do best to let them carry on with their work."

"I know it's a terrible imposition, Drew, but couldn't you come up to the Lodge? Just for a few days? You could have a look about and tell me what you think. You and your wife, of course. Maybe it is just poachers and the vicar's death has nothing to do with it. Either way, at least Sabrina would know something was being done."

Drew glanced at Madeline, and she could see that little spark of eagerness in his gray eyes. It had been a long time since they'd had a case, and she knew he missed the challenge.

"Why don't we talk it over in the morning?" Drew suggested. "It's late and you look all in."

Beaky was immediately on his feet. "I know I've already been a terrible imposition. Is there a convenient time I could call on you in the morning?"

"Breakfast is at nine," Drew said. "I can have Denny wake you an hour before, if you like."

"But . . . Oh, no, I couldn't possibly."

Madeline took his arm. "Of course you can. Don't be silly. We have a very nice guest room, and I will definitely be offended if you refuse to stay in it."

"I, well—"

"You might as well agree," Drew advised. "There's no use your going back out tonight. I'll have Denny bring in your things, and you can turn in. We'll talk over breakfast. Fair enough?"

He looked as if he might protest again, but then he merely looked relieved. "Fair enough. And thank you."

Drew was silent until after Denny came to show Beaky upstairs. Then he sat on the sofa and settled Madeline at his side.

"So what do you think?"

There was a glint in her periwinkle eyes. "You want to go."

He chuckled. "You know me far too well."

"It's been rather quiet since we were in Beaulieu. Actually, I didn't think it would be this long before you stumbled onto another case."

"I did no such thing."

She pursed her lips. "What such thing?"

"Stumble. I did not stumble onto this case. It has been thrust upon me."

"I see."

He squeezed her hand. "I never could leave poor Beaky in whatever muddle he'd gotten into at school. He was always good-natured about it, I must say, though he was bullied most abominably. I hate to let him be taken advantage of now. I'd at least like to know what's going on."

Her eyes were warm as she smoothed the hair back at his temple. "And what do you think is going on?"

He shook his head. "Hard to say at this point. I know what I'm afraid of."

"It's his wife, isn't it?" she asked, her expression suddenly bleak.

"Sabrina. You never met her, but she and Bunny were an item for a short while. He was smitten of course, but even he could see she wasn't serious. She enjoyed the attention, no doubt, and the parties and the clubs, and he was quite extravagant with the gifts, but eventually she moved on. Bunny dodged a rather costly bullet in that one, I'd say."

"And now she's married to Beaky." She glanced toward the stairs. "After he'd come into the family money."

"Precisely. Old Beaky's a good fellow, kindhearted, reliable. I daresay he'd stick by a friend, or a wife, through the worst of times, but, well, you've seen him. He hasn't got much personal appeal. Not for a woman like that."

She shrugged. "I don't know. It's hard to say what makes someone attracted to someone else. It's not always what you'd think."

"True," he admitted. "I haven't seen her more than three or four times, and that was before we went to Beaulieu. It's not fair to make assumptions with no facts, is it?"

She tapped his lips with one slender finger. "And you want to be fair."

He kissed her finger and then gave her a questioning look.

For a moment she looked reluctant, and then she grinned. "Let's do it."

— Two —

'm freezing," Madeline whispered, huddled up next to Drew in the front seat of Beaky's Bentley.

Drew tightened his arms around her. "Perhaps we should have taken our own car."

"No." She glanced toward the telephone box, where Beaky was making a call. "It didn't seem right to have him make that long drive by himself again. And he's so happy to have us."

"Shouldn't be much longer. We're nearly in Harrogate and I think Bunting's Nest isn't too many miles farther on, and the Lodge after that. And there, my darling, there shall be a blazing fire and tea and toast and after that a hot bath and then a fine dinner and finally a warm bed."

She looked at him with helpless wide eyes. "You don't suppose we'll get there and find a baleful old housekeeper with nothing to give us but barely warm gruel while her almost-deaf old husband quotes Old Testament fire and brimstone at us because I have on lipstick, do you? And there'll be dogs and pigs sleeping in the dining room, which is the only room in the house with a smoky fire already laid. And after the gruel, we'll be taken up to a drafty old bedroom with damp sheets and ice in the washbasin."

"Yes, yes," he said dismissively. "And there will be no indoor plumbing or electricity or even gas laid on. And Beaky will, of course, have a mad wife up in the attic, though she's bound to roam the corridors at night, setting fires and such, and signaling to escaped axe murderers and mental patients."

She giggled and snuggled against him. "So long as I have you to protect me, I suppose that will be all right, too."

"Bad connection," Beaky said as he slid behind the wheel once again. "But it's all arranged. I've told Miss Windham to have tea waiting when we get in. Sabrina's taken Raphael walking, but they should be back before us, at any rate."

"I'm eager to meet them both," Madeline said. "Does she know we're coming?"

Beaky started the engine and then eased back onto the road, not looking at her.

"She doesn't, I take it," Drew said.

Beaky still stared at the road, but he raised his voice to be heard over the clatter of the engine. "We . . . discussed having you come up, Drew. She thought it might not be a good idea. I told her I had some business I had to see to in London, and that was true, but I took care of it yesterday before I came out to Farthering St. John." He glanced over at Drew and Madeline. "I didn't think it would hurt to talk to you about coming. Once you're there, I'm sure she won't mind. She'll like you, Madeline, I'm sure of it. There aren't that many ladies for her to social-ize with around the Lodge. Not on her level, you know. Not like you."

Madeline patted his arm. "I'm sure we'll be fine friends. And how did the two of you meet?"

"Well, uh, looking back on it, I suppose it looks rather awkward. Her father was one of Uncle's business partners. She came with him to Uncle's memorial service and we got chatting and well . . ." Beaky shrugged, looking blissfully foolish. "I never thought she'd accept, you know, not after only a month, but she did."

"Right after your father died," Drew said quietly. "And you were married two months later."

"Two and a half," Beaky corrected. "And not an instant too soon, if you ask me. I don't know how I ever did without her."

Madeline's smile was warm. "I think she got quite a catch herself."

Beaky's ears turned as red as his hair. "I don't know about that. But, um, well, we've gotten on rather well until recent events. I spent most of my holidays up at the Lodge when I was growing up, but she's not really accustomed to country life, especially in such a remote place on the moor. I'm sure she'll grow used to it in time. And we do go down to London now and again, dancing and dining and shows and that."

Drew nodded. "Tell me about the vicar. You say there's no motive for the murder?"

"Nothing anyone can figure, poor man. He'd been vicar here since my father and his brothers were young. Well before the war at least. Hadn't any money, of course. No children, and his wife had passed on ages ago. Fairly much all he had was his parish and his memories."

"Pity. Do they know where he'd been before he was killed?"

"That's the odd bit of it," Beaky said. "It was a nasty night. His housekeeper said she'd left him at home in front of his fire, eating her potato soup and listening to Ray Noble on the wireless. She couldn't imagine him getting out again before morning."

"And no one saw him going to the church or talking to anyone?"

"No." Beaky slowed at a signpost and took the road turning northeast. "It wasn't till after dawn the next morning that he was found there on the steps."

Drew considered for a moment. "There haven't been any other unexplained murders, have there? I mean in these past few weeks you've noticed things being odd."

"Good heavens, no. In Bunting's Nest? I daresay there hasn't been anything worse than poaching here for the past fifty years."

Drew nodded, not quite sure he believed him.

"But what does your wife say?" Madeline asked. "Who would be following her out on the moor? And why?"

Beaky winced slightly. "I'm not entirely sure there is anyone, to be honest. Not that I think Sabrina isn't telling me the truth. She's not the type to lie, you know. But she has been rather nervous lately, and she is new to the moor. I know when I used to wander about there when I was a boy, and with the mists and the sounds of the wind and the loneliness, my imagination would run wild. I couldn't tell you how often I hared back to the house with my heart in my mouth because I'd seen a headless ghost or a white lady or man with a hook for a hand. Uncle, God bless him, would listen to all my wild tales and then tell me about what he and his brothers had seen playing out on the moor when they were boys. Then he'd give me a handful of Peace Babies from the jar on his desk to settle my nerves."

"Sounds like a grand fellow," Drew said. "Even if he did go to Cambridge."

Madeline frowned at him. "That's all very nice, but I'm pretty sure Mrs. Bloodworth is not a little boy of ten. Do you really think she's just imagining everything?"

"Not everything," Beaky admitted. "There are things I've seen for myself, but Delwyn tells me it's just poachers. He claims he'll weed them out before long, as well."

Drew nodded. "He's your gamekeeper, I expect."

"Precisely. Took over for Mr. Caswell about two years ago, I'm given to understand. I expect Uncle wanted a younger man, someone who could get about the land and really see what was going on. Anyway, he knows his job well enough, so I don't have to. And I'd think he'd know a bit more about the moor than my London-bred wife, though I haven't gone so far as tell her that."

By the time they wound their way through Bunting's Nest, there was a drizzle of cold rain. When they actually reached Bloodworth Park Lodge, it was a veritable downpour. It was impossible to see much of the house in the storm, but just as Drew had predicted, awaiting them inside was a warm fire and the intoxicating aroma of hot tea.

"Glad to see you've made it, sir. Just as the storm's hit, as well. Mr. and Mrs. Farthering, do come in, if you please."

A pair of maids took their sodden hats and coats, and sturdy, middle-aged Miss Windham sat them down before the sitting room hearth and poured them tea.

"Just the thing," Beaky said, sitting in an overstuffed armchair that was clearly his own special province. "And Mrs. Bloodworth?"

The housekeeper's brow furrowed. "She hasn't come in, sir. Johnson's boy's gone out looking for her."

"What?" Beaky leapt to his feet. "Why didn't you tell me that right away?"

"It had only begun to get bad just before you arrived, sir. But we thought madam might have lost her way and all and sent young Will right out."

Drew gave Madeline a reassuring pat on the hand and then stood, too. "Perhaps you and I had better have our coats again, Beaky, old man."

Before Beaky could do more than open his mouth, a door banged open somewhere in the back of the house, accompanied by the shriek of the wind and the high yips of a small dog.

"Oh, thank God," Beaky breathed. "Sabrina!"

He darted out of the room with the flustered housekeeper behind him. Drew and Madeline followed them through the corridor and into a large stone-floored kitchen. Sitting before the roaring hearth fire was a slight figure with a man's wool coat bundled over her own and with her bobbed blond hair wet and slick against the back of her slender neck. Her still-yipping terrier capered around her feet. The dog bolted toward Beaky and then, seeing two strangers, began growling and barking furiously.

Beaky held up a forefinger. "Raphael. No."

His growl turning into a whimper, the little dog sank down at Beaky's feet, still with a welcoming wiggle in his hindquarters as Beaky leaned over to pat his bedraggled head.

"Oh, don't scold him, Beaky." Sabrina Bloodworth looked at her husband with dark, wide eyes. "We've had enough of a fright already, haven't we, Raffie?"

With a panting doggy smile, the terrier leapt into her lap and licked all over her already wet face.

"Allow me, madam," Miss Windham said, taking the dog from her as Beaky came to her side. "It's time he had his supper."

She carried the squirming terrier into what Drew assumed was the pantry and shut the door. There was a moment of muffled barking and scratching, and then it quieted, no doubt once Raphael was given his dinner.

Beaky stroked one hand down his wife's wet hair. "You had us worried."

She shrugged, pulling away from him just the slightest bit, smiling apologetically at Drew as she did. "I see he dragged you up here after all, Mr. Farthering. It is good of you to come. I suppose this is Mrs. Farthering."

"Madeline," Madeline supplied. "And we're happy to help however we can."

"If we can, Mrs. Bloodworth," Drew said with a slight bow, and then he turned his attention to the lanky man slouching against the kitchen door in just his shirtsleeves, wet to the skin, his coat no doubt the one wrapped around the girl's shoulders. "I'm glad Will found you without much trouble."

The man straightened and touched the brim of his flat cap, his eyes dark and wary in his swarthy face. "Beg pardon, sir, but Will's gone back to bring in the sheep. I'm Delwyn, gamekeeper here at the Lodge."

There was a Welsh lilt to his name and his accent and the wildness of the mountains in the tangled mane of dark hair, wet and clinging to his neck.

"Lucky thing you found Mrs. Bloodworth when you did then," Drew said.

The gamekeeper looked more than a bit smug. "No luck, sir. I happened to see the lady out walking a bit before. When the weather turned so all of a sudden, I thought I'd best make sure she made it back to the Lodge."

"You have our thanks," Beaky told him, looking fondly at his wife.

"Just my job, sir, and happy to do it." Once more the game-keeper touched his cap. "Now if you'll all pardon me, I'll get back to it."

"Your coat." Sabrina shrugged out of the dark plaid wool, re-vealing a stylish if impractical cape in cream-and-black hounds-tooth check.

"You'll need it out there, Delwyn," Beaky said, handing the garment to him. "I can't say the storm hasn't turned even worse now."

"At least it's had a nice warming," Delwyn said, grinning as he slipped into the coat. He pulled up his collar and, head ducked low, vanished into the driving rain.

"Are you all right?" Beaky asked his wife once the man had gone. "Tell me what frightened you."

"Oh, I don't know." She put a hand to her flushed cheek, darting a quick glance at Drew. "Really, Beaky, I don't know if it's right to bother your friends with my foolishness."

"Don't be silly," Madeline said, briskly cheerful. "How's my husband going to get to play detective if you don't let him take your case?"

The merest hint of a smile crept onto Sabrina's face. "Well, if you're sure."

"We would like to know what frightened you," Drew said. "Delwyn said he'd seen you walking earlier and—"

"And you ought to let her change into something dry before you start asking questions," Madeline said.

"Right as always, darling."

"That's all right." Sabrina took off her cape and draped it over an unoccupied chair. "I'm dry enough now, though I'm simply perishing for some tea."

"Miss Windham had just brought it into the sitting room when you came in," Beaky said, offering her his hand. "Shall we see if it's still hot?"

Fortunately, it was. Hot enough, at any rate, to warm them all up.

Sabrina Bloodworth huddled close to the sitting room fire. "I can't seem to get the chill out of my bones."

"Shall I get you a shawl or something?" Beaky offered, but that only made her laugh.

"How about my cardigan? I believe I left it in the library. A shawl makes it sound as if I'm one of the old cottager ladies, mobcap and all. Next you'll expect me to knit scarves or crochet lace."

There was a hint of amusement in Madeline's eye. "I'm rather fond of crocheting lace myself. It's awfully pretty on a collar or handkerchief."

The other woman merely looked indulgent as her husband hurried out of the room. "I just don't have the patience for handwork. And I don't like being cooped up inside for hours at a time. Even on beastly days like this one, Raphael and I must get out."

"You must enjoy the moors then," Drew said. "Quite a change from London."

"Yes, it is. Not that we don't get into the city from time to time. No reason we can't enjoy both."

"Not at all. Madeline and I often drive up. My best wishes on your marriage, by the way." He kept his eyes steadily on her. "Beaky's a fine fellow, and he deserves a fine wife."

He watched her face, pleased to see it turn warm, though

the eyes themselves appeared cold. His meaning hadn't been lost on her.

"And I've got the finest." Beaky hurried back to his wife's side and draped a heavy cream-colored cardigan around her shoulders. "Better?"

"Much." She picked up her cup, warming her hands around it. "I'm sorry to have frightened everyone. I didn't expect the storm to hit so quickly, and then I suppose I got turned around somehow and headed the wrong way."

"I hear the moor can be tricky like that," Drew said. "Beaky says there have been a number of unexplained incidents out there. What exactly have you seen?"

Sabrina glanced at her husband and then looked into her tea. "This will very likely sound foolish. I know you already think I am."

"Of course we don't," Madeline soothed. "Even if it's not what it seems, you still saw or heard something. We just have to figure out what it was."

The other woman nodded. "I can't remember the exact date when things started happening."

"About three weeks ago," Beaky said, pulling up his chair next to her at the fire. "I remember because I'd been to buy more sheep, and Mr. Butterworth always takes some to market the last weekend of the month."

Drew nodded. "So the end of September."

"Right."

"And what did you see?"

"I didn't see anything actually," Beaky said, "but it was past sundown when I got back. Sabrina came running into the house at the same time, scared out of her wits."

Drew lifted an eyebrow. "What frightened you?"

"I—I can't quite say." Sabrina pulled her cardigan a little more snugly around her shoulders. "It was rather a foggy night and I wanted to get back in before Beaky came home and scolded me for being out so late."

Beaky shook his head indulgently.

"Anyway, Raffie and I had gone farther than usual that day, out towards Westings, and I . . ." Sabrina looked at Madeline. "Haven't you ever felt as if someone were following you?"

"Yes," Madeline said. "I get that prickly feeling down the back of my neck."

"Exactly. There aren't many places to hide on the moor. You can see for miles in every direction, but I swear every time I'd stop there would be a little rustle just after."

"But you never saw anyone?" Drew asked.

"No."

"What about the dog?"

She started, but just the slightest bit. "The dog?"

"What was he doing?"

"Oh, barking, of course." She laughed softly. "Raffie nearly always does. Not that he could protect me from anything."

"What kind of barking?" Drew pressed.

Beaky pushed his thick spectacles up higher on his nose and frowned. "His usual yipping, I expect. Why?"

"But what was the rest of him doing? Was he excited? Afraid? What?"

Sabrina considered for a moment. "Excited, I suppose. He wasn't growling."

"Then it was likely someone he knew," Drew said.

"I thought the same, but I got no answer when I asked if anyone was there. I tell you it was unnerving there in the fog and the darkness. Who would do that?"

Drew studied her face again. Big brown eyes, intelligent and sardonic, wispy golden hair, a spoilt mouth quick to smile or pout or turn hard. He could see her again on Bunny's arm, wearing the diamond earbobs and mink wrap he had given her, drinking in his adoration like fine champagne. What was she doing buried here in the Yorkshire moors? And how long would she put up with the quiet monotony of the country before stirring up her own excitement?

"Nothing else happened that time?" Drew asked, eyes narrowed. "You hadn't . . . met anyone while you were out? Hadn't seen anyone?"

"Not a soul. That's what was so unsettling about it." Sabrina shuddered. "Someone had to have been watching me. Creeping along behind me. Ugh."

"You said that was the first time. How many others have there been?"

She bit her lip. "There was only one other time I thought I was being followed. That was a morning about two weeks later. I still never saw anyone. But there have been other things, too."

"Johnson, our head gardener, has seen fires out on the moor three or four different nights," Beaky said. "He thought it was likely poachers or perhaps some fool who'd left a campfire, but he and his boy went out looking and never found anything. Not even the place where a fire had been."

"So the fire was carried and not laid. Torches or lanterns or such. Hmm . . ." Drew paused, then added, "Mrs. Bloodworth mentioned before that she'd been out towards Westings?"

"That's the manor house just over the rise from us. Northwest of here." There was a touch of wryness in Sabrina's expression. "Our neighbors, if you'd like to call them that."

"We'll get it straightened out," Beaky said. "It's nothing that can't be mended, I'm sure."

Drew chuckled. "Come along, old man, give us the sordid truth."

"I'm not sure I know all of it," Beaky said. "It's something from when my uncle came into the place. He never married, which is why he was always so generous with me, but I've heard tell he was once engaged to the lady who eventually became Mrs. Carter Gray."

"I see. And who is Mr. Carter Gray?"

"Don't be silly," Madeline said, eyes shining. "He's the owner of Westings. He must be."

Beaky nodded. "You've got a clever wife, Drew. She's got it in one."

Drew merely looked smug. "And you thought I married her for her looks."

"Behave," Madeline said, poking him in the shoulder. She turned again to Beaky. "That would explain why there was a feud twenty or thirty years ago, but why should the man dislike you now? He got the girl he wanted, didn't he?"

"True," Beaky said. "But I'm afraid the mischief began with Uncle all those years ago. You know the sort of thing, damming up streams, pulling down fences, general nuisance. Gray reciprocated and it went back and forth like that until Uncle was too ill to carry on. When he died and then my father died soon after, well, as soon as the estate was settled I went to talk to Gray. I told him I wanted to end the dispute, that I was willing to pay whatever it took to put right anything my uncle had ordered done."

"Sounds reasonable," Drew said.

"It was more than reasonable," Sabrina huffed, her dark eyes snapping, "considering the damage Gray's people have done to Lodge property, and the old devil ordered Beaky off."

Beaky patted her hand. "You make it sound worse than it was."

"He was going to set his dogs on you!"

"He's never actually done it, you know, and I can't tell you how many times over the years he's made the threat. I wouldn't be at all surprised if he's tired of the whole thing by now."

"Surely he wouldn't have been out on the moor following your wife about," Drew said.

Beaky laughed. "He's nearly seventy and laid up with gout. I don't think he could manage it even if he wanted to."

Sabrina's mouth tightened. "And the sheep were just a prank, I suppose."

Drew glanced at Madeline. "Sheep?"

"Two of them." Beaky's expression was grave now. "Left out on the moor with their throats torn out. Left, mind you. Not eaten as if wild animals had gotten at them. Poor things. They were just lambs really."

Madeline breathed out a little "oh" of pity.

Drew clenched his jaw hard. "Do you think it was just made to look like an animal did it? Perhaps this Gray was responsible. Maybe not personally, but he could have had it done."

"I just don't know," Beaky said. "He's done some rotten things, I can tell you that, and Uncle had, too. But neither of them had ever gone that far. I don't know why he would want to escalate things now. It's really been rather quiet since Uncle died. I thought he'd given up on mischief making."

"But who else would want to kill those lambs?" Drew took a sip of his tea and grimaced to find it cold. "An animal would have eaten them. A thief would have taken them off and at least

32

sold the wool and the mutton. Why kill them and leave them if not for spite?"

He opened his mouth and then closed it again, seeing the fear in Sabrina's eyes. No need to frighten her more than she already was, but he couldn't help wondering if those sheep weren't left there as a warning. Or perhaps a threat.

"I don't know," Beaky said, looking out into the night. At least the rain had stopped.

"And you're sure? They weren't killed by predators? Foxes perhaps?" Drew smirked. "Not a great iridescent hound out on the moor?"

Sabrina's eyes widened, and Beaky frowned.

"We have a wild dog about. At least I think we do. I haven't seen it in months, but it's been heard. Nothing like that silly Baskerville nonsense, so you needn't make any wise remarks."

"No, of course not." Drew half wanted to laugh and half wondered if there was truly something odd going on. "But you said the lambs couldn't have been killed by animals."

"Perhaps not couldn't have been." Beaky looked at his wife, clearly not wanting to upset her more. "But it does seem un-likely."

"What does any of that have to do with the vicar?" Madeline asked, breaking the momentary silence. "What were relations like between him and Mr. Gray?"

"They weren't enemies, if that's what you mean," Beaky said, "but there was nothing between them. As far as I know, they knew each other to speak to, but that was all. Mr. Gray is rather . . . outspoken about his views of the church, and has no use for, as he calls it, the perpetrators of religion."

Drew couldn't hold back a quiet laugh. "That must have gone over well with the vicar."

Beaky shook his head. "Poor Mr. Miles, he was never one to take offense. He even went over to Westings when old Gray came down with the grippe last winter."

"Let me guess. The old boy set the dogs on him."

Beaky sighed. "Threatened to, I heard. To tell you the truth, I'm not sure what Mrs. Gray saw in the old crosspatch. Except where Gray was concerned, my uncle was a jolly fellow. I think she'd have been happy with him."

"No accounting for ladies' affections, I suppose. Is she a churchgoer?"

"Was, I believe," Beaky said. "But she passed on some years ago. Her husband said it was all a load of claptrap and wouldn't even go to her memorial service since she had wanted it to be in the church, but funnily enough, my uncle did."

Madeline sighed, a wistful look in her eyes. "That's terribly romantic and terribly sad."

Beaky shrugged. "Anyway, I never heard of any other incidents between Gray and the vicar. And I never felt there was anything personal in it on Gray's part, nothing about Miles himself. He'd have felt the same about any vicar we had, I have no doubt of that. And another vicar might have been offended by Gray's views, but old Miles never was. He said it was his job to tend to his flock and preach the gospel. What people decided to do with the information was their own lookout."

"He sounds a fine fellow," Drew said. "Pity someone else didn't think so. What do the people in the village say about the murder and the other goings-on?"

"The whole gamut," Beaky said, "as might be expected. Bolsheviks and poachers and any kind of superstition you could name. I'm afraid nobody knows anything."

"I'd love to listen in at the local pub," Drew said thoughtfully. "There's always something worth hearing."

There was a moment of silence, and then Beaky cleared his throat. "I'll, uh, take you round there if you like. To see the . . . place."

"That would help," Drew said once he'd taken note of Madeline's subtle nod of agreement. "If the police don't object, perhaps we could take a look tomorrow. Weather permitting."

— Three —

St. Peter's was a long medieval structure with a square tower and stone steps that led from the front walkway up to the carved wooden door. Drew stopped just in front of the door to examine a dark stain, one that ran down the top step and onto the two steps below it. There was a smaller stain just to the right of the first. The steps showed signs of vigorous scrubbing, but it was unlikely the marks would ever be completely washed away.

Drew knelt down to study the place. "And this is where they found him?"

Beaky nodded. "I didn't see him myself, of course, but they said he fell facedown and so hard that his glasses cut into his cheek. I reckon that's what made the little splotch next to the big ones."

"I expect." Drew looked down at the walkway, quick to find the gap in the stones that bordered it. They were light-colored stones, rather round, a good size to fit into a man's hand and from the look of them heavy enough to do the job. "And the police took away the murder weapon, did they?"

"Never found from what I've heard."

"He was killed this past Wednesday night?" Madeline asked, examining the gap where the stone had been and then the discoloration on the steps. Then she pulled her coat more closely around herself.

Again Beaky nodded. "The way the church sits back from the road, the light falls right on the steps here during the day, but towards evening those trees shadow everything. People might have passed right by that night and never noticed a thing."

"He was found the next morning?"

"By Mr. Blackstock. He's delivered the milk in the village since old Robs passed on in January." Beaky glanced toward the road. "He was out not much past sunrise, as usual, and thought something looked amiss and so went to see what it was. Unfortunately it was the Reverend Mr. Parker Miles. Blackstock went straight for the police, and that, as yet, is all anyone knows. The whole village is shaken."

"No doubt," Drew said, looking up at the bare trees. "Tell me, had the vicar gone inside the church? Before he was killed, I mean."

"I don't know. The lights weren't on in the morning, so if he had been inside, he'd finished his business and come out again."

"Or someone went in and turned them off after he'd been killed." Madeline looked over the sodden churchyard. "Might we go in?"

St. Peter's was as unremarkable inside as it was outside. There was a quiet solemnity in the place, and Drew thought of the many words of truth and comfort and blessing that must have come from that aged pulpit, from the heart of the aged vicar. Who would have wanted to kill such a man? A man who, as Beaky said, had nothing but his parish and his memories?

Hat in hand, and Madeline on his arm, Drew walked the aisle and laid one palm against the pulpit, breathing a quick prayer for the dead man and those who grieved his loss. Then he and Madeline went back to where Beaky waited, clutching his own hat by the brim.

"Any help?"

Drew shook his head. "Unless the police have tidied something up, the killer either wasn't in here or made sure to tidy after himself."

Beaky tried to look hopeful. "I'm sure you'll find something. You always were clever."

"Not all that much."

"What about Tinker and Pomeroy?"

"Ah, the memorable Christmas of '22." Drew gave a wistful sigh.

"I bet old Stinker Tinker never forgot it, eh?" Beaky said.

There was a sudden glint in Madeline's eye as she waited for Drew's response.

He clapped Beaky on the shoulder. "Everybody at school knew they were smuggling in cigarettes. I just figured out how."

Beaky smirked. "And started switching them out for party crackers."

"You didn't," Madeline said with a giggle.

"That bit was Nick's idea," Drew said, grinning in spite of himself.

"Brilliant, if you ask me," Beaky said. "If you'd seen Stinker's face when he opened that first box . . ."

"That," Drew admitted, "was one thing I always regretted missing. But at least Nick and I led him a merry chase that term. I don't know if I had such good sport until I got to Oxford."

"I'm not sure he and Pomeroy ever knew who was deviling them, but at least it gave them less time to bully the other boys." Beaky sobered. "But I expect that was your aim all along."

Drew turned him toward the exit before he could get maudlin and Madeline could demand more details. "That was twelve years ago, Beaky, old man. Long past. We have a rather more serious problem to solve just now." By then they'd reached the door. Drew opened it, letting Madeline go first and then stepping from the dimly lit church and back into the bleak churchyard. "I've just remembered I need to telephone down to Farthering Place, if you'll both excuse me. Estate business. Won't take but a minute."

Beaky pointed out a telephone box round the corner, and leaving him with Madeline for company, Drew loped over to it. He was back a moment later.

"Sorry about that. I need my estate manager to see to something for me and it couldn't wait. Now back to the problem at hand. Do you think we ought to meet the constable on the case? Or would he be the type to resent our interference?"

"Well, there's an Inspector Rawlings who's technically in charge of the investigation, but we haven't seen much of him round the village. It's our Constable Trenton who'd be your best chance of finding anything out."

"And what's he like?"

"Not by any means a clever man," Beaky said, pulling his coat collar a bit more snugly round his neck against the sudden bite of the wind. "But a practical one. Born and bred on the moor. Knows everyone. Knows his job. I daresay you'll like him."

As it happened, Drew did like him. Trenton was perhaps fonder of the pub and the dinner table than he ought to have been; his generous belly was an unimpeachable witness to that. But he welcomed Drew into his cluttered office with a hearty and rather bone-crushing handshake.

"No need to tell me who you are, sir. I've heard how Mr. Bloodworth gone down to fetch you up to Yorkshire to see if you could make what's what out of the mess we've got. And your missus as well." He pumped Madeline's arm up and down. "Lord love you, ma'am. It's good to have you here in Bunting's Nest."

"We wouldn't want to interfere in your investigation," Drew assured him, trying not to snicker at Madeline's startled expression.

"Nonsense. It's only me and Teddy here, sir, and sometimes young Pennyworth. And my wife is going to give us another little Trenton any day now, so we know when to be thankful for a fresh pair of eyes and some willing hands." Trenton tapped the side of his nose. "And if extra help comes free, well, sir, you won't find me kicking over it."

Drew laughed. "That's certainly a refreshing change from being warned off of cases at every turn. And congratulations on your blessed event."

"Thank you, sir," Trenton said and then rolled his eyes. "I've told Jimmy time and again he ought to be grateful for whatever help you give him, but he's mule stubborn, that's what he is, and I've said so more than once."

Drew glanced at Beaky, who had taken a seat on the corner of Trenton's desk. "Jimmy?"

"Sure," Trenton said, giving him a shove on the shoulder. "Jimmy. Jimmy Birdsong. We had a bit of a talk about you when the families were together last Christmas. He won't admit it, but I can tell he's that fond of you and your missus, no matter what grief you give him."

Drew turned to Madeline. "The families?"

"Oh, didn't I say?" Trenton looked a trifle smug. "My wife and his are cousins. So when Grandfather and Grandmother Hawkins have everyone for Christmas dinner, naturally Jimmy and I have a nice talk about our work. I told him I wouldn't mind having a bright young gentleman to help me untangle the worst of my cases, and so I don't. You are welcome, sir."

He shook Drew's hand again, and Drew didn't know if he was more astonished by the enthusiastic welcome or by the idea of the dour chief inspector of the Hampshire police sitting about with a bevy of cousins and aunts and uncles and all their offspring caroling round the family hearth in a paper crown and eating plum pudding.

"I'll try to be what help I can," Drew said once his hand was free. "Beaky here's told me some of the basic facts of the case, but I'm sure you can tell me a great deal more. We were just in the church—"

"I expect you've seen the steps, then. It's an outrage, that's what it is." Trenton stood again and pulled up a couple of chairs that very likely hadn't seen paint since King George was in short pants. "Do sit, ma'am. Sir."

They sat.

"About those steps," Drew said after a moment, "I'd very much like to know how the vicar was . . . situated. When you found him, I mean."

Constable Trenton blinked at him. "Lying there with his head bashed in, sir. I can't tell you much plainer."

"Yes, but how was he lying? Faceup? Facedown?"

"Facedown. Can't very well cosh a man on the back of the head and have him land facing up, eh?"

"Very true. Now was his head towards the church or away from it?"

"Towards it. We reckon he'd met someone there and was going to go inside with him."

"Or perhaps he never saw the fellow at all," Madeline suggested.

"Might not have, missus," Trenton said. "We didn't find any sign of anything out of place inside the church. Nothing missing. Nothing disturbed. Might be they never were inside at all."

Drew nodded, thinking. "Beaky tells me he was found by the chap who delivers the milk."

"He was. Not long after dawn on the Thursday morning."

"And your suspects?"

The constable shook his head. "None as yet. Seems rather senseless if you ask me. Who's to profit from it? Could be simple mischief, someone with a grudge against the church. Who can say? There were gypsies on the moor not two days earlier, but they went away before I could find out what they were up to. Can't see what they would have done it for. Weren't nothing stolen. Not even the money in his pockets, nor his pocket watch."

Drew considered for a moment. "Tell me about this milkman who found the body. Local fellow?"

"Came up from Kent," Trenton said. "Not a bad little fellow. Lost his wife not long ago and decided a change of scene would do him good. Likes the quiet, he says, but friendly enough if you meet him. Likes a single malt whisky now and again, but not one to overindulge."

"What about the vicar? Were they friends?"

Trenton shrugged. "Generally acquainted, I believe. Never heard of any trouble between them."

Drew glanced at Beaky. "And where might I find him this time of day?"

"I'll drive you," Beaky said. "He ought to be finished with his rounds by now. I need to pop over to the post office and then we can be off. Or would you rather come?"

Drew squeezed Madeline's hand and gave her a look anyone else would have missed. The corner of her mouth twitched just slightly before she turned big blue eyes up to Beaky.

"May I come with you? I need some stamps and things."

"Of course." As usual, Beaky blushed. "Do you want to come, Drew?"

"That's all right," Drew said. "I'll just chat with the constable for a bit longer, if he doesn't mind. I think I'd like to know a bit more about our Chief Inspector Birdsong at Christmastime."

Madeline gave him a pert kiss on the cheek and then took Beaky's arm. "Let's hurry or they'll start talking about pistols and fingerprints and that sort of thing and we'll never get away."

Beaky chuckled. "Won't be but half a moment."

"Actually," Drew said once the two of them had gone, "I'd rather ask you about Mr. and Mrs. Bloodworth."

Trenton blinked. "You had, sir? You don't think one of them—"

"No, no, of course not. I just want to know, strictly between you and me, what your professional opinion of them is."

Trenton rubbed the back of his neck, his mouth in a reluctant frown. "I don't know, Mr. Farthering, sir. It might be a bit awkward, you know, if what I said were to get back to the Lodge. I've got to live here."

"It won't come from me," Drew assured him.

The constable relaxed slightly. "Not that there's anything bad to be said, sir. Mr. Bloodworth used to come up to the Lodge to stay when he was a boy, during the school holidays and such. Always minded his manners." He shook his head, suddenly wistful. "I was a bit of a boy myself, those days, just starting out in the force after the war, but here I am, and young Bloodworth's a man grown, lord of the manor and with a wife to boot."

"He did return to the old home place in fine style, didn't he?" Drew said with a chuckle.

"He did that." Trenton whistled low. "I can see how he'd be taken with a woman like Mrs. Bloodworth, though. Not meaning any offense, of course, but we didn't expect a London-bred lady like that would come up to the Lodge to stay. Not permanent anyway. But still, young Bloodworth is proud as a peacock with his hen, though she's easily the more decorative of the two birds."

"And everyone else at the Lodge? How did they take to her?"

Trenton shifted a little on his feet. "Bit different for Miss Windham, now, isn't it? With another woman in the house, running things and all? Not like when old Mr. Bloodworth was alive." He leaned closer. "Mrs. Bloodworth has modern ways, you know."

Drew fought a smile. "I see."

"But I'm sure we don't fault her for that. She'll learn our ways before long, I daresay."

"Oh, to be sure," Drew said. "After all, she hasn't been here a year yet. I understand the moor can be a tricky place."

"It is that, sir. I was born here and I can tell you it's no place to trifle with. I understand Mrs. Bloodworth got herself turned around in the storm, and Rhys Delwyn had to bring her in."

Drew nodded. Everyone knew everything about everyone in these little villages, he was well enough aware, but it still surprised him how quickly even the most innocuous bit of gossip spread.

"He seems an interesting fellow."

"Not too bad for a Welshman," the constable allowed. "Lives like the devil, of course, but he knows his job. If you were to ask me, though, and I see as how you haven't, he'd do well to stay out of trouble. There's things on the moor and things a bit closer to home a wise man keeps clear of."

Before he could say anything more, Beaky and Madeline came back into the police station, ears and noses red with cold, but smiling.

"It's looking a bit threatening out there, Drew," Beaky said. "We might better get along to Blackstock's if you still want to speak to him." He looked at Trenton. "Sorry, have I interrupted?"

"We were just chatting," Drew said. "I thank you for your time, Constable. Perhaps we could talk later?"

"Any time you like, Mr. Farthering." Trenton beamed at him once again. "It's a pleasure to have you with us in the investigation. Teddy means well, you know, but sometimes I think I'd be better off with a bull pup."

"Teddy?"

"My sister's boy, God love him. He's a fine chap. Works hard and follows orders to a T. Well, we'll make a policeman out of him yet, eh?"

They made their farewells and settled into Beaky's car.

Beaky looked at his watch. "Blackstock ought to be at Morton's still. We'll have a look."

They drove a little way out of the village and finally turned down a narrow road that ended abruptly at a large barn and fenced pasture. Out front, a middle-aged man, bearded and stoop-shouldered, was currying a disgruntled-looking brown horse. A freshly painted cart, white with delft-blue letters touting the virtues of Morton's Hygienic Dairy Farms, stood in the nearby shed.

"Mr. Blackstock," Beaky called as they got out of the car and walked toward the man. "Good morning."

The man squinted for a moment behind his thick spectacles and then smiled faintly. "Why, it's Mr. Bloodworth, is it? Good morning." He looked Drew over. "Is this your London detective and his lady, then?"

Drew gave him a nod. "Drew Farthering. And it's Hampshire, actually."

"Dear me, and I'm sure Mr. Clifton said it was London. Can't trust gossip these days, eh, Maisie?" He gave the horse a swat on the rump, and she looked at him with a baleful eye as he took the hand Drew offered. "I suppose you're here about poor Mr. Miles. A bad business." He tugged his cap. "Mrs. Farthering."

"Good morning, Mr. Blackstock," she said politely. "Thank you for talking to us."

"Yes, it's very bad business," Drew said. "I understand you were the one who found the body. Would you mind telling us exactly what you saw?"

Blackstock stroked his graying beard. "I had a funny feeling all that morning as I was about my rounds. Maisie here must have been feeling it, too. She was shying at every little thing." He stroked the mare's neck, and she jingled the bridle when she tossed her head. "Anyway, I saw something heaped up on the steps when I drove by that morning. At first, I thought it was a bundle of clothes left for the parish charity. Well, my eyes are a bit weak, but I saw it was all sort of strewn about, and I thought maybe animals had got into it. I started to go on, but it just didn't strike me right, if you know what I mean, so I went up to take a look." He shook his head, looking a bit queasy. "Blimey, it was as ugly a sight as ever I've seen. The parson was lying there stone dead with his blood half run out and frozen solid. And that stone he was clipped with, it was lying at the bottom of the steps, just left there bold as brass."

"Did you pick it up?" Madeline asked.

"Me?" Blackstock's eyes went wide, and he jerked his head back. "No, ma'am. I went for the police straight off."

"In your cart?"

"I didn't stop for that. The station's just the next street over. I went through the churchyard and out the other side. Quickest way there. We came back the same way." Blackstock glanced around as if someone might overhear what he said next. "Funny thing is, when we got back, that stone was gone."

"That's what I'd heard," Drew said. "And how long did it take you to get to the police and come back?"

"Not much over five minutes, I don't think. Less than ten, I'm certain of that. And, no, sir, I did not see anyone out on the street that morning. Don't think the police didn't ask me that fifty different ways. But I hardly ever see anyone that early, unless it's old Jem Nealy staggering home from whatever alley he'd passed out into, not that I'm to judge."

"Any other footprints when you came back?"

"None. That's what made it so very odd. You could see mine there in the mud and then on the path, and you could see where that wicked-looking stone had been sitting, but it wasn't there no more. I couldn't imagine how it were done, but P.C. Pennyworth had a thought on that, and I expect that's why he's

47

with the police and I'm not." The man grinned, lightly elbowing Drew's ribs and then quickly sobering and tugging the brim of his cap. "Beg pardon, sir. No offense meant."

Drew did not smile. "And what did the constable think?"

"He was of a mind that whoever it was took that stone had stepped right into my footprints, neat as you please, right up to where the vicar lay, and took away what he done the murder with. And when we looked at the footmarks, bless me if he didn't get it spot-on. Whoever it was was a shifty rascal, no denying it, but you could see just now and again where he'd stepped on top of my footprint."

"And that was just up to where the vicar was, was it?"

"That's right, sir."

"Not past that and across the churchyard or anything?"

Again the man's eyes widened. "You mean as like he was following me? No, sir. Not at all. Bad enough that he must've been lurking somewhere, watching." He shuddered and then collected himself again. "No, the constable looked at the steps and the path and where I went round the church to get across to the police station. Those prints were just my own. Pity we've had such weather since then or you might've had a look for yourself."

"Yes, a pity."

"Did they happen to take photographs?" Madeline asked.

"I couldn't say as to that, ma'am. You might better ask the constables."

"We'll certainly do that," Drew said. "Anything else you noticed at the time or recalled since you last spoke to the police?"

"Not anything, sir, and I truly wish there was."

"Yes, well, if you think of anything, no matter how small, you let someone know. I'll be at the Lodge. You can always leave a message when you bring the milk. Or tell Constable Trenton."

"Right you are, sir. The very minute."

"Good man.

It was only a short drive back to the Lodge, and after a couple of attempts at conversation, Beaky had grown silent. Madeline, perceptive as always about her husband's moods, also said nothing. Drew sat thinking all the while of what he'd seen, wondering what the connection, if any, might be between the murder and the other things that had been going on out on the moor and at Beaky's home. He tried to keep from drawing conclusions until he had more evidence, but he couldn't help but wonder about Sabrina Bloodworth. She was as beautiful as he remembered, and as hard.

He'd seen it when she had gone round with Bunny nearly two years ago. It wasn't anything very obvious, but it was there all the same. He'd seen her pull away from Beaky when he touched her, a subtle but visceral reaction, and she had seemed more annoyed by his solicitousness than appreciative of it. And that Delwyn was a handsome brute, earthy and untamed, the kind society women sometimes fell for when they grew bored with their privileged lives and went looking for trouble. Drew had noticed Sabrina had not looked at him. Was she afraid to lest she give herself away?

Drew glanced at Beaky, steady, good-hearted Beaky, and then looked up the road. Bloodworth Park Lodge was just ahead, and he could see it clearly now. "I say, old man, could we pull up here a minute? I'd like to get a good look at the ancestral home."

Madeline raised one questioning brow and then smiled. "Oh, yes, let's."

Beaky grinned and let the car slow to a stop. The sky was blue and bright, the sun glinting off the rain-washed windows of the old house. It was done in the Jacobean style with a large central section flanked by two long wings. Drew could tell from here that the north wing was indeed abandoned. Even in daylight, there was something sadly forlorn about it, and yet there didn't seem to be anything particularly sinister about the place. Just empty and neglected.

"I suppose it looks a bit dowdy to you," Beaky said.

"No," Madeline insisted.

"Not at all, old man." Drew shaded his eyes to see it better. "Barring the north wing, which I'll admit needs a bit of work, it's admirable. I'd wager it's a stunner in the springtime."

"Sabrina says it's dowdy, but I think it's got nice lines. Needs some work here and there, a bit of updating, and of course that wing will need a massive dose of wherewithal, but I think it could be quite grand again."

"Bathrooms," Madeline said decidedly, and Beaky chuckled.

"Good heavens, yes. I've already been told more than once that the place hasn't enough of them. It seems you ladies are most particular on that subject. But the mistress of the manor is going to have to wait until spring before we can start work. Remind me and I'll show you what we have planned. And if you think of anything we've forgotten, please chime in."

"I'd love to see," Drew said, looking over the house once more. "But it's really Nick you should talk to about plans. He's quite keen on electrical systems and furnaces and drains and that."

"Pity he couldn't have come up with you two." Beaky put the car into gear and pulled back onto the road. "I'd like to have seen him."

"Oh, I expect he'll be up here sometime or another. When

he is, the three of us will have a good long chat about school and how glad we are that we're not there anymore."

Beaky didn't say anything else until they pulled up in front of the house. Madeline hurried inside, but Beaky was walking very slowly. Not wanting to get to the house quite yet, no doubt.

"Have you ever been too happy?" he said finally, still looking straight ahead. "Like you've been given something that's outrageously more than you deserve, something you never dreamed you could ever have?"

"You mean Sabrina," Drew said, and inside himself he prayed desperately that God would help him keep his mouth firmly shut on this particular subject.

"Sabrina." The name was somehow glorious when Beaky said it, and for an instant his plain face was transformed into something vividly alive. Then he coughed and turned faintly red. "I just . . . I never thought I'd find anyone at all, much less someone like her."

"I know what that's like," Drew told him, glad that, at least on this subject, he didn't have to guard his words. "One meets so many girls, and then you meet one and all at once something just drops into place and you know that she's the one for you. And it's rather a miracle that she'll have you at all."

Beaky half smiled. "No. You think you know, but you really don't. I've seen them, all the girls, simply throwing themselves at you. And why shouldn't they?"

"I wouldn't say that." Drew felt his own face turn warm. "Not all of them, surely."

"I heard there was a certain Miss Pomphrey-Hughes who was just perishing to be Mrs. Farthering."

Drew winced. "How ever did you hear that?"

"Sabrina told me when I mentioned asking you and your

wife up here. She said she wondered that you were married to a Madeline and not a Daphne."

"I didn't think she and Daphne had ever met."

"I believe she heard it from Bunny Marsden-Brathwaite. When the two of them were an item."

Drew fought to keep his expression blank. Beaky was certainly nonchalant when discussing his wife's former lover. But then Drew had only his assumptions to go by concerning Bunny's relationship with Sabrina Prestwick. Clearly Sabrina had convinced Beaky there was nothing but innocence in it or Beaky wouldn't have brought it up so casually. Knowing his infatuation with her, perhaps she hadn't had to do much convincing at all.

"Anyway," Beaky said, "which particular girls they were doesn't matter. The point is that you're Drew Farthering and I'm Beaky Bloodworth, a carrot-topped bean pole who can't put two words together talking to girls." His mouth twisted into a wry grin. "And to top it all off, I've got this monumental snout no one will ever let me forget."

"Listen, old man, when we called you Beaky, I don't think anyone ever meant—"

"Don't be silly," Beaky said. "You don't know how comforting it was back in school to have my friends call me that. It made the actually cruel remarks not sting so badly."

Drew merely waited for him to go on.

"So, no, Drew, you're a capital fellow and all that, but you really have no idea what it is to be someone like me. And then to have someone like Sabrina love me, I mean truly love me, it frightens me sometimes. It makes me wonder when it's going to all come crashing down around me." There was just the tiniest bit of a quiver in his voice. "Or when I'm going to wake up and find it's all been just a cruel joke."

"That would be unthinkable," Drew said, trying to sound reassuring, knowing Beaky had suffered more than his share of cruel jokes when they were in school simply because he was awkward and plain. But to himself Drew swore he would find out whether or not his friend was being deceived and by whom.

— Four —

Madeline huddled into her coat, certain that her nose and cheeks were frozen solid. The sky was an unrelieved gray, and she was sure it was cold enough that, if there were precipitation, this time they would get snow rather than rain. The moor stretched out in all directions, hills and dales but no trees, only heather and gorse and the leavings of the ever-present sheep.

"I wish you had borrowed a pair of my boots if you were going to come out with us today," Sabrina told her, not slowing her brisk stride as they tried to keep up with Raphael, who was trotting a few yards ahead of them. "We'll have to go into the village and find you something this afternoon. We might have to go into Harrogate if you want something even remotely stylish. You may as well be comfortable while you're here."

"That's a good idea. I don't know why I didn't think to bring anything like that with me. I suppose I'm still getting used to my new country."

Sabrina looked her over, just the hint of a smirk on her red lips. "If I can get used to this, I suppose you can, too. Do you miss it? America, I mean."

"Sometimes very much," Madeline admitted, lengthening her stride as the dog began trotting faster. "I have two aunts and an uncle in Chicago I'd love to see again. Letters are never quite the same, are they?"

Sabrina shook her head.

"And sometimes I just miss being back there," Madeline added. "I miss the sounds and the smells and the taste of it. I miss the great bigness of it. But then again I love it here in England." She looked down at her low-heeled shoes that were all wrong for walking on the moor. "Now wherever Drew happens to be is home to me."

Sabrina snickered. "You sound like one of those oh-so-sincere stories where the factory girl meets the handsome young mechanic who turns out to be a duke in disguise." She took Madeline's arm. "I'm glad you two came up to see us. I don't know how much either of you can do about our difficulties, but Beaky's enjoying it at any rate. And I have to admit it's good to have another woman to talk to. Besides Miss Windham, I mean. Raphael! Not so fast!"

The terrier came back, sniffing the ground and then panting up at her, eager-eyed and adoring, before trotting ahead once again.

"Don't you like Miss Windham?" Madeline asked, hurrying again to keep up.

"That's not really it," Sabrina said. "Miss Windham, if you must know, does not approve of me."

"Really? Why would you think that?"

"Because it's true. None of the people who were here when Beaky was a boy know what to make of me. Not that they'd say anything. We all have a very . . . cordial relationship. But unless I want to spend my days in the company of the cook and the scullery girl, my options for girl talk are rather limited here in Bunting's Nest."

They walked on for a while. The only sounds were the wind on the moor and the panting dog. Soon they passed a stone marker engraved ROAD TO BUNTING'S NEST with an arrow pointing back the way they had come.

"I suppose your husband told you we met a time or two in London a while back," Sabrina said, keeping her eyes on Raphael, who had gone farther ahead than before.

"He said you knew his friend Bunny."

Sabrina shrugged. "You know how those things are. Bunny and I had some laughs a couple of years ago. He's decidedly got more money than sense, but we parted friends as far as I can tell. I met Beaky a few months later and decided it was time I settled down."

"No one in between?" Madeline asked.

Sabrina laughed almost inaudibly. "That's old news. I'm happy here, even if the only nightlife I get now is listening to the dance bands on the wireless." The dog was scurrying even farther ahead of them now. Sabrina put her hands on her hips. "Come back now, Raffie. Raphael! Not down there. Raphael! Come back!"

But the little dog had disappeared down a mostly overgrown path that turned sharply to the left and into a deep hollow.

Sabrina was half running now. "Raphael!"

"What's over there?" Madeline was hurrying beside her. "He's not going to get into something he shouldn't, is he?"

Sabrina looked annoyed, but Madeline couldn't tell if there was another emotion in her expression. Anxiety? Fear?

"Raphael!" Sabrina snapped. "Come on now or you can just spend the night out here."

They rushed around a clump of trees and came upon a ruin of worn stone and weathered wood that looked as if it had been there since Anglo-Saxon times. Perhaps before. It was hardly more than a couple of battered walls jutting out of the side of the hill and only halfway up now, one wall with a broken opening where a window must have been, along with a little square tower with a wooden door. Several large stones lay half buried in the ground around it, cracked and battered from centuries of sun and storm.

Sabrina stood watching as Raphael sniffed along the ground of the ruin, whining softly.

"What is it?" Madeline asked. "Or what was it?"

"I heard it was once an old church, but I'm not sure exactly. If it ever was a church, I think it was abandoned and used for something else later. Maybe it's just this place that gives me the creeps. Like Merlin Hill."

"What's that?"

"Oh, it's nothing really. Just a bluff that looks over the house. The locals say it was one of the pagan high places a long while back. It's nothing but bare rock now." Her mouth tightened at Madeline's inquisitive look. "No, I haven't ever seen anything unnatural out there. And I don't think our north wing is haunted either, no matter what Beaky says. He never knows when I'm teasing him. Raphael, come back here right now or I'm going to be very cross with you."

The dog made a yipping sound but did not look back at her, his attention fixed on whatever scent he had picked up. Madeline looked at Sabrina, wondering why she didn't just go pick him up before he wandered out of sight.

"I'll get him," she said, but Sabrina caught her arm, holding her back.

"He'll come back. I'd rather you didn't get too close."

Madeline drew her brows together. "Why not? What's the matter?"

Sabrina shook her head, but her attempt to look scornful failed miserably. "Nothing. I just don't like the look of the place. Never have. Raphael! Where did you go?"

The dog was nowhere to be seen now.

"He must be on the other side," Madeline said. "I can get him."

Before she could change her mind, she took long, quick strides toward the ruined church. Halfway there, Raphael let out a high yelp and came tearing around the corner. Madeline caught him as he tried to dart past her and then almost dropped him again when he snarled and snapped at her.

"Raphael!" Sabrina came close enough to take the dog from her and then looked back at the old church, her eyes wide. "Come on. Really. I don't think we should be here right now."

With the still-growling dog clutched against her, she led Madeline out of the hollow and across the moor. The looming dark shape of Bloodworth Park Lodge was a welcome sight when it came into view. Even more welcome was the sight of Beaky's car pulling up to the house and then Drew and Beaky getting out of it and walking over to them.

"Hullo, darling." Drew wrapped Madeline in his arms and kissed her forehead. "Miss me?"

"You don't know how much."

He pulled back from her, looking into her eyes. "What is it? You look as if you've seen a ghost."

"No ghosts," Sabrina said, her expression snide and superior.

"Raphael spooked himself over by the stone church, that's all." She lowered her head and nuzzled the squirming terrier in her arms. "Isn't that right, Raffie, darling? There wasn't anything there."

Beaky came over and put a hand on her arm. "Are you sure? Are you both all right?"

She hugged the dog closer, pulling away from her husband. "Of course we are. We're just cold and tired and want our tea. Come on, Raffie."

Beaky gave Madeline an apologetic smile. "I meant you and Sabrina, not her and the dog. Sorry about that."

"That's quite all right." Madeline took Drew's arm and started them toward the door. "She spoke for me as well as Raphael."

"Poor darling," Drew said. "Are you certain you didn't see anything?"

"Nothing, although Raphael was on to something. He was trailing a scent, but there must have been something that scared him because he tore back the way he had come. I was afraid he'd bite me, growling and snapping the way he was."

"That's not like Raphael," Beaky said. "Poor little chap."

"But you didn't actually see anything," Drew pressed, escorting her through the front door after Beaky opened it for them. "Nothing out of the ordinary?"

"No. But I didn't like the feel of the place, Drew."

"Well, never mind," he said, settling with her before the fire on the drawing room sofa. "I'll have a look out there when I can."

"Not alone," she urged. "I don't want you to go alone. Please."

He looked at her strangely.

"I think I've spooked myself with all this talk about strange happenings on the moor." Madeline took a deep breath and smiled. "It's all right. Really."

Drew didn't look at all convinced.

☕

Dinner that night was quiet. Afterward the two couples played bridge, but no one seemed very interested in the game and it broke up early. Not very much later, they all went up to bed. Drew was glad. He had wanted to talk to Madeline in private about what had happened earlier that day out on the moor, though she had made it clear she didn't want to say anything more about it in front of their hosts.

He lay back against the pillows, watching her as she prepared for bed. Usually he had to wait until her maid had finished undoing whatever it was that had to be done up to make her presentable for dinner, but they had left maid and valet behind for once. Now he could silently admire the graceful movement of her body as she stepped from the bathroom to the dresser to the wardrobe in just her slip, the little pout of annoyance when she couldn't find some folderol she wanted, and the tinge of pink in her freshly washed face.

"You're wishing you'd brought Beryl along by now, I daresay."

She made a face at him in the mirror. "Shows what you know. Actually, I was just thinking how nice it was for it to be just us in the evening for a change without anyone else around."

"It is, isn't it?"

"It's in the morning that I really miss having a maid, especially doing my hair. I can't believe how clumsy I've gotten in little more than a year and a half."

"Beryl will be glad to know she's been missed. I'm just glad Plumfield can't see me now. I'm certain the tie I had on today was just the wrong shade of charcoal to go with my smoke-colored waistcoat and slate jacket."

She laughed. "He's probably spending the time we're away organizing your socks and ties into perfectly coordinated sets."

"Plumfield and Beryl both deserve a bit of time away from us, don't you think? They both have such lovely tempers, we wouldn't want to spoil everything by being around too much. Speaking of spoilt things, how are you and Mrs. Bloodworth getting on?"

She scowled at him. "Be nice now. You were going to be fair, remember?"

"Yes." He sighed. "Yes, I was. She just . . ."

He trailed off with a shrug and another sigh, and she gave him a look that was all love and understanding.

"She reminds you of Fleur."

He nodded. Fleur and Sabrina looked nothing alike, *were* nothing alike, except they were both stunning beauties, both stylish and self-possessed, both heedless of any casualties left in their wakes. No, he was going to be fair. He didn't know Sabrina, not really. He wasn't eighteen anymore, and Fleur wasn't toying with his unwary heart. It was ridiculous to suspect every woman just because of one. It wasn't fair.

"She hasn't done anything to make you think badly of her," Madeline said gently.

Sabrina, not Fleur. Fleur was in the past.

"Oh, I suppose not." He sat up and punched the pillow a time or two to get it into just the right shape and then lay back again. "Anyhow, how are you two getting along? Any shocking confessions or hitherto undetected clues?"

"Nothing you don't know." Madeline got into bed beside

him. "It may take longer than I thought to get her to confide in me. She's not the type."

"Did you ask her about the north wing?"

"We talked about it." Madeline pulled the coverlet up to her chin and turned to nestle under his arm. "She says she was only teasing about it being haunted, but I'm not so sure about that. She looks, oh, I don't know, unnerved whenever she talks about it."

"But why? What's she seen? Headless cavaliers? A weeping White Lady? A smuggler's grinning skeleton?"

"Nothing as dramatic as that," she assured him, toying absently with one of the buttons on his pajamas. "Just some noises now and then. Nothing she can quite put her finger on, yet they shouldn't be there. Nothing should be there."

"You saw it when we were driving back from the village. Why anyone should be afraid of the place, I can't begin to imagine."

"Well, we saw it from the road in broad daylight. It has to be very different when it's right on the other side of a wall in the middle of the night and you're alone and still not quite used to the country."

"I happen to know Beaky's had some of his men look over the whole wing more than once, and they haven't found a sign of anything but mice. Oh, and a family of squirrels in the box room. They didn't find any of them particularly terrifying."

She huffed. "Fine. But if we find out later there's a secret room haunted by the ghosts of the murdered brides of some eighteenth-century Bloodworth Bluebeard, I am certainly going to say I told you so."

"Whatever we're dealing with, my imaginative darling, it's almost assuredly not ghosts."

"There were pagans here once, you know. There's a precipice that looks over the Lodge and all the Bloodworth land, Sabrina says, that used to be one of their high places. Makes me shudder, no matter how long ago that was."

He pulled her closer. "Well, if you're menaced by any pagans, ghostly or otherwise, you send them straight to me. I'll familiarize them with the tale of Elijah and the prophets of Baal and let the Lord answer for me."

"My hero." She gave him a smacking kiss and then slipped her arms around him and nuzzled his jaw. "You're so nice to have around, I may just keep you after all."

"Cheeky," he breathed, but whatever else he might have said was lost in her kiss.

The next day, when Madeline and Sabrina went into the village to buy Madeline a pair of boots, Drew made his way to the study that was just off the library. Beaky was sitting at the desk, his chin resting on his hand, frowning at a stack of papers and opened envelopes.

Drew tapped on the doorframe, making him jump.

"Drew. With all this talk of ghosts and devils and murders, you really ought to learn to tread a bit heavier."

"Sorry, old man. What have you been about?"

Beaky waved a dismissive hand over the desk. "Bills, bills, bills. And then there's always someone asking for money. Do you get those?"

Drew chuckled. "All the time. Many of them are quite worthy. I wish I could send along more than I do."

"That's true, and I feel the same, but there are just so many." Beaky filed through the handful of letters on one corner of the

63

desk. "Charity hospital, orphans' home, home for the blind, for disabled servicemen. I feel as though I'm spitting in the ocean for all the difference it makes."

"It makes a difference. Perhaps not to the whole world, but to those you can help it makes a world of difference."

Beaky shook his head, studying one of the envelopes. "Even an insane asylum."

Drew's eyebrows went up. "You got one from an asylum? Poor devils. What's it say?"

"Evidently Uncle Hubert had been supporting them and all these other places, too. This one wants to know if I would consider carrying on."

"Nearby?"

Beaky looked at the return address on the envelope. "Someplace in Norfolk. It's the farthest afield of the lot."

"You ought to look into it before you send any of them anything."

Beaky nodded. "I'll see what Rogers has to say about it. He's managed the finances at the Lodge since before the war. If Uncle really did send these places money every year, then they're all right."

"Good idea. But I was rather hoping you might want to take a breather from all that. What do you say to the two of us having a talk with the vicar's housekeeper. Mrs. . . . ?"

Before Beaky could supply the name, the telephone rang. Beaky glanced toward the study door, and a moment later Halford appeared.

"Telephone for you, sir. Mr. Treadwell from the bank."

Beaky excused himself and picked up the telephone on the desk. "Mr. Treadwell, good morning."

Drew started to leave the room to give the man some privacy, but Beaky shook his head and held up one finger, indicating he didn't expect the call to take long.

Drew studied the room while he waited, only half hearing Beaky talking about additional funds needed for making the north wing habitable. Uncle Hubert's study was probably little changed from when he had left it. The wallpaper was old, a cream-colored print that had aged to a nondescript tan, darkened still more by smoke from the fireplace and from the collection of pipes that was still in the stand on the desk.

On the bookcase was a photograph of what Drew assumed was the old boy himself, a jolly-looking fellow of portly middle age with a great walrus mustache and pince-nez eyeglasses and what looked to be the flaming red hair of the Bloodworths. Further over was another photograph, this one much older, of three boys in Eton jackets, the two eldest standing behind the youngest, who sat on an iron bench with his top hat in his lap and his large light-colored eyes fixed on something far off.

The oldest of these boys was Uncle Hubert, though the mustache and spectacles on the more recent picture had made Drew skeptical at first. The middle boy was undeniably Beaky's father, as tall and gawky as Beaky had been at that age and possessed of the same memorable nose. The third boy must be another brother, judging by the resemblance between the three, although this younger one's hair looked fair, his nose more in proportion with the rest of him. Drew smiled thinking how little Eton had changed in the past forty years. If it hadn't been for the age of the photograph itself, he could have well believed these boys were from his own days there or even from the present.

"A motley crew, eh?" Beaky said as he rang off. "My old

governor, Uncle Hubert and Uncle Sylvester. Eton men, brave and true."

"I didn't know you had another uncle." Drew squinted at the faded photograph. "Do you stay in touch?"

"I'm afraid not. He was killed in Amiens in '18." He pointed Drew over to a photograph of a young man in uniform, the same man from the Eton picture but a bit older, a man with a firm chin, gentle mouth, and light-colored eyes. The Victoria Cross hung on a ribbon over the corner of the picture frame. "I don't remember him much."

"Pity. I remember my father doing some work for the Home Office during the war. I was always afraid he'd be called to France or some other horrid place to fight, but he never was."

Beaky nodded. "I thought my father would go too, but he was getting a bit past the age by then and had a dodgy ticker. And Uncle Hubert was too old, too. They both did their war work here at home." He bit his lip. "I remember feeling very wicked indeed when I was glad it was Uncle Vester who was killed and not Father."

"Perfectly understandable for a boy of nine."

"The sad bit is that he was a capital fellow and I worshiped him. He'd play cricket with me—well, a sort of cricket we made up between us—when he was home, and he told the best bed-time stories, not just with funny voices but acting them out and everything." Beaky touched a finger to the photograph, smiling faintly. "My mother used to scold him for it, saying they were more likely to keep me awake than put me to sleep at night. I felt a perfect beast being glad he was dead."

"Be fair," Drew said. "It's not as though you were actually glad of it, were you? That's a different thing entirely from just not wanting to lose your own father."

"It took me a while to see that," Beaky admitted. "Funny how one can feel two entirely opposite ways about the same thing at the same time."

"We're funny creatures." Drew clapped him on the shoulder, not wanting to revisit a particularly repugnant time in his own past when he, too, had felt that way, unwilling to dredge up Fleur again. "But I think we can agree that there is nothing good about the murder of your vicar and that his killer ought not to get away with it, eh?"

"Oh, certainly. Right. You were asking about Mrs. Tansy."

"The housekeeper, yes."

"That's right. Shall we go round and see her?"

— Five —

The Tansy residence was an indifferent little row house on an indifferent little street. There was no answer to Drew's knock. According to the woman at the house next door but one, Mrs. Tansy had gone off to stay with her sister, being that upset about Mr. Miles's murder. The woman did not have the sister's name or address.

"Well, that's a bust," Drew said, scowling at the door that had just been closed on him.

"I expect the police got a full report before Mrs. Tansy was allowed to leave the area. I doubt she knows more about the murder than I do. Or you now, for that matter."

"I suppose so. I've just found that people often remember more than they think they do if one asks the right questions."

"Sorry, old man." Beaky thought for a moment, and then his expression brightened. "We could go round to the police station and ask to see her statement. Trenton won't mind."

While Trenton was extremely helpful, the statement itself was not. Mrs. Tansy had left the vicar eating soup before his fire, just as Beaky had said, and knew nothing more of the matter.

"What now?" Beaky asked.

Drew looked at his watch. "What do you say to a bit of lunch at the pub? Madeline said she and your missus wouldn't be back at the Lodge before tea."

"Ah, yes. I expect they'll be at Milbury's. Shall we see if we can catch them up? Or would you prefer the pub?"

"The pub, I think. Some of these tea rooms are too ladylike for my taste. I like to know I've had lunch once I've actually had it."

Beaky chuckled. "The Hound and Hart, then. Straight this way."

They left the car where it was and walked from the police station down the high street toward the pub. Halfway on, Beaky stopped to buy a newspaper as Drew walked a few feet ahead, stopping to admire an Alfa Romeo roadster, a fire-engine-red two-seater parked in front of the post office. She was flashier than he typically cared for, but she was a sweet-looking machine for all that. He leaned closer, admiring the automobile's sleekness, imagining racing it full throttle up the road toward—

"A bit of all right, isn't she?"

Drew started and turned at the deep voice. "Sorry. I was just having a look. Is she yours?"

"I suppose, being asked, it's not bragging. Yes, she's mine. Isn't she a stunner?"

The man was fortyish, not very tall, rather thin and pale. Bookish. Nothing like his voice. And if this was his car, he must be rather well off.

"Morris Gray, I take it."

The man blinked once behind his glasses, and then a smile brightened his face as he shook the hand Drew offered. "Why, yes. How'd you know? Someone told you this was my car, did he?"

"Actually, I reckon one would need quite a bit of ready cash to afford a motor car like this one, and I knew you weren't a Bloodworth. That leaves only the people at Westings. You are obviously too young to be Mr. Carter Gray, but I would imagine just the right age to be his son. Ipso facto, you are Mr. Morris Gray of Westings, Bunting's Nest, Yorkshire."

"Then I would venture to say you're the London detective Bloodworth has staying up at the Lodge."

"Drew Farthering, yes. But I come from Hampshire, not London. And I have come up to have a look about, if only in an unofficial capacity."

Gray nodded. "Then you did come to see about the vicar. I told her that was why."

"Her?"

"Oh, my wife, of course. My wife. Awful thing to happen, the vicar. Nice chap."

"So I've heard," Drew said. "You don't have any theories, do you?"

"None, I'm afraid. Not that we're a hotbed of iniquity here, but if anyone in Bunting's Nest was to be murdered, he would be the last one I'd peg."

"Rather a shock in a nice quiet village, eh?"

Gray's face clouded. "Beastly hole, if you ask me. Miserable winters."

"I suppose it's a treat in January, eh?"

"It is that." Gray smiled abruptly. "Have you ever been to Nice? Or Venice? Or even Guatemala?"

"Not quite so far as Guatemala, but I've been to the others."

"Glorious places, aren't they?" A wistful longing came to the older man's eyes. "Drenched in warm light and beauty."

"Lovely places. I went a couple of years ago on my honey-moon."

Gray sighed. "My wife and I went to Brighton."

"Oh . . . well, I'm sure it was very nice."

"Frances said it was practical."

"I thought you and the Alfa Romeo would meet up in time." Beaky walked up to them. "Good afternoon, Gray. Good to see you."

"Bloodworth. Just having a chat with your detective here." The neighbors shook hands.

"We have yet to make any brilliant deductions," Drew said. "But if neither of you is in a particular hurry, I'd very much like to know a bit more about recent goings-on."

"No hurry," Gray said. Then he looked at the sullen sky and pulled his collar up closer to his ears. "But someplace a bit cozier, eh? Come along, then."

Beaky and Drew followed him down the street to a low brick building, the sign swinging above it bearing the image of a dog and a stag in fine medieval style. As they approached the entrance, the door opened and a trio of laboring men spilled out into the street. A fourth, shabbier than the other three, stepped inside as they left, coughing out a hoarse apology when he stumbled against Drew and then hurried over to a group of roughs gathered at a table near the pub's dart board.

"We seem to have idlers from everywhere these days," Gray said as he led them to the back of the room. "Scots. Welshmen. Heaven help us, the Irish. Afternoon, Williams."

"Mr. Gray, sir," the barman called back. "Gentlemen. Won't be half a moment."

"Good old Hound and Hart," Gray said, finding them a table as near the fire as possible and then shifting his own chair even closer. "If nothing else, Mr. Farthering, you can count on Williams here to look after you."

It was a good time of day to come. The men had had their dinner and mostly gone back to their work. It was too early for the evening crowd. Just a few old duffers with their pipes and checkers and no trouble. They ordered shepherd's pie, and afterward Gray leaned forward, arms on the table, fingers tented in front of him.

"I suppose Bloodworth's told you about the . . . difficulties between his family and mine."

"Only a bit," Drew said. "Perhaps you ought to tell your side of it."

"My side?" Gray chuckled. "I don't have a side. I think it's all perfect rot. Two grown men acting like absolute infants over nothing? Ridiculous."

"I don't suppose it was nothing to them," Drew said, "or to your mother."

"Mother, God bless her, wanted no part of any of it. And if she regretted her choice of husband, she made sure no one ever knew it. But that was ages ago. She's gone now. Old Bloodworth's gone. My father's little better than an invalid. I expect I'll be master of Westings before long, and then who'll care about the old days?"

"And when the place is yours?" Drew asked.

Gray shook his head. "If I had my way, I'd sell the old barn and be done with it, but Frances would never stand for that. She wants to 'make something of the place.'"

"She sounds quite industrious."

"Oh, she is." Gray smiled into his drink and then drained it in a gulp. "She was never one to go on about da Vinci or Proust, but if the sheep are looking a bit dodgy or the pipes are plugged, she'll figure out why, you can be sure of that."

"Rather handy to have about," Drew said.

"Good afternoon, Mr. Farthering."

Drew looked up to see Blackstock, the milkman, standing at his elbow, cap in hand. The group of men at the table by the dart board turned to gape at the newcomer and then huddled together again, no doubt gossiping like old women.

"I do beg your pardon, sir. Mr. Bloodworth. Mr. Gray." Blackstock bobbed his head at each of them in turn, squinting in the low light. "Don't want to interrupt, but might I have a private word, Mr. Farthering?"

With a quizzical glance at Beaky, Drew stood and stepped away from the table. "Yes?"

"I wouldn't want to bother the other gentlemen, sir, and I won't disturb you but a moment, but I was just wondering if you'd found out any more about our vicar?"

"Not just yet," Drew replied. "Have you thought of anything else we ought to know?"

"No, sir. Makes me nervous, though, doing my rounds in the early morning with no one about, knowing there's someone out there not above doing murder. Makes me afraid to go watching my birds of a Sunday afternoon. I go just about everywhere round these parts. Who knows what that I might see something I ought not and have to be put out of the way?"

"I shouldn't worry, Blackstock. There's no reason anyone would want to kill you, is there?"

The milkman huffed. "No reason anyone ought do for the vicar either, is there? I ask you, sir."

"I hope we'll get this all sorted before there's any more trouble." Drew gave the man a sovereign. "Have something to eat. Nothing's going to happen here in the middle of the day."

"I suppose not, sir. Thank you." Blackstock bobbed his head again. "Sorry to have bothered you."

Drew studied him, considering what he had said about being everywhere and seeing most everything. "No bother at all. I can use a man like you, in point of fact. You're all over the village. And if you're a bird watcher, I daresay all over the moor."

The milkman's bearded face lit up. "I am that, sir."

"Just between you and me, keep your eyes open and come see me up at the Lodge if you see anything untoward, eh? I'll make it worth your while."

Blackstock held up his hand. "No, sir. Not for money. It's my duty and no less."

"Very good of you."

"Happy to be of service however I'm able, sir," the milkman replied. He then nodded toward Drew's table. "Now if you gentlemen will pardon me," he said, raising his voice, "I see Mr. Williams has your dinner." He held up the coin Drew had given him. "I'll drink this to your very good health, Mr. Farthering, sir."

He ducked around the tray the barman was setting down on the table and took a seat at the far end of the bar with a couple of other men from the village, who welcomed his company.

"Good fellow, Blackstock," Beaky said once the barman had served their shepherd's pie, steaming and well-browned on top. "Everything all right?"

"Oh, yes." Drew sat down and put his napkin in his lap. "He was just wondering if we'd found out anything about the vicar's death."

"Must have been quite a shock," Gray said, looking as if discerning the contents of the shepherd's pie was of far more interest to him. "Finding a body like that on his morning rounds.

Of course, in his trade he must see lots of things the rest of us don't."

"Rather interesting," Beaky said, "if you think about what servants and tradesmen must see and keep to themselves."

Gray stared at him for a moment before returning to his examination. "Oh, quite. Quite."

They all tucked in, the companionable silence broken only by the clatter of crockery and the muddle of voices from other conversations. The bunch near the dart board glanced over at them again, nudging each other over something one of them had said, something they obviously found humorous. Drew stopped still, his fork halfway between his plate and his mouth, as they burst into laughter. Beaky's ruddy complexion was redder than ever now, and Gray evidently couldn't get his napkin situated in his lap properly.

Drew's mouth tightened. "I see I'm not the only one who heard that."

Beaky managed a weak smile. "You're new in the village. They don't see many fashionable personalities up here. You can't expect them not to talk."

"It's more than that," Drew said, his voice low and tight. "If it weren't, you both wouldn't look as if you'd swallowed your forks sideways. What have they been saying?"

"I wouldn't know," Gray said, glancing covertly at Beaky. "I haven't been in here in days."

Drew's eyes flashed. "Beaky?"

"Let's not have a scene over it," Beaky said. "I'll tell you about it later. Back at the Lodge. But please, not here. You'll only make it worse."

"So there is something. About my wife?"

Beaky nodded, turning again to his food. "Don't make

it more of an issue than it is, Drew. Please. It was less than nothing."

Drew exhaled slowly. "All right. Sorry about that, Gray, and no real harm done, eh?"

Beaky took a hearty bite of his pie. "You know, Gray, speaking of wives, you and Mrs. Gray ought to come round to the Lodge and have dinner. It would be just me and Sabrina and the Fartherings, of course, but you two might like to get out for the evening. I'd say bring your father, but I have a feeling that might not be as well received as we'd like, eh?"

Gray chuckled, more relaxed now. "I think we'll just skip that bit, if you don't mind. What the old fellow doesn't know won't put him out of temper."

"That's settled then. We'll expect you and the missus, say, Thursday evening. Eight o'clock. Fair enough?"

"Done."

"Oh, Beaky, did you absolutely have to?" Sabrina rolled her eyes and blew cigarette smoke out through her nose as she paced before the drawing room fire. "And I thought we were all getting along so well as we were."

"It's just one evening," Beaky said. "I thought it would be nice to have guests while the Fartherings are here."

"Yes, but those guests? He's all right enough, I suppose, though I don't know how he manages to stand upright, spineless as he is. But you know she despises me."

"Now, darling—"

"Now nothing. You know she does. You can tell by how very polite she is with her prickly remarks. How he's stayed with her for the past fifteen years, I couldn't possibly tell you." She puffed on the cigarette once more and then ground it out in the marble ashtray on the end table beside the sofa. "You might have talked to me first."

Beaky looked at Drew and Madeline, wincing almost imperceptibly. "Sorry, old girl, I really didn't think about it. Drew and I were just talking to Gray and it just seemed the right thing to do. How will we ever mend things between us and Westings if we don't start somewhere?"

"It would be helpful if we could spend a little time with them," Drew added when it was clear she was not going to reply to her husband's question. "They may say something that would shed light on the investigation."

Sabrina drew a startled breath, half choking on it and then quickly turning it into a laugh. "You're not saying you suspect Morris Gray of being a murderer?"

"I would doubt that of him," Drew said coolly, "but it's far too early to rule anyone out. I'd just like to find out a bit more about him. Him and his wife."

Sabrina's mouth twisted up at one side. "Anything for the cause. If you can figure out what's going on here, I suppose I can put up with Frances Gray for one evening."

"You're a topper," Beaky said, beaming at her. "And you'll see. Farthering here will sort this whole thing out in half a jiffy."

"I'll give it my best," Drew said. "There's a lot here to be sorted, from what I can tell."

"I wanted to go look at the north wing when we got back from the village," Madeline said from her seat in the wing chair near the hearth. "But Sabrina told me it wasn't a good idea."

"I'm not sure how sound those floors are anymore," Beaky put in. "And the old gas lighting is probably unsafe. We use it now and then when we have to go in there, but to be honest I'm surprised there's any gas left. We can all give it a look tomorrow if you like, though I'd rather neither of you went in there alone."

"So had I." Drew gave Madeline a faintly stern look. "Though I expect there'll be little enough to see."

"Well, come on, Madeline," Sabrina said, standing. "We just have time to dress for dinner. Beaky, you two don't be late."

"We'll be right up, my dear," Beaky assured her, and he and Drew stood until the ladies had left the room.

"Now," Drew said, taking his seat on the sofa once again, "I want to know what those men in the pub were saying. I heard enough to know they were talking about a woman, and I could tell by how they were looking towards our table, specifically at me, that it must have been about Madeline."

Beaky glanced toward the door Sabrina and Madeline had just gone through and sighed. "It really was nothing, old man, at least not what I heard. A lovely woman like your wife comes to a place like this, and the men from the village are bound to comment, especially the ones from off the farms, sheepmen and the like. They may not have much refinement, but I doubt that anything that was said was very bad. Most likely little more than open admiration."

Drew crossed his arms over his chest. "And what did you hear specifically?"

Beaky squirmed slightly. "It was more foolish than offensive."

"What?"

"One of them said he'd like to be a detective too, if he could turn up a pip like that."

Drew scowled. "I'll grant you, that's not so much. But I can't say I care for my wife to be spoken of in such a way and in that sort of place."

"I expect it will be quickly forgotten, if you let it be."

"I suppose that's probably true. Still, I want to know who started it. Which one of them was it?"

"I'm not certain. But whoever it was, I don't doubt he was one or two over the eight. Mostly they're all just good village lads who'd mind their manners if they were sober. Let it be," Beaky repeated. "Don't we have much more pressing matters to see to just now?"

"True," Drew agreed, "but I still mean to have a word with whomever is responsible."

— Six —

It was busy inside the Hound and Hart when Drew returned the next day, cheerfully raucous but early enough in the evening that it was still relatively quiet. The barman was a different fellow than the one he had met when he came in with Beaky and Morris Gray.

He came over to where Drew stood. "Evening, sir. What can I get you?"

"Cider, if you please."

"Coming right up."

The barman put the glass on the counter in front of him. "Fourpence, please, sir."

Drew put a half crown on the bar. "Keep the change."

"Very kind, sir. Very kind."

The barman tugged at the coin, but Drew held it where it was. "Perhaps you can give me a bit of information as well."

"If I can, sir."

Drew glanced around the bar, looking for anyone he might recognize. "I understand someone here's been rather free with a certain lady's name the past few evenings."

The barman gave a nervous little shrug. "Might be, sir, no matter how we try to keep things respectable. Which lady would that be?"

"A Mrs. Farthering."

"Ah, yes . . . I have warned the fellow to keep a civil tongue in his head, but you understand, sir, when a man's in his cups . . ." The barman again shrugged. "This lady a relation of yours?"

Drew gave him a cool glare. "I am Mr. Farthering."

The barman winced. "As I said, sir, we try to keep things respectable. I can't guarantee every man comes through my door knows his manners. Nature of the business, and none of my doing."

"Just tell me which one." Drew looked around the room and saw he'd drawn the attention of a number of the barman's customers. "He's here, isn't he?"

"Not a regular, sir. My regulars are most of 'em good working men. Family men. Nothing much I can do about the strays that come round."

"Which one?"

The barman pointed with the wet towel he had wadded in his hand. "That one. Just there."

The man just there was sitting at a corner table, bent over a glass of what was probably whisky, his cap tugged down over his brow and his collar pulled up at the back of his neck. A tattered knitted scarf that had once been red hung over his shoulders.

Drew narrowed his eyes. "I see. He was careless enough to bump into me last time I was here." Drew released the coin and strode over to the shabby man's table. "I beg your pardon. My name is Drew Farthering."

"No need to ask my pardon," the man growled, not looking up. "I didn't name you."

A few of the onlookers snickered, and Drew clenched his jaw. "Might I ask your name, sir?"

The man shrugged, still not looking up. "Suppose you might. Don't mean I'm giving it out for free."

Drew gave him a cold smile. "You keep it then. I haven't anything smaller than twopence, and I doubt you have enough on you to make change."

The man lifted his stubbled chin. "We weren't all born toffs, you know. Some of us have to earn what we get."

"One needn't be born a gentleman to have good manners. I'm given to understand they cost nothing."

"Oooh, la-de-da," the shabby man mocked. "But I don't know what you have ruffled your feathers over. Ask anyone. Nothing I said was anything but complimentary to the lady. Fine woman, if you ask me. Wouldn't mind having her to tea, eh?"

There was something nastily insinuating in his grin. The eavesdroppers all around laughed, then gasped as Drew seized the man by his shirtfront and hauled him to his feet.

"Gentlemen! Gentlemen, please!" The barman hurried over to the table. "No trouble now. No trouble."

The shabby man shoved Drew's hands away and tugged his coat straight once more. "Don't you worry about that, mate. His type don't have nothing but talk." Again he grinned. "Just maybe that fine woman would be interested in something more, eh?"

Drew shook his head, his breath coming hard and heavy. "Evidently no amount of reason can make a cad into a gentleman. I will put this in terms you can understand then. If I hear of you again making even the slightest mention of my wife in a public house, or anywhere else for that matter, I promise I will deal with you in more than just words."

The man chortled, slapping the table with his hand. "Did

you hear that, lads? He's going to teach me a lesson. Maybe I'll have to write lines and everything."

Drew took a step forward, and the barman immediately put himself in the way.

"Please, sir."

"No need to worry. If our friend here would like to discuss the matter further, I'll be glad to speak to him outside."

"Oh, yeah." The man settled his cap more firmly on his head and wrapped his dingy scarf around his neck. "Lead on, mate. Lead on."

"You'd better ring the p'lice," someone said to the barman.

"No need to trouble them," Drew said.

"Toff's right," the other man muttered, glaring at Drew. "We all know who ends up taking the blame when one of us has a set-to with the gentry. And don't he know it. That quits it for me. I'm not going to hang about in the alley waiting for his like."

Drew opened the door for him. "Perhaps another time."

"You can bank on that, mate. And soon." The shabby man removed his cap and made an elaborate bow before stepping into the darkness of the street.

Drew sat himself at the vacated table, drank his cider in leisurely fashion, and afterward went around to the narrow alleyway at the back of the building. The yellowish bulb above the back door lit the shadowy figure slouching against the grimy brick wall.

"All right then," Drew said, crossing his arms over his chest. "Your punishment is to write five hundred times 'I will not make Drew laugh when he's supposed to be righteously indignant.'"

Grinning, Nick pushed back his battered cap. "I do rather enjoy playing the rogue now and again."

"Comes a bit too naturally, if you ask me."

"Manners," Nick reproved. "And I was so pleased you took the time to telephone me right after you'd visited the murder scene."

"All right, all right. Tell me what you've found out."

Nick exhaled heavily. "Not as much as I'd hoped. I did have a nice chat with one fellow, who seemed more than a bit dodgy. He's definitely got something going on, playing the big man round the pub when he's usually stone broke, standing everyone to drinks. I let him know I'd take it as a favor if he heard of anyone wants a job done, and I wouldn't be too particular what it was so long as it paid."

"And?"

"He allowed I was a good fellow and he wouldn't forget."

Drew frowned. "Not exactly a contract for employment."

"No. And he may well have had no recollection of it once he sobered up, but I can always try again tonight. Or tomorrow."

"Name?"

"Jack Midgley. He has a cottage out on the moor somewhere. Says he's a man-of-all-work, though he says it with a wink and a nod. The word round behind his back is that he makes his living poaching off the local estates. Been here for years and never once caught at it."

"Not born here?"

Nick pulled his coat closer against the October wind and shook his head. "To hear him talk, I'd say Irish, yet he must have come to Yorkshire when he was still a boy. Most of the brogue's worn off him."

"Not much in that to think he'd murder a vicar. From what I can tell, the old man liked his hearth when he wasn't about his pastoral duties. I can't imagine him out on the moor watching for poachers."

"True," Nick said, "but he might have something to do with what's been going on out there. There's no reason to think the murder and the mischief are connected, is there?"

"That mischief's been going on for years now. No deaths, unless you count a couple of lambs." Drew shrugged at Nick's questioning look. "It was made to look like something wild killed them. I'm not so sure about that, however. I suppose there are the requisite legends about a demon hound out on the moor."

"Not that I've heard about so far, but give it a day or two."

"Beaky's gamekeeper, Rhys Delwyn," Drew said. "Says he's looked into it, but he's found nothing."

"Delwyn, eh?"

Nick chuckled, and Drew raised an eyebrow.

"What?"

"The lads at the pub are of two minds about that one, from what I hear. On the one hand, he's all hail-fellow-well-met, buy you a pint and drink it with you."

"And on the other?"

"On the other, they don't care for the idea of him left alone with their wives and daughters."

Drew thought back on when he'd seen Delwyn at the Lodge, when he and Madeline had first arrived. Just the sort of rogue who rarely, if ever, was told no. "Is he attached to anyone in particular at the moment?"

"Not that anyone's said."

Drew saw something more in Nick's expression. "And?"

"Just the usual pub gossip. Some of them say he needn't come into the village if he wants company. I expect there are a number of girls employed at the Lodge who wouldn't object."

Drew narrowed his eyes, not liking what came to mind. "But there wasn't a particular name brought up?"

"No. Are you thinking of anyone specific?"

Drew looked up at the naked lightbulb over the backdoor. It didn't shed much light on the alley's dark corners. "Beaky's wife."

"What? Oh, good heavens, is that what they were smirking over? Are you sure?"

"Not in the least. What exactly did you hear, Nick?"

"I . . . really, it's nothing in particular. More like a secret they all knew and sniggered about whenever Delwyn was mentioned. Poor Beaky. But how do you know?"

"I don't know," Drew said. "I don't know at all. You remember how she was."

Nick looked mildly puzzled. "I do?"

"Oh. You don't know yet, do you? Beaky married Sabrina Prestwick."

Nick whistled under his breath. "So that's where she landed. Well, maybe she's grown up a bit."

"One can hope. Still, Sabrina Prestwick. With Beaky Bloodworth? It boggles the mind."

"I don't know. She and Bunny got on all right."

"Until she decided to break things off without warning. I still don't think the old boy knows why."

Nick chuckled. "Well, he's better off, isn't he? Getting on all right isn't the same as being in love. And if she was just after money, why wouldn't she have stayed with him? At least until they married and divorced and she got a nice settlement. He's much richer than Beaky."

"He's much richer than everyone," Drew admitted. "And I suppose that is a point in her favor. Well, as I said to begin with, I don't know anything. Maybe I'm just making assumptions I have no business making. Still, keep your ears open about

Delwyn and whomever he might be calling on. Just for Beaky's sake. What do you hear about Westings?"

"Nothing much. There's some who think whatever's been happening on the moor is more of the same as when Beaky's uncle was alive. There's others who say it's not the same at all. One old duffer says there's a bluff overlooking the Lodge that's been haunted since the pagans used it, however long ago that was. Swears blue he's seen them up there calling down curses on the lot of us for taking up Christian ways. The others don't pay him much mind, though they do say there have been some strange happenings up there, especially in the past few weeks."

Drew shrugged. "There are always strange happenings on moors, aren't there? Half the books written in England wouldn't exist if it weren't for that."

"Not half, surely."

"Well, if you hear of anything tangible, let me know right away. Any local gossip could come in handy as well." Drew glanced toward the opening of the alleyway. "Perhaps we'd better let you get back inside. No good having someone find us talking. Anything else I should know for now?"

"I'll get word to you should something turn up."

Drew looked at him thoughtfully. "Perhaps it wouldn't hurt if it looked as if we finished our discussion after all. That is, if you're going back inside."

With a sigh, Nick wadded up his cap and stuffed it temporarily into his coat pocket. Then he used both hands to muss his hair and rumple his clothes. Finally he bent down and patted his hands in a muddy puddle and used them to redden his face and soil his shirt more than it already was. That done, he replaced his battered cap and presented himself for inspection.

"Very nice," Drew said, looking him up and down. "But

maybe you ought to roll about on the ground. Just a bit. In case someone happens to look back here, we'd want him to see that pleasantries have indeed been exchanged."

Nick huffed. "I suppose we couldn't both make it look authentic?"

"Come now, old man, you wouldn't want to worry Madeline, would you? And you know it would worry her if I came home looking like . . . well, like you."

Nick scowled but dropped to his knees in the blackish puddle. He threw his shoulder against the grimy brick wall twice and lightly scraped his knuckles against it for good measure.

"Excellent," Drew said. "Nothing barbaric. Just a nice discussion, eh?"

"And you fresh as a daisy. You'd better be off. You don't want anyone from the pub to see you that way."

"Very true. All right, you keep me informed when you can. Where are you staying in case I need to hunt you up?"

"I've taken a garret room at a Mrs. Denton's in Partridge Row." Nick looked slyly pleased with himself. "Under the name Selden."

"You're incorrigible."

"The house is off Trelawney Lane off the high street. Anyone should be able to direct you. I'm sure she must have somewhere around eighteen to twenty-five children, all of them between the ages of one and twelve."

Drew laughed. "All right. If I need you, I'll send a message under the name Stapleton. The more you can find out about this Midgley, the better."

Nick saluted. "Right-o. Best to the missus."

"I'll tell her you're behaving as well as can be expected."

Drew gave Nick a swat on the shoulder and then, making

sure he wasn't being observed, hurried out into the dark street. When he got to the corner, he stepped into the shadows and watched as Nick went back inside the Hound and Hart. Then, turning up his collar against the wind that whipped cold over the moor, he walked toward the lights of the Lodge.

"Explain to me how that's supposed to help?" Madeline demanded. "You said Midgley wasn't even there."

"It's even better that way." Drew warmed his hands at the bedroom fireplace, then pulled her close and kissed her. "Even if Midgley wasn't there to see him, word will no doubt get back to him about the enmity between the London toff and the new ruffian in town. It seems much less like a setup this way, don't you think?"

She sighed. "Oh, I suppose."

"I don't like doing this in the first place, not even as a setup."

"So you've said."

He gave her a stern look. "A lady's good name—"

"Can be sullied only by the lady herself. Besides, it was my idea in the first place."

"We should have thought of a better idea," he grumbled.

"We couldn't think of a better idea." She teased his lower lip with her finger, trying to make him smile. "I can't imagine Nick would say anything outrageously bad anyway."

He chuckled in spite of himself. "It was so mild, I had a hard time being properly incensed when I finally dragged it out of Beaky. And he, poor fellow, was mortified to have to repeat it."

"Beaky's a dear. I'm glad you're looking after him and that you did back in school. Most young boys aren't that considerate, you know."

"I'm not in a position to be beatified quite yet," Drew said, regretting the memory. "Beaky's a stout fellow, believes the best and all that, but I didn't set out to champion him right off. In fact, I was the one who started the lads calling him Beaky, and it wasn't meant as a sign of jolly comradery. Not then at least."

Madeline pursed her lips. "Not nice, darling."

"I know. Never tell him, but at the beginning I stood up for him not because I was kind, but because I wanted to devil that swine Tinker and his toady Pomeroy. They were always bullying the younger boys and anyone they thought they could terrorize. They started in on Nick once, as soon as they found out his father was just a butler, but we soon put a stop to that. It became rather a war between us at that point, and I wasn't about to be bested."

"I'm sure the other boys were grateful, no matter your motive."

"I daresay they were, Beaky most of all. And after a time, I grew genuinely fond of him. He's a good fellow. Good enough to forget our early acquaintance."

"I'm glad," Madeline said. "But now what do we do?"

"Now we let young Mr. Dennison do his work behind the scenes while we carry on in the spotlight and see what comes of it all. How are you and Mrs. Beaky getting on?"

"Well enough. She's definitely one of the smart set. I must seem very naïve to her."

"I wouldn't say that, darling. Unspoilt is a better word. Not jaded." He gave her another brief kiss. "It's rather attractive."

She squeezed him tightly and then pulled away. "Well, even if she does think I'm quaint and provincial, I think we're getting along fine. She's friendly, though she doesn't want to talk about herself much."

"What did the two of you do today?"

"I bought some hideous boots for walking on the moor, and the most delicious yarn. One of the local women spins it and sends it to the shop to sell. I bought all there was."

He feigned horror. "We'll have to hire a lorry to haul it all back home."

"It was only five skeins," she said, scowling, "and they were very reasonable. The lady at the shop said she should have more in the next day or two."

"Then we really will need the lorry."

"Oh, hush, or all you're getting for Christmas is knitted ties."

He shuddered. "Pax, darling. Buy all the yarn you want. I suppose Mrs. Bloodworth is a great knitter, as well."

As he expected, Madeline laughed. "Not at all."

His smile fading, he sat on the upholstered bench at the foot of the bed and let the warmth of the fire seep into his bones. "Do you think she and Beaky get along all right? I mean, truly?"

"You mean do I think she really cares for him?" There was a little pucker between her brows. "It's hard to say yet. I think we all need to get better acquainted, don't you?"

"We should be able to do that to great advantage when the Grays come to dinner Thursday." He pulled her into his lap. "But I'll leave the lonely-hearts column to you, darling. Just keep your eyes open for clues."

Thursday evening was drizzly and cold, and the Grays were late for dinner.

"Come in. Come in," Beaky said when Halford at last showed the couple into the drawing room, and he shook Gray's hand. "We were beginning to worry."

"Terribly sorry," Gray said. "The roads can be tricky in weather like this."

The woman beside him offered a brittle smile. "I believe the problem is not so much with the roads as it is with someone not coming home to dress until nearly seven o'clock."

Gray's mild expression did not change as he shook Drew's hand. "Good evening, Farthering. Do allow me to introduce my wife, Frances. My dear, this is Mr. and Mrs. Drew Farthering."

Drew made a slight bow. "A pleasure, Mrs. Gray."

Madeline took the woman's hand in both of hers. "So good to meet you, Mrs. Gray, Mr. Gray. Do call me Madeline."

Mrs. Gray blinked at her. "You're American, aren't you? Morris didn't tell me."

Madeline gave Mrs. Gray her usual pert grin. "English now. By marriage at least."

"I always wanted to go to America," Gray said, his pale eyes wistful. "All that wide open space and so many different things to see. Palm trees and orange groves and—"

"Do spare us the travelogue, Morris," Mrs. Gray said. "We're keeping everyone waiting as it is."

If Gray was pinked by her gibe, he didn't show it. "I do apologize. Mrs. Bloodworth, I hope everyone's dinner isn't spoilt by my thoughtlessness."

"Of course not, Mr. Gray," Sabrina said, giving him a dazzling smile as she swept up to them in a gown of red and gold that turned her blond hair to flame. She turned to Mrs. Gray. "It's very good of both of you to come on such an awful night. Oh, dear, and it looks as if the rain has ruined your dress. I'm so sorry."

Mrs. Gray wore a gown of green silk, exquisitely cut even if it did appear a bit awkward on her angular frame. Startled, she looked down at the lush fabric and then gave Sabrina a pinched smile.

"It's watered silk."

"Oh, how silly of me." Sabrina took her arm, patting it as she did. "Of course, it's meant to be that way. It's certainly lovely. Do come and have a cocktail. Beaky, do get something for Mr. Gray and then we'll go on in."

Dinner was exquisite, and despite Mrs. Gray's almost-constant annoyance with her husband, reasonably pleasant. They were in the middle of the fish course when Halford came to stand beside Beaky's chair.

"Beg pardon, sir, but Miss Patterson is on the telephone for you."

"That's very odd," Beaky said.

Sabrina frowned. "Good heavens, Beaky, this is hardly the time to deal with village matters. Halford, tell her Mr. Bloodworth is entertaining and will ring her in the morning."

"I have done, madam," the butler said. "She asks Mr. Bloodworth's pardon for the imposition and says she wants only a moment of his time."

"In the morning, Halford." Sabrina's tone did not invite further discussion.

"Very good, madam." The butler bowed and disappeared.

"I hope it's not urgent," Madeline said.

Gray glanced at his wife. "Old Miss Patterson? I shouldn't imagine it is, Mrs. Farthering. Funny she should ring up this late, though, don't you think, Bloodworth? What in the world could she want?"

"Oh, it's probably about the drains or something," Sabrina said.

Madeline gave Beaky a puzzled smile. "Would she call you

about drains? Shouldn't she get a plumber or someone like that?"

"She's never called me about drains before," Beaky said, "but I do own the house she's living in just now. I suppose it could be something of that sort."

"Cheeky to ring up like that," Mrs. Gray said, picking at her fish as if it might have gone bad.

"Do let's talk about something else, Beaky," Sabrina insisted. "You can see to Miss Patterson tomorrow if you must. It's hardly something our guests want to hear about, is it?"

"Quite right, darling. Sorry." Beaky gave her hand a squeeze and earned a faintly annoyed little huff in return.

"Beaky and his people," Sabrina said to the table at large. "I don't know what they would do if he didn't look out for them."

"They don't ask much," Beaky said, his ears growing rather pink, and then he turned to Gray. "Did you ever find out what happened to the things taken from your garage? Drew might want to hear about that as well."

"Another mystery?" Drew asked.

"I doubt it's anything to do with what you're asking after," Gray said. "Just a few things gone missing. I wouldn't be surprised if our chauffeur put them up somewhere and forgot where. It's hardly anything."

"If someone's come onto our property and stolen our things, I think that is *not* hardly anything," Mrs. Gray said. "They'll be in the house next and helping themselves to the silver, I shouldn't wonder. And I swear there's a bottle of wine missing. Cook was keeping it for a French recipe she was keen to try."

"That is troubling," Drew agreed. "Might I ask what all was taken?"

"It was next to nothing," Gray told him. "Some things we had in the car during the summer and then stored in the garage—blankets, an old lantern, two camp chairs. Not worth much, the lot."

"It's not their value that matters," his wife protested. "It's that they were taken at all. I don't like the thought that someone's been lurking about. What if I were to come upon someone like that when I was alone?"

"I don't think it's anyone dangerous, my dear," Gray said. "We can buy new, if you like. Anyone desperate enough to steal that sort of tat ought to have it, hadn't he? And Cook probably put that wine somewhere so it wouldn't accidentally be served, and now she doesn't remember where."

Mrs. Gray's lips were primly tight. "It was those gypsies if you ask me. Can't open your mouth to tell one of them good morning and not risk your eyeteeth."

"Be fair, Frances. They only camped on the moor a night or two. They didn't hurt anything or anyone."

"Because I told them to clear off. What they would have gotten up to if I hadn't seen to it, I can't tell you." She gave the rest of the table an apologetic smile. "I expect they'd have made themselves at home if Morris had had his way about it. Just give the whole place away and not a look back." She sniffed. "I don't know where he'd be if not for me."

Gray looked down into his wine and muttered what sounded like "the south of France."

"Oh, do speak up, Morris, if you mean to say anything at all."

"It was nothing, my dear," he said mildly. "I merely thought you might have given them a chance."

"A chance to rob us blind is all." She turned away from her husband, and her expression became pleasant and indulgent.

"Well, well. Good thing one of us is practical, eh, Mr. Farthering? I expect you're the practical one in your family."

"Not at all, I'm afraid," Drew replied. "I spend my time careering about the country, poking my nose into other people's business and annoying the police. Madeline here's the practical one."

Madeline gave him a cheeky grin. "You haven't had the latest bill from my dressmaker yet."

The conversation shifted to the outrageous cost of nearly everything these days and then to the cost of refurbishing the north wing, which took them through the remainder of dinner and into the drawing room for cards. Not long after, the Grays took their leave.

The three couples walked out toward the Grays' Bentley, but Morris Gray hung back.

"Oh, I say, Farthering?"

Drew slowed beside him while Beaky was settling Mrs. Gray in the passenger seat.

Gray cleared his throat. "I—well, since you are here to investigate, I expect I'd ought to own up."

"Own up?"

Gray looked both amused and embarrassed. "About those things that were taken. The ones the wife claims were stolen by gypsies. Utter nonsense, of course. They merely spent the night on the moor. Their own wagons. Their own food. I daresay they might have gotten away with some water from the stream, but that's the most of it. If they did somehow take the other things, they're more than welcome, as I said. But one thing they didn't get was that bottle of wine. I'm afraid that one was me."

"You?"

Gray nodded. "Frances doesn't like me to drink. That is, besides the one glass at dinner and only if we're in company. But hang it all, sometimes I need a little bit of something. Steady the nerves and that. It's not as if I need to have it."

"No, to be sure," Drew said, not sure at all.

"I usually get something on my own from the village and don't bother the stuff from the kitchen, but I suppose I thought that bottle wouldn't be missed, not just the one time. I should have known better." His shoulders went up in a halfhearted shrug. "Frances never misses anything."

"Perhaps you should let her know," Drew suggested. "Then she wouldn't be worried about intruders lurking about."

"Oh, uh . . . no. No, I think she's all right. Now that she's sent the gypsies off, I don't think she's too worried anymore."

"You know best, I suppose. But the things that were stolen, do you have any theories about that?"

"Silly thing to worry about, isn't it? I don't care about the stuff, and I don't think the gypsies are going to murder us all in our beds, no matter what Frances says."

"Morris!" Mrs. Gray leaned over toward the window on the driver's side of the car. "Do hurry. It's getting colder by the minute."

He looked at the starless sky with a sigh. "Yes, I do believe it is."

He got behind the wheel and, with a final farewell to his host, drove away.

The following morning was bright and sunny with not a cloud in sight. As usual, Sabrina slept in, but Drew and Madeline found Beaky already at the breakfast table, squinting into a newspaper.

"Good morning, old man," Drew called as he picked up a plate from the buffet. "Anything interesting?"

The newspaper rustled down to the table.

"There you are." Beaky's freckles were more prominent than usual against his pale skin. "I have some dreadful news."

Madeline glanced at Drew, taking the chair he pulled out for her.

"What is it?" he asked.

"I'm afraid there's been another murder."

— Seven —

The Burrows was a narrow little house just off the high street, not far from the church.

"This is where she lived?" Drew asked.

"It was, sir." Trenton opened the door and then stepped back to allow Madeline, Drew, and Beaky to go in first. "She was found just there."

His close-set eyes bright and eager, he indicated an overstuffed chair opposite the unlit hearth. It was covered in a fussy floral fabric, the crocheted doily that had no doubt been draped over the back now lying torn on the polished floor. There was no blood. Only the torn doily, a broken teacup, and a disarranged rag rug gave evidence of a struggle. Evidently it didn't take much to snuff out the life of one elderly lady.

"It's not much to go on, I'll grant you," the sergeant said, "but with your experience, sir, it might be you could help us sort things out a bit. We don't have much by way of murder here in Bunting's Nest, and now two in less than a week, well, it's more than we know what to do with."

"I haven't actually—"

The sergeant held up his hand. "It's no use being modest, sir. I've read the accounts about you and your missus, and if Mr. Bloodworth says you're the article, you're the article."

Beaky watched with anxious eyes. "If you could help at all, Drew . . ."

"She's the one who telephoned you last night, isn't she?"

"Yes. Halford said she seemed rather flustered about something. A letter she'd sent."

"A letter?"

Beaky nodded. "She said she'd sent me a letter and then decided it was a foolish matter and called to say I should pay it no mind, that she had merely imagined something fanciful and I needn't worry over it."

"And did the letter come?"

"Not this morning," Beaky said. "Not that I'm aware of."

Drew looked around the shabby little room, feeling more than a bit out of his depth. "Tell me about her."

"A Miss Millicent Patterson, spinster, aged seventy-three," the sergeant read from his notebook. "Was in service as a nursery maid for a good long while, from when she left school until she retired some ten or fifteen years ago. Had a nephew in Caerphilly, another in New York City. No other family to speak of."

"Did she always live in Bunting's Nest?"

"Born here, as I understand, sir, and lived in Bunting's Nest a while before going down to London to work. Then came back about six months ago."

There was a bit of unfinished needlepoint in the basket next to the chair, an old-fashioned picture of roses and cherubs, but the colors were off in several places.

"Did she have poor eyesight?" Madeline asked, fingering a skein of rose-colored wool.

"She wore spectacles, ma'am," the sergeant said. "I'm sorry to say they were broken when she was—well, during the incident."

"And who found her?" Drew asked.

"It was Mrs. Pence come with her laundry early this morning. More to check up on her, as she generally did. She wondered why the milk was still on the step, seeing as Miss Patterson was always early up. Found the poor old lady slid down off her chair and onto the floor, huddled over like a broken doll." The sergeant frowned contemplatively. "Neck broke, of course. They get brittle at that age, you see, and it doesn't take much. The doctor says it was likely done the evening before. And her old tabby cat was sitting pressed up close to her, just as sad as if she knew what had happened."

"I trust the cat's been seen to."

"Oh, yes, sir. Mrs. Pence took her. Said it was the least she could do for Miss Patterson now she was past being helped."

Drew nodded and looked around once more. "There wouldn't seem to be a financial motive for the killing."

"She hadn't two beans," Beaky said. "Just a small pension." He seemed reluctant to go on.

"A pension?" Drew asked.

"For service, you know. She tended rather a lot of children in her time, I reckon. Seems only right for one of those families to look out for her when she was past doing that sort of work."

She hadn't been Beaky's nanny, Drew knew that much. He remembered too vividly the stories the boy had told about the very strict Mrs. Bowden and her threats to pinch his head off if he made so much as a peep. Could this Miss Patterson have once been at Westings?

"She wasn't Morris Gray's nanny, was she?"

"That was before my time," Beaky said. "She might have been. But old Mr. Gray's too mean with his money to pay anyone for no work. I, uh, happen to know she worked somewhere else before she was pensioned off."

Again he hesitated.

"What aren't you telling me?" Drew asked finally. "Who was paying her?"

"Well, actually . . ." Color flamed into Beaky's face. "I was."

Madeline's eyes widened, but she didn't say anything.

Drew glared at Beaky. "You? Why? You had the Bowden, I remember it distinctly."

"I did. But when Sabrina's father passed on, I took over the payments for him. We couldn't just let Miss Patterson go to the workhouse, you know."

"Sabrina's . . ." It all clicked into place. "She was your wife's nanny. I see."

"We had her brought up from London, Sabrina and I, once we were married. She was in a wretched little flat in Ealing." Beaky looked faintly embarrassed. "I suppose I ought to have given her more. I—I never thought about it, to tell you the truth. I never met her, and I'd never been round here to . . . to see how she lived."

Drew clasped his shoulder. "Perhaps it isn't much, but the place seems cozy enough."

"I think it's very sweet," Madeline said. "She had her cat and her sewing, and it doesn't sound as if she was friendless and alone."

"No, ma'am," Trenton put in. "I'm given to understand four or five of the old ladies played whist together every Thursday afternoon. Other than that, she went to church, and sometimes she and the ladies would go to tea at Milbury's in the village, but that was all."

"Not much reason for anyone to kill her." Drew examined the floral chair, the faint signs that Miss Patterson had ever even been there. "Any theories, sergeant?"

"None, I'm afraid. That's why Mr. Bloodworth thought you might be able to help." There was something almost apologetic in the officer's mild expression. "We don't have this sort of thing happen much, not in Bunting's Nest."

Drew nodded. "I suppose her nephews would inherit whatever it was she had to pass on."

"Right, sir, but I wouldn't much think they'd have done it. Not rich men, I understand, but comfortable enough. In business, families of their own, all that. Wrote now and again, Mrs. Pence says. Out of duty, I suppose, but it couldn't have benefitted either of them to kill her."

"Rather far to come, too," Beaky added. "At least for the one in America."

"Still, one can't know for certain, I always say. Might be some family grievance that's been festering all these many years." The sergeant's eyes brightened once again. "I did have a thought, sir, which I shared with Mr. Bloodworth earlier on. I'd like to know what you think of it."

Drew gave Madeline a subtle wink. "Certainly. You never know what's going to spark an idea."

"Just as I always say." The officer gave Beaky a nod. "I thought that if it were to be one of the nephews, the one from America most like, seeing as they have peculiar ways he might have picked up, he might have come over in disguise and strangled her in the night and then slipped off quiet as you please back to New

York to wait for the sad news. Mightn't he, sir? I say it's well within the realm of possibility."

"I suppose it is." Drew glanced at Beaky, who only shrugged in reply. "But why would he do it? If she had nothing to leave him, and that seems rather evident, why go to all that bother?"

The sergeant sighed. "Just a thought, sir. One doesn't know for certain in these matters."

"Very true. Very true. My advice on that line of investigation is for you to contact the police where the two nephews live to see if they're unaccounted for at the time of the murder. That ought to settle it for you posthaste."

"Yes, sir, and we've done that. The younger one, the one in Caerphilly, has been the speaker at a convention of dentists all this week. Seen by a good three hundred people during that time and was giving a speech on proper oral hygiene at the assumed time of his aunt's death. We're waiting to hear on the other one. That's why I thought you might want to hear my theory. Might not be so fanciful as it first seems."

"Well, you keep it handy," Drew said. "If it turns out we need it, we'll ask for the loan of it with thanks."

There was little to see at the house, and before long Drew, Madeline, and Beaky were headed back to the Lodge.

"Were you going to tell us?" Drew asked after they had driven a few minutes in silence.

"What?"

"About this Miss Patterson having been Mrs. Bloodworth's nurse and you being the one paying her pension?"

Beaky gaped at him. "Of course I was. Why shouldn't I? We've nothing to hide."

"Then why didn't you tell us straight off?"

"I didn't think of it, to be honest. It's unsettling enough to have someone in one's own village murdered, let alone two, but that's nothing to do with me or my wife."

"She was Sabrina's nurse in London?" Madeline asked.

"Yes. Until she went off to school," Beaky said. "Sabrina's father pensioned Miss Patterson off after that, and when he passed on, it seemed only logical to move her back up here. The house has been in our family for ages, but it had been standing empty for some months before. It seemed the perfect solution for everyone to settle her there."

"Until now," Drew reminded him.

When they returned to the Lodge, Sabrina was waiting for them at the front door.

"Patty's dead, is she?" She blew out a curling stream of cigarette smoke. "It's too bad. She was never very interesting, but she was generally kind. I'm sorry."

"Would you like to talk about it?" Madeline said, sympathy in her gentle expression.

Sabrina scoffed. "It's not as if we were close, you know. I'm sorry she's dead. It's an awful thing to happen to anyone, but I can't say I'm terribly cut up over it. Come tell me what you found out, and I'll show you the new gown I got for the Mayfield bash next month." She hurried Madeline up the front stairs.

Beaky shook his head, watching them go. "Apart from when she went to see if Miss Patterson was well settled in the house this spring, I don't think she'd seen the woman since she went off to school." Once again, his ears and cheeks had reddened. "I'm sure she doesn't mean to come across as unfeeling."

"Of course not," Drew said as he followed Beaky into the study.

Beaky immediately pounced on the stack of mail on his desk, rifling through it until he came across one addressed in an old-fashioned, spidery sort of script. On one corner, in heavier strokes, the letter was marked *Personal and Confidential.* He slipped a finger under the flap and took out a folded piece of notepaper.

"She was just like poor old Miles. Never harmed a fly. Hardly someone anyone would bother with, if you ask me. Who'd kill either of them?" He opened the paper and scanned it. "I'm sure neither of them had been out making mischief on the moor in the middle of the night. The idea of their taking a lamb and . . ." He paused, his brow furrowing.

"What is it?" Drew asked.

Beaky handed the note to him. "What a perfect swine I am."

It was the letter, the one Miss Patterson had called about the night before, the one she had wanted Beaky to disregard. Drew read it.

The Burrows, Bunting's Nest, Yorkshire
12th October, 1934

Dear Mr. Bloodworth,

I am reluctant to trouble you, but I feel I cannot repay your continued kindness to me by keeping from you something that concerns you intimately. I have debated for some while whether or not it is my place to speak of such a delicate and potentially damaging matter, but if I do not, especially in light of recent events, it seems to me it would be a greater wrong than keeping silent.

This is not something I can trust to a letter or a telephone call. Please do me the favor of calling upon me at your earliest convenience in this matter of great importance.
Until then, I am

Yours faithfully,
Millicent Patterson

Beaky looked miserable. "I should have returned her call. No, I should have taken it at the time instead of putting her off and then completely forgetting about it. The poor woman."

Drew scanned the letter again. "What do you think it means?"

"I just don't know." Beaky dropped onto the straight-backed chair near the desk, shoulders slumped. "I hardly knew the woman. What could she have wanted to talk about that involves me intimately?"

"And the bit about recent events?"

Beaky shrugged, looking as bewildered and helpless as he once had when trying to explain to the French master how an indecent translation of Rabelais had ended up in his copybook.

Drew paced for a moment, thinking. "I have to assume Miss Patterson's murder and the vicar's are related, wouldn't you?"

"In a place like Bunting's Nest? I daresay it is. Two murders within days of each other? They must be linked somehow, but how? I mean, she went to St. Peter's, naturally, but most everyone does. I don't think there's anything in that."

"Doesn't narrow it down much, eh?" Drew said, and Beaky's grave expression did not change.

"I'm hanged if I know what she could have wanted to talk to me about. Why me? If it had to do with the parish or the church, why should she have told me about it in particular?"

"You were supporting her," Drew said. "Perhaps she thought you were the most logical one to come to if she needed help."

"But she didn't say it was to do with her. She said it was to do with me. *Intimate*, *delicate*, and *damaging* were her words."

Drew nodded, stopping to stare out of the mullioned windows that overlooked the drive and the canary-yellow Austin Ten parked there. Intimate. Delicate. Damaging. He didn't like what he was thinking, but he could hardly think anything else. No wonder the woman had changed her mind about talking to Beaky about it. It wasn't her place any more than it was Drew's, but still, a man ought to know, oughtn't he?

"What are you thinking?" Beaky asked after a bit.

Drew shook his head.

"No, there's something, Drew. I still remember when we were at Eton and you'd get that look. You know something or think you do."

"I don't know," Drew admitted. "But I can't help but wonder."

"What?"

Drew didn't turn. He didn't want to see Beaky's face just now. "I . . . well, you know how it is, especially in these small villages. People talk. It doesn't take anything sometimes, especially when there's not much else to do."

Beaky snorted softly. "'Enter Rumor, painted full of tongues,' eh?"

"Exactly. And when someone new comes along, especially someone privileged and young and beautiful, well, there has to be something to wonder about. And if there's the slightest basis for conjecture . . ." Drew turned, looking at his friend at last. Beaky's face was taut, the freckles strewn across it stark against its pallor.

"What are you saying?"

"Nothing, old man. Just wondering what this Miss Patterson might have thought. Or heard."

"About Sabrina?" Beaky's voice was low, strained. "Are you saying she wanted to tell me something about Sabrina?"

"I'm only trying to reason it out. From what the lady wrote in that note, it seems whatever she wanted to say had something to do with you specifically. Something personal." Drew managed a smile. "It's rather cliché, isn't it? But I suppose it's human nature that scandal is the first thing that springs to mind."

Beaky gave a grudging nod. "Might be."

Drew steeled himself. "I have to ask you, have you ever heard anything? Ridiculous as it might be, has any gossip gotten back to you about your wife? Anything at all?"

"Oh, good heavens, Drew." Beaky's pale face was purplish now. "Of course I have. Did you think a girl like Sabrina could suddenly show up here looking the way she does and be mistress of the largest estate in the county and there not be talk?"

"I understand that. But I would think this Miss Patterson would as well. If she spent most of her life looking after the children of the gentry, living in their homes and everything that entails, she had to have spent a great deal of time ignoring baseless gossip. If she went so far as to write to you about this, she had to have seen or heard something that made her think you needed to know."

"If she did, I couldn't tell you what it might be. I've never heard anything that was remotely believable."

The hardness in his eyes and the set of his jaw dared Drew to question the statement. "But what have you heard?"

Beaky threw up both hands. "Oh, monstrous, ludicrous things."

"Tell me. About her and Delwyn?"

"Why him?" Beaky demanded.

"He'd be the obvious choice, wouldn't he? Handsome. Brooding and mysterious. Welsh. More than a few of the fair sex are fascinated by the Heathcliff type, aren't they? The rogue only the love of a good woman can tame?"

"Perhaps."

Drew nodded. "I don't know the man, but I hear he has a reputation for being something of a Lothario."

"That's as may be," Beaky said. "What's that got to do with my wife?"

"I'm not saying anything except perhaps they were seen talking. In the village or even out on the moor. Maybe he was even bold enough to approach her."

"Are you saying Miss Patterson was out on the moor?"

"No, of course not. I'm just saying, no matter how innocently it might have started—"

"I think you had better stop right there, Drew. If you're going to make assumptions about my wife based on—based on nothing, that's where I must strongly object."

"No offense meant, Beaky, old man." Drew gave him an apologetic grin, knowing it would be no good if he were ordered off the estate before he'd even started to investigate. "Obviously you know Sabrina much better than I do. But if she weren't your wife, you'd say I wasn't much of a detective if I didn't ask."

Beaky merely looked stern.

"Admit it now. You know you would."

Finally Beaky cracked a smile. "I suppose it had to be asked. But you're right. I know Sabrina better than you do. She's a good egg, even if she does try a bit too hard to be modern and sophisticated. Be fair now and you'll see."

"Can't ask for more than that," Drew said, clapping him on the shoulder.

He would be fair. He just hoped he wouldn't have to hurt his old friend in getting at the truth.

Once Sabrina had shown Madeline her new gown, a dazzling confection of shell-pink taffeta, she insisted that Madeline come walking with her and Raphael again.

"It's so nice to be able to talk to someone like this," she said as they tramped along. "I didn't realize how much I missed it until you came to visit."

Raphael sniffed and rooted in the heather at her feet, making satisfied little snuffling noises as they walked. Madeline looked out over the endless fog-shrouded emptiness in front of them and smiled faintly.

"I'm glad we could come. I've always wanted to see Yorkshire. I suppose the Brontës are to blame."

Sabrina's mouth twisted into her habitual smirk. "I never liked Brontë. The moor's depressing enough by itself without reading about unlikable people."

Madeline chuckled. "You mean Heathcliff and Cathy. They were rather unhappy, weren't they?"

"And Rochester. He was beastly to Jane and didn't at all care."

Madeline didn't respond right away, and for a moment there was only the sound of their boots on the muddy pathway.

"I always felt rather sorry for him," she said at last. "He'd been treated very badly by his family when he was young. I think he felt he deserved to do as he pleased, right or wrong, to have the woman he loved."

Sabrina looked far into the distance, silent, and then she

frowned. "Come along, Raphael. There is nothing particularly interesting about that rock."

The dog ignored her and finally routed out a startled and angry lapwing, but there was nothing he could do but bark and leap at the bird as it flew out of sight.

"I'm sure the moor is glorious in the spring and summer," Madeline said after she had brought Raphael to heel again and they'd gone a bit farther. "I'd love to see the heather in bloom. But you're new to Yorkshire, I take it. London?"

"Oh, yes. I lived there until Beaky and I married. There's always so much to do in London, nightclubs and theatres and cinemas. I thought it would be nice to go to the country where it was quiet."

Madeline looked around, breathing deeply of the cold, bracing air. "It's wild, beautiful and untouched."

"But it's *so* quiet." Sabrina looked behind them suddenly and moved a little closer. "I heard something in the north wing again last night."

"You did?"

"I told Beaky about it, but he said he hadn't heard anything and that I must have dreamt it."

"I think—" Madeline stopped, looking at her for a moment before plunging ahead. "I think we should take a look ourselves."

Sabrina blinked at her, and then a wicked grin crossed her face. "Really?"

"We'll have to wait till the boys are gone and we'll have to be extra careful. We don't want to crash through a floor or something."

Sabrina snorted. "Beaky's had men looking in there several times. There wasn't any crashing, not even once."

"So?" Madeline raised an eyebrow. "Shall we?"

"Definitely. So long as it's during the day." A flicker of wariness then came to Sabrina's eyes. "I sometimes feel as if there's no one else in the whole world when I'm out here. And sometimes . . ." Her voice dropped lower. "Sometimes I'm sure there's someone watching me. Following me. Especially when it's foggy like this."

Madeline felt a tingling down her spine. "Have you ever actually seen anyone out here? Or any*thing*?"

"Not really, no," Sabrina said. "Just a light out in the middle of nowhere some nights. Beaky says it's nothing and I shouldn't worry."

"Maybe you shouldn't come out alone."

Sabrina looked faintly horrified. "And stay penned up in the house all day? I'd go stark staring mad, I promise you. Besides, Raphael needs his walk, don't you, my angel?"

Hearing his name, the little terrier gave her a panting doggie smile and then led them on across the rocks.

"Maybe Beaky could walk with you until they find out what's going on," Madeline suggested. "Have you asked him?"

"Beaky? Good heavens, no. He'd want to chatter the whole time, and that would spoil everything. How can I think or even breathe with him standing right there every minute?" Sabrina looked very intently for a moment, and then that smirk returned to her lips. "We get along well, Beaky and I, but in small doses." She put her arm through Madeline's, picking up the pace. "You know how it is. Familiarity and contempt. I always think it wise to keep a little mystery in a relationship. Men are so easily bored, don't you think?"

"I wouldn't like to think I had to be constantly entertaining," Madeline said. "Not with Drew."

"You'd better not let that one slip through your fingers, my dear. He'd be snapped up like French couture at the church jumble sale." She looked around and then frowned. "Where's Raffie got to? Raffie? Raphael!"

They reached the top of a rise, bare rock but for some wiry grasses that grew out of the crevices. Below, the moor stretched out before them, gray and white and brown. It was shrouded in mist, though she could still make out the Lodge and, farther on, the shops and houses of Bunting's Nest huddled cozily together, the smoke from their chimneys drifting up and quickly lost in the fog and the slate sky. There was no sign of the dog.

"Raphael!"

"What's that?" Madeline asked, pointing to a large dark shape a good distance beyond the village, its windows mere pinpoints of light. "Is that Westings?"

"Yes." Sabrina was silent for a moment, and Madeline wondered if she was laughing to herself. "They're a rather pitiful pair, aren't they? The Grays?"

Pitiful was perhaps the perfect word for that union, but as she had told Drew, "It's hard to say what makes someone attracted to someone else."

Sabrina's mouth twisted slightly at the corner as she continued to scan the area for her little terrier. "I don't know how they were when they first met, but I can't imagine two people less suited for one another." She put her hands on her hips. "Raphael, you are a very naughty boy! Anyway, if I have to hear him sigh over the beauties of sunny Italy one more time, I'll—"

She broke off with a low gasp. Before Madeline could ask her what was wrong, she heard it herself, a shuffling sound in the dead undergrowth. She made her voice as sternly imperious as she was able. "Who's there?"

There was perfect silence.

"Who's there?" Madeline demanded again. "I know there's someone there."

Sabrina shrank closer to Madeline and gave an almost inaudible shriek when a dark figure stepped out of the shadow of a craggy bluff as if it had risen, incorporeal, from the moor itself.

— Eight —

You oughtn't to walk out here by yourselves," the man said. "You might lose your way and never get back."

He stood there grinning at them, bandy-legged and barrel-chested, his unshaven face ruddy and lined, his hawklike nose bent at the bridge and pushed to one side, and his gimlet eyes sharp under half-closed lids. A greasy lock of black hair fell over his forehead.

Sabrina drew herself up, glaring at him. "What are you doing out here, Jack Midgley? This is Lodge property."

He tugged the brim of his battered tweed hat, not looking the least bit respectful. "No harm meant, missus. I musta lost my way. Or maybe you've lost yours." He looked both women up and down. "It's easy to get lost out here these foggy days, and I know my way better than most." He narrowed his eyes. "You ladies had best stay off the moor. There are things out here you don't want to know about."

"Mrs. Bloodworth's dog got away," Madeline said, making her tone just short of contemptuous and trying her best not to shrink away from him. "He's a white terrier. Have you seen him?"

"A terrier?" Midgley gave a humorless bark of a laugh. "Why, a little dog like that wouldn't be no more than a mouthful for whatever might get him."

"What do you mean?" Madeline demanded.

He leered at her, his heavy-lidded eyes bright with malice. "Furrin, are you? Likely you never heared talk of the barghest. Take care you don't meet him. Unawares like."

"What do you mean?" she breathed.

"Don't listen to him," Sabrina said. "He's drunk, like as not."

"You'd best go on home, Mrs. Bloodworth. You're not likely to see your little dog again." He gave her an impertinent wink. "Might even find an unexpected visitor a-lyin' across your threshold when you get there."

"That's a nasty thing to say," Sabrina snapped, though there were sudden tears in her eyes. "You know there's nothing out here."

"Just as you say, missus." Midgley tugged the brim of his hat again. "Just as you say."

"We'd better go back to the house," she said to Madeline, pulling her away from him and toward the way they'd been going.

Midgley snorted. "You'll be a long time getting there, ma'am, if you go that way."

Madeline glared at him, realized she was turned around, not knowing if he was telling the truth or if he might just be nasty enough to steer them wrong in the fog. He must have read the thought in her eyes because he grinned again.

"That way, ma'am." He pointed behind them. "You can just see the Lodge chimneys down below."

Madeline squinted into the dimness, not sure at first if she saw anything at all, but then she made out a billow of smoke, barely thicker than the fog itself, and then the dark shape of the house. She took Sabrina's arm.

"This way. Don't worry. Raphael is probably already in the kitchen having his supper."

Sabrina hurried alongside her, but she glanced back at Midgley. "You'd just better clear off our property. If anything's happened to my dog—"

"Come on," Madeline hissed, and she could have sworn she heard the man snickering behind them.

They trudged on in the wet for a few minutes, and everything was silent but for the rustle of dead grass and their own panting breath. Then Madeline looked back again. Midgley was nowhere to be seen.

"Do you think he was following us?"

Sabrina hurried her pace. "I don't know."

"But who is he?"

"The devil, if you ask me." Sabrina's eyes darted from side to side as she stalked forward. "Come on, Raffie. Where are you?"

Madeline scurried after her, almost slipping. "Sabrina."

Sabrina didn't turn, didn't slow. "He's just a poacher. I'm tired of him nosing around where he doesn't belong. It's too bad they don't allow flogging anymore. Raphael! Come on, boy! Come on!" She stopped, listening, then called again. "Come on, Raphael!"

For a moment there was only silence, followed by a faint yip ahead of them. Madeline wasn't sure she'd heard it at first, but then it was repeated, and Sabrina caught her breath.

"Raffie? Come on, boy! Come on!"

They hurried toward the sound, almost at the house again,

when someone stepped around the corner of one of the out-buildings.

"Mrs. Bloodworth."

It was the gamekeeper, with the dog squirming in his arms and whining to get to Sabrina.

"I found him headed back to the Lodge," Delwyn said, handing him over. "He looked as if something frightened him, but he doesn't seem hurt. I thought you ladies might have lost your way in the fog."

"Raffie," she scolded as the dog whimpered and wriggled and licked all over her face, and then she hugged him close. "You're a naughty, naughty boy."

"Thank you," Madeline said. "We were worried about him. He bolted before we knew it."

Delwyn's dark eyes flicked toward Sabrina. "Then something did frighten him."

Sabrina tossed her head. "I thought it was your job to keep poachers off our land. What's Midgley doing out there, I'd like to know?"

"Midgley? That—" Delwyn snapped his mouth shut and glanced at Madeline. "Beg pardon, ma'am, I didn't know he was about. Where did you see him? On Lodge property?"

"Up on Merlin Hill." Sabrina lifted her chin, mouth taut. "That was Lodge property last I heard."

"Yes, ma'am," the gamekeeper said with a sullen duck of his head.

"Then why is a notorious poacher allowed to run wild all over it?"

"I do my best, ma'am. Lodge property covers a lot of acres."

"Then maybe I should tell my husband to engage a game-keeper who can handle the job."

For a moment, Delwyn stood with his lips pressed tightly together, saying nothing. "You should do as pleases you, Mrs. Bloodworth, ma'am," he said at last. "I'm only a hired man and it's not my place to say."

"Is he dangerous, Mr. Delwyn?" Madeline asked when Sabrina's only reply was a disdainful sniff. "I mean, he wouldn't actually hurt anyone, would he? He's just a poacher."

"It's hard to say what a man might do, Mrs. Farthering. But I'd be happy to know you ladies weren't going out on the moor alone anymore. At least until we know who's doing what. It's not safe going out there. It's not wise." He fixed his eyes on Sabrina until she was forced to look away, and then he turned to Madeline again. "It's not wise."

"I want to know," she said. "What's out there?"

Sabrina's eyes widened, and she clutched her dog more closely. "It's all old wives' tales. I told Midgley and I'll tell you, Rhys Delwyn, there's nothing out there. Nothing that hasn't always been out there. Nothing you can't see in the daylight as well as during the nighttime."

Delwyn nodded slowly, dark eyes hooded. "I daresay, ma'am, but that doesn't make them any less dangerous."

"Then it's your job to see to them, isn't it? Come on, Madeline. It's time for Raphael's dinner."

Sabrina swept into the house without another word.

"Good afternoon, Mr. Delwyn," Madeline said, and she scurried after her.

Delwyn tugged his cap. "Ma'am."

"There you are." Drew padded down the back stairs and into the kitchen and took Madeline into his arms. He hadn't wanted her to go out in this weather in the first place. "You're freezing. Come by the fire and get warm. I was about to come looking for you two. Where's Sabrina?"

"Looking after her dog. He got away from us, and I thought we'd never find him." She shivered against him. "I can see why she'd start to feel like the place is haunted. It's almost like a nightmare out there in this weather, one of those where you're trying to get somewhere or trying to find something and you never can. I don't know what frightened Raphael, but I'm sure it was something besides his imagination. And then this horrible man just popped up out of nowhere and said—"

"Wait a minute." He turned her face up to him. "Who popped up?"

"I don't know. A poacher. Sabrina said his name was Jack Midgley."

Drew frowned. "Midgley was out there? What did he say?"

She wriggled away from him so she could hold her hands over the fire. "Not much. Just that Sabrina and I should stay off the moor, and that if Raphael ran away, something had probably already eaten him. It was nasty of him, even if Mr. Delwyn did say almost the same thing. Not about the dog, of course."

"Delwyn was there, too? You have been busy."

"No, he wasn't there when we saw Midgley. Delwyn was later. He'd found Raphael and was coming to look for us."

"And he told you to stay off the moor, as well?"

Madeline nodded. "A bit more respectfully than Midgley did. I'm afraid Sabrina wasn't very—"

"Wasn't very polite?" Sabrina stalked into the room, a freshly lit cigarette in hand. "Wasn't very gracious? To our gamekeeper?"

"I was going to say you weren't very happy about Midgley being over there. What did you call it, Merlin Hill?"

Sabrina looked wary for a moment, and then she laughed half under her breath. "Yes. That's the rocky hill that overlooks the house. Beaky tells me it used to be some sort of high place for the pagans. Gives me the creeps. I don't know what Midgley was doing up there, but something needs to be done about him." She looked at Drew almost defiantly. "And she's right about Delwyn, too. I wasn't polite, and I wasn't gracious. He's an insolent dog, if you ask me. Thinks he's God's gift, and everyone in skirts should be throwing themselves at his feet."

Drew glanced at Madeline, reading mild surprise in her expression. Clearly she didn't agree with Sabrina's assessment of the man.

Sabrina paced in front of the hearth, puffing on her cigarette. Then she managed a brittle smile. "Why don't you two go into the drawing room? I'll see the cook about our tea. Won't be a minute."

"Lovely. Thank you," Drew said, tucking Madeline's arm into his own. "Come along, darling."

He escorted her into the hallway that led to the main part of the house. They'd walked about halfway to the drawing room before he took a look behind them.

"'The lady doth protest too much, methinks,'" he quoted, voice low.

"Well, I didn't think he was anything but respectful and trying to be helpful."

"So why should she tear into him like that?"

Madeline pursed her lips. "I think she was scared. I know I was."

He wrapped her in his arms and pressed a fervent kiss into her hair. "I'm glad nothing happened. Please, darling, until we know what's happening, couldn't you stay a bit closer to the

122

Lodge?" He thought he felt her giggling against him and turned her face up to him. "Please? For me?"

She looked around, making sure they were still alone, and then touched her lips to his. "For you."

That evening after dinner, Drew borrowed Beaky's Bentley and went again to the Hound and Hart. He found the game-keeper at a table with four other men.

"Good evening, gentlemen. Delwyn."

"Mr. Farthering." The Welshman's eyes narrowed. "Was there something you wanted?"

"A moment of your time, if I may. Will you join me?"

His friends looked at Drew warily, but Delwyn only winked at them. "Won't be half a tick, lads, and then I'll tell you about the trout I caught back in '29. Long as your arm, I swear." They jeered at him good-naturedly as he followed Drew to an empty table and made himself comfortable.

"What'll you have?" Drew asked.

There was a flare of belligerence in the gamekeeper's eyes. "So please you, Mr. Farthering. I'd have thought you'd do your drinking up at the Lodge."

"I'm not much of one for drink, to tell the truth," Drew said, taking the seat opposite him. "But I'm not averse to an evening spent in good company."

Delwyn laughed softly. "Nothing like the devil's brew to loosen tongues, eh? Well, the pump is well-primed. What would you like to know? There's nothing much I don't see or hear about round these parts."

"Looks as if I've come to the right place, then."

The gamekeeper gave him an almost-regal nod.

"How is it you ended up here?" Drew asked. "You can't deny the Welsh in your voice."

"Nor would I," Delwyn said, his accent suddenly more pronounced than usual. "God didn't make a truer, wilder, more beguiling place in all His green earth for a man to live and die."

"And yet you left it."

"My mother came back to her people when my father died." The fierce passion in the swarthy face faded. "I was a boy yet, and when I got older, I had her to look after. And after her there was . . ." He shrugged negligently. "I've lived here near fifteen years. It would be a strange thing if I hadn't any attachments by now."

"Attachments that can't leave Yorkshire?"

"Or won't," Delwyn said.

"Attachments with their own attachments." Drew nodded. "I see."

"Do you now?" The gamekeeper's eyes gleamed with dark humor. "Do you indeed?"

A cheer from the other side of the room broke the moment.

"The very man!" someone shouted, and they all gathered round a weathered, stoop-shouldered fellow with lank black hair and a ferretish look to him. Beside him was the rogue Tom Selden. Drew made sure not to look his way, but later he would have to find the time to meet with "Tom" to hear about what he'd discovered so far.

"If there's mischief on the moor," Delwyn said, leaning closer to Drew as the ferretish man ordered a round for his friends, "he's the one behind it."

"That's Midgley, is it?" Drew studied him a moment. "Seems he's everyone's darlin' just now."

"Oh, to be sure. You can buy any number of friends with fourpence."

"He must do well for himself if he can afford that many friends."

Delwyn's eyes narrowed again. "Sure sign he's up to something. Usually he hasn't two bob to keep each other company. Mostly he don't get a drink unless someone takes pity on him or just wants him to go away. But I'd just about swear in church that if there's something bad going on, he's back of it somewhere."

"Such as what?"

Delwyn shook his head. "That's something I can't say. He might be more rotten than last week's fish, but he's a sly devil. The whole county knows he makes his living poaching from Lodge property and from Westings', but he's never once left so much as a whisper behind him." He took a deep drink of his ale and made a wry face. "I spent a whole month one summer determined I'd have him, and what do you think?"

"Nothing?"

"Not hide, hair, nor feather. Not Jack Midgley." Delwyn darted a glance toward the boisterous group at the bar that surrounded the man. "Why, butter wouldn't melt in his mouth, he was that cool. 'Come inside, Rhys,' he'd tell me. 'Have some tea or stay to supper. It's chicken done up in a pie today.' And I knew it weren't no more a chicken than I am, but pheasant and grouse and whatever else he'd took from Lodge land, but by then there were no proving it, and he knew it. I've been near a year trying to catch him out for all the good it's done."

On the other side of the room, Midgley cursed the fog. "Well as I know the moor, hang me if I didn't end up more than a mile out of my way today. I wonder I didn't go off Merlin Hill, it was so hard to see. Never know what you might see in such weather." He smirked in the general direction of Drew's table. "Or who."

"There's worse as happens at sea," one older gent said. "I recall a time back in '87—"

A groan went up from the others, along with some indulgent catcalls as the man launched into his well-worn story.

Drew shifted his attention back to the gamekeeper. "I understand I am in your debt."

Delwyn looked momentarily puzzled, and then he shrugged. "Not really. Though Mrs. Farthering might be wise to stay off the moor on days like this. Mrs. Bloodworth as well, though she's not one to take advice." His mouth twisted into a sneer. "Not from the likes of me anyway."

"She does seem rather determined to have her own way," Drew said. "What do you think she might run into out there? Or perhaps I should ask, what *did* she run into out there?"

Delwyn snorted. "There's nothing out there. Nothing that's not perfectly ordinary."

"No hound?"

"Foolishness. All of it. Folk like to scare one another with tales of ghosts and demons. Always have."

"My wife says Midgley mentioned a barghest."

The gamekeeper nodded. "That's what they call him round here, the demon hound. Sometimes he's headless. Sometimes he's invisible altogether and rattling chains. Haunting the crossroads where the gibbets used to stand. Or where murders were done. Particularly fond of strangers wandering the moor at night."

"I see."

Delwyn rolled his eyes. "Utter rubbish."

"I don't doubt my wife when she says they heard something following them."

"I won't argue the point with you, sir. I found them afterwards and couldn't say what they might have seen or heard by then. But if there was something, it's likely got a reasonable explanation."

"Such as?"

"Might have been Baxter. He was old Mr. Bloodworth's mastiff, big as a child's pony and black as night. Ran off after the gentleman passed on and been wild on the moor since. I haven't been able to catch the rogue, and he's a wily one. If Mrs. Bloodworth's little terrier had wandered into his path, there mightn't be anything left but a handful of white fur and the collar."

"You've seen it?" Drew asked.

"A time or two," Delwyn said with a frown. "From a distance, and that's months ago. He wasn't letting me near if he could help it. He never had much use for anyone besides the old master even at the best of times."

"And that's what started the tales of a demon hound on the moor?"

Delwyn smirked. "I'd wager those have been around a bit longer. At least since that Sherlock Holmes fellow's tale got about. Probably before. This wasn't always a God-fearing land. Perhaps it isn't yet."

"How about you?"

"Me?" Delwyn laughed, but there was a flush of color in his swarthy face. "Nah. Interferes with my drinking, eh?" He drained his mug and thumped it on the table. "Mr. Jenkins, if you please."

"Same again?" the barman called back. "Right you are."

Delwyn grinned at Drew, a certain boyish mischievousness in his usually brooding expression. "Drinking and other things."

"Like Mrs. Bloodworth?"

Delwyn sniggered at that. "You want to lose me my job."

"Not I, I can assure you. That's left up to your own wise choices. Or lack of them."

"Mrs. Bloodworth." Delwyn's mouth twisted up on one side. "Nothing soft about her. Still, who'd say no to that if asked?"

"And were you? Asked, I mean."

The gamekeeper grinned slyly. "A man ought never tell tales of a woman, sir. Isn't gentlemanly. But then you'd know that without being told, eh?"

"And of course you're against poaching."

"By trade, sir. By trade. But is it poaching when the pheasant comes to you?"

Drew gave him an indifferent shrug. "One might point the poor creature back toward its nest and no harm done."

"I'll leave that sort of thing to you God-fearing men," Delwyn said without rancor. "For my part, I let Him alone, and He fairly much doesn't bother me. I expect we both like it that way."

Drew lifted an eyebrow. "Fairly much?"

"You're a persistent devil . . . sir."

"Just curious."

Delwyn chuckled as the barman replaced his empty mug with a fresh one. "Life story then, eh? All right. My mum took me to church. Obviously it didn't stick. Too many 'thou shalt nots' for my taste. What's God care if we have a bit of fun?"

"I expect it grieves Him to see how we treat one another," Drew said. "And ourselves."

The gamekeeper looked studiedly bored.

"Did you never see someone you care for persist in doing something that couldn't bring anything but pain?" Drew asked. "To others, of course, but more to that person himself?"

Delwyn's expression turned grave, and for a moment he said nothing. Then he gave a curt nod. "I suppose I have."

"I daresay you'd tell that person not to do it, if he'd listen," Drew suggested, wondering who might be on his mind just now. "Not for your sake, but for his."

"Yeah," Delwyn said. "If he'd listen." He was silent a moment, and then a sardonic little gleam came into his eyes. "And maybe, after I'd given my sermon, I'd take up a collection, too. If I could get it."

Drew laughed. "From what I've heard of him, I think the vicar would have liked you."

"He did," Delwyn said, his expression turning grim. "He was a good man and we got on well, religion or no. It's a dirty shame someone had to go and kill him."

"Who do you think might have done it?"

Delwyn frowned. "Hanged if I know, sir. Nor about the old lady either. I can't say I wouldn't like it to have been Jack Midgley there and have him swing for it, but I can't see how. There'd be nothing in it for him, and he's not one to work up a sweat when there's no profit to be had."

Drew glanced over at the poacher. "I hadn't considered him. No motive, as you say. Do you know for certain he couldn't have killed the vicar or Miss Patterson?"

"I can't say about the vicar," Delwyn said after a thoughtful pause, "but he couldn't have done for the lady."

"Why's that?"

The gamekeeper shook his head, making the thick curls at the back of his neck brush his collar. "He was here that night from suppertime till past midnight, drunk as five lords, not in a fit state to hold his head up much less murder anyone."

"Here in the Hound and Hart?"

129

Delwyn nodded.

"You don't think he might have pretended? To give himself an alibi?"

The gamekeeper laughed low. "I saw myself what he put away. There's nobody could have drunk that much and not felt it."

"And then he went home?"

"Trenton let him sleep it off in the jail."

"I suppose that lets him out," Drew said with a sigh. "As you say, there was no reason for him to kill her in the first place. But maybe he knows something about the guilty party. I'd like you to introduce me to Mr. Midgley. If he's in back of the local mischief, I'd like to have a word or two with him."

The gamekeeper looked faintly disgusted. "You're a gentleman, sir. It would be an insult for you to be acquainted with his sort."

The surrounding chatter abruptly died, and Drew looked around to see Midgley himself staring in their direction.

"Minding my business for me again, are you, Delwyn?" The poacher rose and came across the room, eyes glazed over and a spot of red in each weathered cheek. "I'll make my own introductions, I thank you. Mr. Farthering, my name is Midgley. Jack Midgley, jack of all trades, at your service, sir, and your lady wife's. If I might tell you friendly in your ear, you ought keep better watch over her if you don't want something unfortunate to happen."

Drew got to his feet, but before he could open his mouth, Delwyn stood and pushed him aside.

"You shut your mouth, Midgley," the gamekeeper spat. "You know nothing about how a decent man treats a woman. Nothing."

"And what would you know, Rhys Delwyn, about how a

decent man does anything?" Midgley laughed. "You take your morals from Jenkins's tomcat."

He flinched as Delwyn lunged toward him, but Drew caught the gamekeeper's arm and pulled him back.

"Don't let him bait you into a night in jail."

"Come back and have another drink, Jack," Nick said in his guise as Tom Selden. "Let him toady for the toff if he likes. What's that to you?"

Midgley snorted. "True enough. True enough. Wouldn't want to waste my knuckles on his like."

"Come on," Drew said quietly, turning Delwyn back to the table. "I want to know—"

Without warning, Midgley struck the gamekeeper with a crushing punch to the jaw. Delwyn went down in a heap, and there was a sudden commotion. Nick pulled Midgley away as the barman hurried over, his heavy face red and shining.

"None of that! None of that, Jack Midgley! I've warned you before."

"I was provoked," Midgley said. "You heard him. All these lads will say the same, eh?"

There was a general murmur of agreement, but the barman shook his head. "You hadn't ought to hit him from behind." He looked nervously at Drew. "Do we need to have the doctor in, sir?"

By then Delwyn was struggling to sit up, muttering darkly, clearly woozy.

"How is it, Delwyn?" Drew asked. "Do you need a doctor?"

"Doctor?" Delwyn huffed. "For the likes of him? No fear."

Drew hauled him to his feet. "Come on. You'd better go home and lie down."

Protesting, Delwyn let Drew help him outside and into Beaky's car. He managed to give Drew clear enough directions to get them to the cottage that had long been the residence of Bloodworth Park Lodge's gamekeepers. Drew turned off the engine, hopped out of the car and went round to the passenger side, but Delwyn was already struggling to his feet.

He threw off Drew's helping hand. "I'm all right." He swayed as he stumbled toward his door, and Drew caught him. "I'm all right," Delwyn muttered again, but then leaned heavily against Drew's shoulder until they'd reached the armchair that sat before the fireplace. He sank down into it, throwing his head back against the worn floral print and closing his eyes with a groan.

Drew took a moment to scan the room. It was tidy, though far from immaculate. There weren't many books, but what was there was worth the reading. Drew had to hide a smile when he noticed a well-worn copy of the adventures of Sherlock Holmes, including *The Hound of the Baskervilles*. It took him a moment to notice the little tabby shrinking back between two volumes of Victor Hugo's works.

"Hullo, sweetheart," he said gently. "Don't worry. I won't bother you."

He stepped back, slow and careful, and she watched him with wide sea-green eyes, ready to bolt at the slightest provocation.

"Oh, don't be such a numpty, Lizzy," Delwyn told her. "Nobody's after you." He shook his head and immediately regretted it. "She hardly sees anyone but me, and sometimes I think she's sure I'm going to roast her and eat her."

Drew chuckled and turned to Delwyn again. "Come on. I'd better help you get to bed."

The gamekeeper glared at him blearily. "I said I was fine. I don't need any help."

He was certainly feisty enough. That ought to be a good

sign. "Is there anything I can get you?" Drew asked. "Anything I can do for you?"

"No." Delwyn managed to focus on him for a moment. "You should have let me see to him in the first place."

"Maybe so. I didn't think he'd blindside you like that. I'm sorry I interfered."

Delwyn grinned faintly. "It's your job, isn't it? Interfering?"

"I suppose it is. Well, if there isn't anything I can do, I suppose I ought to be getting back to the Lodge." Drew started to leave, but then turned back to Delwyn. "Oh, I say, I don't suppose you can tell me where that blighter lives, can you? I'd love to catch him at something. Something punishable by fine or imprisonment or both."

Delwyn's grin widened, and then he winced and put his hand up to his jaw. "He's got a cottage out on the moor. Hold on."

He steadied himself, sat up straighter, and took a pencil and a used envelope from the small table to his left. With a few swift strokes he drew a map showing the Lodge and the stream that ran across the moor toward Westings and the cottage that stood about halfway in between.

"It's not hard to find," he said. "Just take care. Midgley's a sly devil." He gestured to his swollen face. "As you see."

Drew folded the map and secured it in his waistcoat pocket. "I'll do that. Put a beefsteak on that if you've got one."

"I'll get one," Delwyn said.

Drew went to the door and then turned, meaning to tell him to make sure he did. But then he saw the tabby creep over and settle herself in Delwyn's lap, so he very quietly let himself out.

— Nine —

Drew took a long time to make the short drive back to the Lodge from the gamekeeper's cottage, trying to sort through the tangle of questions in his mind. At first he tried to focus on the murders. The vicar and the nanny. Both of them old, both leading quiet lives, possessed of little more than enough to keep them alive and decently comfortable. Who would kill either of them, and why?

If it weren't for material gain, perhaps it was for something they knew. A man of the cloth was often confided in, asked advice of, confessed to. Perhaps someone with a guilty conscience had said more than he or she ought and then later regretted it. But why kill Miss Patterson, as well? Had she heard or seen something untoward? What was it she had wanted to tell Beaky? What could an elderly former nanny know that was intimate, delicate, or damaging?

Again Drew couldn't help but wonder about Delwyn and Sabrina. If Delwyn was the scoundrel everyone said he was, it seemed rather strange that he would call Midgley out over his treatment of women. What women, and how had he treated them? He'd have to ask Nick about that once they had a chance to talk again. There might be something he'd heard about the village that would explain things further. At any rate, there certainly seemed to be more than a suspicion of poaching between Midgley and Delwyn, something that must have been festering between them for a long while now.

Drew thought again of how Delwyn's indifferent expression had turned somber and thoughtful while they were talking. Who had he been thinking of? Was someone he cared about hurting himself—hurting *her*self—with the choices he or she had made?

Once more, Drew thought about Sabrina. Delwyn had admitted to having "attachments" here. If he were involved with Sabrina, she was definitely already attached, and it seemed she had no intention of unattaching herself for his sake. But had the idea of her hurting herself and others with her infidelity truly pricked him with regret? Surely, if the gamekeeper was as much of a Don Juan as rumor laid out, he had long ago cauterized the portion of his conscience concerned with the seventh commandment.

Well, as Madeline liked to remind him, he hadn't the slightest proof that Sabrina was seeing anyone, much less who that man might be. He wanted to be fair. He needed to be fair. If he wasn't, Fleur had bested him after all. If he made assumptions about other women because of his memories of Fleur, then it would mean she still had hold of him. It would mean she had won.

He never thought of her with fondness or even, despite her intoxicating beauty, as some forbidden fantasy. She was merely someone who had deceived him, someone who had taken advantage of his naïveté and forever sullied his eighteen-year-old idealism. She was a painful lesson to be sure, but he had learnt it, and then along came Madeline to prove his ideals were not so impossible after all. Fleur was in the distant past and shouldn't be any kind of recurrent memory for him now, unpleasant or otherwise. Then why did she insist on coming back to him? Why was he allowing the thought of her to color his assessment of Sabrina Bloodworth? Were Fleur's red-lacquered nails still buried so deeply into him that he hadn't even realized it?

No, he wouldn't let her best him. He would be fair. To Sabrina and to Delwyn and even to Midgley, he would be fair.

"God," he breathed, looking up at the grayish night sky, "help me see the truth without presuming anything. Help me remember that you are the only one who truly knows what's in someone else's heart. Help me to let go of . . ."

He was going to say let go of the memory of Fleur's deceit, but he saw with sudden clarity that the problem was something else entirely. It wasn't her deceit but his own pride he needed to let go of. He had been taken in by a pretty face and a charming manner. At eighteen, he had thought himself clever and discerning. To be honest, most of the time he thought it still. But when he looked at the facts, when he looked clearly at himself, he knew that wasn't always so. And when Fleur had deceived him so easily, bringing into sharp relief that failure, that deficiency, it had hurt his pride. Not his heart, his pride.

If he were ever to see the truth, he had to let it go. That presumption. That pride. He had to see things as they really were. Everyone involved in the case here deserved as much. The dead most of all.

When he finally pulled up to the Lodge, he had no answers, though he had more questions than he had started out with when he went into the Hound and Hart. But he was going to find the answers, and he didn't have to do it alone. And, God helping him, he would be fair.

It was good to know Madeline was waiting for him inside the house.

After lunch the next day, Drew and Madeline sat down with Beaky to go over Miss Patterson's letter once again, urging him to think of anything, no matter how trivial, she might have wanted to tell him. Poor Beaky could think of nothing.

Drew watched him until he went into his study and shut the door. Then he moved closer to Madeline, keeping his voice low. "What could it be but something about Sabrina? Miss Patterson had never even met Beaky, but she knew Sabrina very well."

Madeline looked at him reproachfully. "And you were going to be fair."

"I *am* being fair. What else can it be? Granted, perhaps it wasn't something to do with another man, I don't want to rule anything out as of yet, but how can it not be about Sabrina in some way? What other connection would there be between Beaky and Miss Patterson? He never even met her. His estate agent arranged for her to come live in Bunting's Nest."

Madeline crossed her arms over her chest. "And what does that have to do with the murder of the vicar?"

He shrugged. "Maybe he saw Sabrina where she shouldn't have been."

She merely looked at him, mild disgust in her expression, and he pressed a contrite kiss to her cheek.

"Don't be cross with me, darling. At least not yet."

"You're about to give me a reason to be cross with you, aren't you?"

"No," he protested, and then he looked even more contrite. "Well, yes. A bit."

Her mouth tightened, and he knew she was trying not to smile.

"I told you about what happened in the pub last night," he said. "I need to go see what I can get out of Midgley. Maybe when he's not drunk and trying to impress his friends he'll be more cooperative."

"And you don't want me to go with you."

"Not there, darling. I don't know what sort of place this cottage might be, and as you know, he's not at all a nice fellow."

She frowned, but she wasn't arguing with him. "You shouldn't go alone, though. Can't you take Nick with you?"

"You know I can't. He's supposed to be Midgley's friend, not mine."

Her frown deepened. "I guess that would spoil everything. What about Delwyn? I suppose he might not be feeling too well after last night."

"I'm not quite sure what to make of him yet, but if I'm going to get Midgley to tell me anything at all, having Delwyn along is probably not the way to go about it."

She put one soft hand up to his cheek, and he leaned into it, breathing in the light scent of lavender.

"Be careful, Drew. I don't like you going out there alone."

Heaven help him, how could he resist those eyes?

He kissed the underside of her wrist. "You needn't worry, darling. Even Midgley's not fool enough to do me any harm when I've told everyone I'm going to see him."

She pursed her lips. "Everyone?"

"Well, you. But if I turn up on the moor with sheep shears in my back, you be sure and tell Trenton who did it."

"That's a terrible thing to say, and not at all funny." She flounced away from him. "You know someone like Midgley is more likely to use the knife he carries to scale fish."

Laughing, he pulled her back into his arms. "I'll be back for tea, so try to behave yourself while I'm gone. And remember, you and Sabrina both promised you wouldn't go walking on the moor alone anymore."

"Yes, yes, we promised. We'll be here when you get back." She hugged him hard. "I'll see what else I can find out from Sabrina while you're gone." For a moment she was silent, and then she turned her eyes up to his again. "I still think we should have a look at the north wing. After what Sabrina's heard—"

"Oh, don't let's go on about that again, darling. Really. Beaky's had his chaps look it over more than once already. There's nothing to see. And the bally floor's likely to come away under us if we go in there anyway."

There was a touch of pique in her expression now. "You're supposed to be the smart amateur sleuth, you know. Not Beaky's hired men. They're not likely to know what's important and what's not. What would it hurt—"

"It wouldn't hurt anything. I just have actual leads to follow rather than wasting my time on a dead end. Right?"

She merely pursed her lips.

"Right?" he urged, squeezing her close.

She sniffed.

"I promise we'll give it a look as soon as I have some free time, all right?"

"All right," she said finally.

He gave her a sound kiss and, before she could say anything more, he was gone.

Drew followed the map Delwyn had drawn on the back of the envelope and was soon at the poacher's cottage. If Midgley was home, perhaps he'd have something worthwhile to say. At the very least, he ought to be sober this early in the day and wouldn't be trying to impress his mates from the pub. If he wasn't home, all the better. There was no telling what a quick look around the place might turn up.

The cottage was more of a shed than a proper house, hardly big enough for one person. But it seemed sturdy enough under its thatched roof, and a steady stream of smoke drifted out of the stone chimney. He studied the door before he made his presence known. A place like this wasn't likely to have anything more than a latch to keep the door shut, much less an actual lock. It shouldn't be difficult if he decided to let himself in.

He lifted his hand to knock, then stopped. Someone inside was humming, but it wasn't the craggy-voiced Jack Midgley. It was a woman's voice. He wasn't familiar with the tune she hummed, though he thought it must be one of the folk songs native to this place. It sounded as old and lonely as the wind on the moor.

So Midgley kept a woman, did he? A wife or someone a trifle less official? Either way, maybe that would clarify Delwyn's comment of the night before, but it would certainly put a damper on Drew's ability to search the place. Perhaps an interview and a chance to have a subtle look about would be just as helpful. Nothing for it but to try.

He rapped sharply on the door.

The humming broke off, and there was a scrabbling sound from inside. "Who is it, please? I do have a shotgun, in case you'd like to know."

"I very much like to know that sort of thing when I come visiting," Drew called back. "I find it so much more congenial when all parties are forthcoming about how heavily they are armed. Now I, for one, haven't anything but my wits about me, and I'm told those are too dull to cause any damage."

"I don't recognize your voice," the woman said, now sounding more annoyed than frightened. "Who are you?"

"My name's Drew Farthering. I'm staying up at the Lodge. May I come in?"

For a moment there was silence.

"What do you want?" Her voice came from just on the other side of the door now, accompanied by the dull thud of what could only be a gun barrel against the doorframe.

"I was looking for Jack Midgley. I understand this is his cottage."

"If he owes you money, you may as well go on back to Harrogate or wherever it is you come from. I haven't got any, and if he has, he's not likely to turn loose of it without a fight."

Drew bit his lip to keep from laughing. The woman sounded rather young, but it seemed she had come face-to-face with Midgley's creditors a time or two before now.

"I assure you, ma'am, I came here for the sole purpose of getting some information. Are you Mrs. Midgley?"

The woman snorted. "I'm his daughter. And there's nothing I can tell you."

Daughter. Well, that wasn't what Drew was expecting. At least there was no romantic entanglement to be dealt with.

"Perhaps there's something I can tell you," he replied. "It costs you nothing to just listen for a moment, eh?"

She made no reply.

"Look here." He made his voice as persuasive and unthreatening as he could manage. "You're the one with the gun. Just let me come in for a moment. I'd like to know what your father's involved with. Whatever it is, if you can convince him to talk to the police about it, it might save him and you a lot of trouble. What do you say?"

Again there was only silence.

"Have a heart, Miss Midgley," he said at last. "It's deuced cold out here, and I'm sure my wife will be waiting tea for me before long."

After another moment, there was the clank of the latch and the door creaked open. The gun barrel nosed out first, followed by a girl of perhaps twenty, dark-haired and slight, wearing a dress that had gone out of fashion at least five years before. She jerked her head toward the hearth, not meeting his eyes.

"Go on and sit down. Say what you want to say and then go back to the Lodge where you belong."

The little house was cluttered, needed paint, and smelled of smoke and boiled potatoes, yet it was scrupulously clean. Drew pushed a low, three-legged stool closer to the fire and had a seat. The girl made her way back to her own stool beside the spinning wheel that filled most of the center of the small room and took up her wool once more, keeping the gun propped next to her.

"Mr. Farthering, is it? I suppose you're the gentleman from London we've heard of. Come about Mr. Miles."

However did she know, penned up out here alone?

"Hampshire, actually, but yes. I did come to see what I could find out."

He watched her for a moment, fascinated by the swift, skilled movement of her slender fingers. She didn't even look at the spindle as the fine yarn flew from it.

"You don't happen to sell your yarn in the village, do you?"

She ducked her head. "It helps make ends meet."

"I must tell my wife I've met you." He smiled, hoping she'd look up. "She bought some of it and said it's the best she's found anywhere. I have a feeling she'd like to take several skeins of it home with us."

"That's very kind of her. Tell her I'll send some more into the village as soon as I can." She did not look up. "Now if you would, please say what it is you came to say. I'll have to get tea on before long myself, and I don't think you'll want to be here when my father gets back."

"All right," he said, standing to look into the little baskets on the table behind her, each one filled with a different color of yarn. "Though I know my wife would like some of this blue yarn. It's just the color of her eyes." He picked up a skein of bright red and held it for a moment. "Perhaps I could buy some of it from you now."

She glanced up and then shook her head, her attention again on her work. "The blue is promised already. If you like, I can have some sent on to you when I have more."

"Pity," he said. "But that will have to do. I'll just give it back to you then."

He put it into her outstretched hand, and she turned and dropped it into the basket with the other blue skeins. So that was it.

He caught her hand as she turned again to her spinning wheel, making her jump. "Forgive my bluntness, Miss Midgley, but you're blind, aren't you?"

She snatched her hand out of his, giving him his first real glimpse of her flashing pale-green eyes. "I don't see what that has to do with what you came to say about my father."

"I beg your pardon. I meant no offense. But it would seem to me that your situation makes it even more urgent for your father to stop what he's been doing and find honest work. If something were to happen to him, what would you do?"

She lifted her chin, a chin as stubbornly cleft as her father's was. "I'd do what I always do, Mr. Farthering. Look after myself."

"Out here alone?"

"I've done it since my mother died. Da was never much help even before then, but we got along. Mrs. Preston at the shop in the village is good enough to carry my yarns, and there's a place in Harrogate as well. What I make off that gets us through."

"And without what your father brings in?"

Her mouth twisted into a sneer. "What he brings in never gets any closer to here than the Hound and Hart."

"I've heard he's been rather generous with the drinks these days," Drew said, watching her expression. "Is that usual for him?"

She huffed. "He's more likely to beg a drink than buy one from what I've always heard. He must have made good on one of his great schemes if he's buying now, but don't bother asking me what that might have been. He never tells me what he has going on, though I do hear things from time to time."

"Really?"

"I'm blind, Mr. Farthering, not deaf. I do have friends, and I do get about a bit. I know my father isn't spoken well of in Bunting's Nest. I expect you've already been told he's a poacher, that he'll do any kind of job so long as he's paid well enough. And so long as he doesn't have to keep regular hours."

"Is that all true?"

She sighed and began spinning again, her white brow furrowed. "I don't know if anyone's as good or bad as gossip paints him."

Drew didn't say anything for a moment, just listened to the whir of the wheel and watched the swift, deft movements of her fingers.

"He doesn't buy what you need? Clothes and that sort of thing?"

"No. It's all I can expect for him to carry my yarn into the village for me. He tells me he has other things need seeing to. He doesn't come home much but to sleep. If that."

"Does he ever talk to you about what he does? Who he sees?" Drew hesitated, watching her fine-featured face. "Who pays him?"

She shook her head. "I don't know that I'd mind so much if they put a stop to whatever it is he does. I don't guess it could be right, not from what I've overheard. Mum would be that ashamed, though even when she was alive he never cared what anybody said."

"You've overheard?" Drew said, and there was a sudden quickening in his blood. "What have you overheard?"

She lifted one slender shoulder just slightly. "I couldn't hear much. Not any of the times. He was out back of the cottage, and the other man was talking very low. A while back I heard him say something about the sheep, and then afterward I heard two lambs were left dead on the moor, made to look as if something had got them, maybe the barghest, talk was. But you can't tell me it wasn't Da."

Drew leaned forward in his chair. "Who was the other man? Did you recognize the voice?"

"No, sir."

"How did he sound to you? Young or old?"

She thought for a moment. "Not young. I could tell that right away, but not old either. I mean, not elderly. Perhaps in his fifties. Maybe not quite so much."

Drew added that to his notes. "And was there anything about his voice that you particularly noticed?"

"Not really. Just a man."

"English? Not American or Scottish or Welsh?"

She shook her head. "He didn't have any sort of accent."

"Not from Yorkshire?"

"I wouldn't say so. At least not from the country. He'd been to school, I could tell that. Gentry, and no mistake." She smiled a little now. "Same as you."

"Was this the first time you'd heard this particular voice?"

"No," she said. "But I don't think it's been but another time or two before that. But I didn't dare move any closer when I heard. Da would light into me if he knew I was listening at all."

Drew looked her over again. She was a slight little thing, possibly pretty if she weren't so pale and fragile-looking. He noticed that there was a bruise on her forearm, as though someone had taken ungentle hold of her.

"Your father"—he didn't know how to soften it—"is he rough with you?"

"No." The color came up in her face. "Not really. No more than a slap now and again. He gets mean when he's had too much to drink. I suppose some men do, but not all." Once more she lifted a thin shoulder. "I try to have his meals ready when he wants them and keep out from underfoot and have plenty of yarn to sell. He mostly lets me alone."

Drew tried to keep the raw, fierce anger out of his voice. "And you don't have any idea what he and this man were talking about? Or what your father's been doing?"

"I'm sorry, no." She bit her lip. "Maybe it isn't right, him being my father and all, but I wouldn't be too sorry if the law took him off for a while. Not a long while, mind, but maybe long enough to make him see he can't go on doing what's wrong. He thinks he's too clever for everyone, and it's going to get him into real trouble one day. I know it will."

146

Drew took a deep breath and released it, careful not to let her hear. "I hope I can find out what's going on before that happens. Meanwhile, if you hear anything more or remember anything, can you get word to me? At the Lodge?"

"Yes, sir." She seemed to relax a little. "I think so."

She reached up to push back the lock of hair that had fallen against her cheek. He noticed her earring, just a small pearl. Tasteful. Expensive.

"Those are lovely earrings," he said pleasantly, and she put her hand up to the one he could see, turning faintly red.

"They were a gift." She ducked her head again and went back to her spinning. "We don't have many nice things, as you can see. It doesn't matter much, I suppose, but I do wish we had a wireless. I'd love to hear broadcasts from all over the world."

"Perhaps you'll have one someday."

That made her laugh. "They cost money, you know, and then there'd be batteries to buy and all."

He frowned. "I guess that would be a difficulty, wouldn't it?"

"That's all right. I hear it when I go visiting sometimes. I love the programs where they describe the sights in foreign places. I feel as if I'm there somehow, seeing everything I've only seen in photographs."

Photographs? "But—"

"Oh, I wasn't born this way."

He wasn't sure if that was better or worse than never knowing what it was to see at all. "That must be very hard for you. I'm sorry."

She smiled a secret little smile. "It's not so terrible. It would be worse to know I had no one in the world, wouldn't it?"

"Yes," he said, wondering if Midgley was indeed better than no one. "I suppose it would."

147

"Anyway, I'm sorry about what happened to the vicar and to the lady from the village, but I don't know anything about it. If my father does, he hasn't told me."

"Thank you for talking to me all the same." He looked about the cottage again, his eyes lighting on the mantel clock. It'd had the glass over the face removed. "I'd best be going. Your father might not appreciate finding me here without his say."

"You're probably right. Sorry about the gun. A girl can't be too careful out here alone."

"No, I suppose not." He went to the cottage door and stopped abruptly. "I don't believe I ever got your name."

There was a touch of wryness now in her expression. "Iris. Rather ironic, isn't it?"

He made sure his smile could be heard in his voice. "I think it's lovely."

— Ten —

Drew tramped back toward the Lodge, conscious of where he was walking only enough to steer clear of what the sheep had left behind them, but his thoughts were mostly on Iris Midgley. He couldn't help pitying her, and yet he couldn't help admiring her, too. She was blind, but she had found a way to earn her own way and, like as not, support her father as well.

Drew's blood turned hot at the thought of the scoundrel raising his hand to her. No more than a slap now and again indeed. The villain. The utter reprobate. No wonder Delwyn had spewed such venom toward him at the pub last night. No man with even a shred of decency would stand for it.

And yet there were those earrings. What exactly was Midgley up to that he was able and, more astonishing, willing to buy something so costly and so impractical for his daughter? Whatever the reason, Drew was glad the girl had at least some trifle to cherish. There had to be something Drew could do as

Murder on the Moon

well to bring her a little enjoyment. He'd have to ask Madeline what she thought, but perhaps—

"Hello!"

Drew started, almost stumbling on the heather near the path, and then squinting to make out who had hailed him from behind some distance away. It wasn't until the man loped closer that he recognized the bearded face.

"Mr. Blackstock. Hello."

The milkman scurried toward him, smiling. "I saw you coming some way off, sir, but I didn't know it was you till just now. It's providence, that's what it is. I was going to come by the Lodge to speak with you before I went back home, and here you've spared me the bother."

"Oh, yes?"

Blackstock scanned the still-foggy moor, but there seemed to be nothing but sheep for miles around. "I was out watching the lapwings. They call them peewits up here, you know."

"No, I—"

Blackstock bobbed his head. "They make that sort of sound, you see. Peewit! Peewit!" He looked rather delighted. "They're a nice bird, don't you think?"

"To be sure," Drew said.

"Almost iridescent blue and green on their wings and that little feather on top of their heads like one on a cavalier's hat, eh?"

"You saw something when you were watching the lapwings?" Drew prompted.

"Yes, well, I was sitting quiet watching one when a fox snapped it up. I leapt to my feet and scared the fox away, and the bird fluttered into one of the old lime kilns. I'd seen the thing a hundred times before, of course, but I never had occasion to go into it. They look rather nasty, half buried as they are, but I went in to see if the bird was much hurt. And what do you think I saw?"

"I can't imagine."

"It was black as pitch inside, so I lit a match to see if the bird was dead. Poor thing, it came fluttering out again when I did and flew off. I'm guessing it wasn't much hurt at all."

"But what did you see?" Drew urged.

"What do you know, but somebody's living in the old place!" The milkman nodded, obviously pleased at the startled look on Drew's face. "Yes. From what I saw, it's been swept out a bit, and there's a cot and a packing crate for a table and a lantern on it, nice as you please. No one was in there just then, of course, but someone had been and not so long ago. I thought you'd better know about it. My look lasted only as long as my match, and then I thought I'd ought to come tell you. And, bless me, here you are."

"But who'd want to live in a place like that? It must be miserable, especially in the cold."

"Oh, yes, I daresay," Blackstock said. "But mightn't it be a good place to hide? If someone meant to do mischief . . . or worse."

His thoughts whirring, Drew looked out over the moor. There was still no one in sight. Mischief or worse. Murder? Would someone really come live under such primitive conditions out on the moor for the sole purpose of killing people at random? It was madness. The ever-present wind seemed to turn colder.

"Where is this kiln? Near Midgley's?"

"Not far, sir. Not far. It's not very noticeable at first glance, grown over for the most part, and has been a good many years

I expect, but you'll see it. Of course, it mightn't have anything at all to do with poor Mr. Miles and that other lady who was killed, but it seems hardly right not to find out. I hope I did right telling you about it."

"Oh, definitely. You've been a great help."

The milkman flushed with pleasure. "Only too happy, Mr. Farthering, sir. Only too happy."

"You'd better get along now," Drew told him. "It wouldn't do for you to be seen talking to me out here. But keep on the lookout."

Blackstock ducked his head a bit as if to keep himself from being recognized. "Right you are. I'll just be getting back home then. You take care if you go out to the kiln, sir. As I said, I don't rightly know who might be staying there."

The man scurried off and soon vanished over a rise. Drew hurried back to the Lodge to make a telephone call.

Mr. Selden and Mr. Stapleton met at the agreed-on place outside the village. Drew told Nick what he had learned from the milkman, and before long they were striding across the moor toward Midgley's cottage. They soon found the old kiln.

From most angles it was invisible, just an overgrown mound, but in the front was a brick archway and a black opening into the hillside. Drew shone the torch into the entrance, his eyes taking a moment to adjust to the dimness inside. As Blackstock had said, there was a cot along one wall and a crate with an oil lamp sitting on it.

Nick lit the lamp, and faint yellow light filled the space. "So this is where the fellow's keeping himself when he's not actually committing murder."

"It may well be." Drew switched off the torch. "Someone's certainly been here recently. And I expect these are the things taken from Westings. Gray told me they weren't worth bothering over, and I see he was right."

A number of books were stacked against the crate. One volume lay facedown on the cot, and he picked it up, straining to read the small print in the meager light.

"Sir, your wife is living; that is a fact acknowledged this morning by yourself. If I lived with you as you desire, I should then be your mistress. To say otherwise is sophistical—is false."

Jane Eyre again.

"Odd choice for a murderer, isn't it?" Drew looked through the other books there on the ground. *Wuthering Heights.* Appropriate for the moor, he supposed. Shakespeare's *Sonnets*, a collection of Byron's poems, and something written in Italian. Odd choices indeed.

There was a tin with some shortbread in it and, half buried in the blankets, a bottle of wine, champagne, half gone. Mindful of fingerprints, he turned the bottle with the toe of his shoe, just so he could read the label. It was a fine old wine. A good year. Expensive.

"An embarrassment of investigative riches."

"Seems our killer is a romantic," Nick said.

"Seems so. I suppose one must occupy one's time somehow."

They looked around a bit more, but there was little else to be seen.

Drew scuffed his boot on the brick floor where it was especially charred and then looked up. There was a square hole that opened to the slate-colored sky. "He must lay his fire here when he's in."

Nick nodded, and then his face changed. "Where do you

suppose he might be just now? I would have thought he'd keep hidden during the day."

"Now there's an interesting question. Presuming he is our man, where could he get to during the day? Trenton says there haven't been any strangers around the village. At least not until that reprobate Tom Selden arrived."

Nick grinned. "But that was after the vicar was killed."

"Right. And if our fellow took the trouble to hide himself in this wretched place, then it doesn't follow that he would show himself around the village. So again we are left with the very pertinent question of where he might be just now."

Nick scanned the titles of the books in the stack. "You don't think this could have nothing whatsoever to do with our murders, do you?"

"That's a possibility," Drew admitted. "Quite a coincidence, but a possibility all the same. Unless . . ." He trailed off as an idea struck him.

Nick frowned. "What?"

"Suppose he has another hiding place. You know, in case he feels this one isn't safe. Blackstock certainly means well, but I can't imagine he doesn't make a great deal of fuss tramping about round here looking at peewits and such. If our murderer has been clever enough to kill two people and not leave a clue behind, he's most likely found alternate lodgings."

"But where?"

Drew blew out the lamp. "Come with me."

Drew and Nick hurried back over the moor toward the Lodge.

"Madeline and Sabrina were out on the moor a day or two ago. They said Sabrina's dog got rather agitated when they got near an old stone church. Perhaps it was because he came across the scent of a stranger."

"I understand the dog took off, terrified," Nick said, scanning the moor ahead of them, and then he noticed Drew's puzzled expression. "Midgley was telling me about it. It amused him to no end."

"Fine fellow," Drew said, despising the man more than he had already. "One day I shall have to tell him how much I admire his choice of pastime."

"That will be satisfying," Nick said. "And think how much more so if it could be done as the police are taking him away to answer for his part in all this."

"But just what is his part in all this?" Drew asked.

"He's definitely keeping that bit of information close. He's very good at 'the pronouncing of some doubtful phrase' that gives away nothing."

"Ah, Hamlet." Drew laughed. "'Well, well, we know,' or 'We could, an if we would,' or 'If we list to speak.'"

"Precisely, though his ambiguous givings out are much less coherent."

Drew lifted an eyebrow. "You mean much less sober."

Nick shrugged. "Unfortunately too sober to give anything away, I can tell you that. And I don't dare press too much or I'll give myself away."

"True. Well, you'll have to be patient with him, Nick, old man. He's got to make a slip sometime, and it's certain that's not his own money he's flashing about."

Drew stopped, seeing an overgrown ruin of stone just as Madeline had described.

Nick looked unimpressed. "Is this it, then? What we've come for?"

Drew nodded as he looked over the area, making sure no one was nearby, and then went up to the stone church. "Madeline told me there was still a sort of tower here with a door. If our man is living in that kiln, mightn't he make use of other abandoned places?"

Nick glanced at the door. "What you reckon? Might he be in there?"

"Only one way to know." Drew examined the door before touching it. "It's very old, but the hinges aren't rusted shut. I daresay the door's been opened, and not too long ago."

Nick nodded toward it. "Well?"

Drew put his hand on the door, took a deep breath, and pushed. It didn't budge. With a huff of frustration, he shoved it with his shoulder. Nothing.

"Put your back into it, man," Nick said, smirking.

Drew glared. "Help me."

At the count of three they made a run at it together. All that got them was rattled teeth.

"It is my considered opinion," Nick said, rubbing his shoulder, "that this door is locked."

"Brilliant deduction." Drew studied the lock more closely. There were a couple of scratches near the keyhole, just little ones, but they were fresh. "Someone has definitely been here, and recently."

"Someone's been *here*," Nick said, suddenly grim as he looked down at the hard-packed dirt at his feet.

Drew went to him, for a moment puzzled as he too studied the ground, and then his eyes widened. "Good heavens, the hound."

He went down on one knee, the better to study the print. It was an animal's paw, most likely a dog's. He spread out one hand to judge the size of it, but his hand wouldn't quite cover it.

"Delwyn says the Bloodworth dog has been running wild on the moor." He looked up at Nick. "How big would you say a mastiff's paw is?"

"Not nearly that size, certainly. You don't suppose—"

"I don't suppose spectral hounds leave footprints, no matter how big." Drew stood, slapping the dirt off the knee of his trousers. "But it is possible that a very tangible one has been nearby. Perhaps it's even been kept here."

Nick glanced at the locked door. "Do you think so?"

"It would seem, given the absence of a proper key, there's only one way to find out."

Drew went back to the door and took hold of the heavy iron ring over the keyhole. With all his might he banged the ring like a knocker against the door. The two of them waited for a moment, but there was no response.

The tower, if it could be called that, was no more than ten or twelve feet wide and perhaps twice that tall. The top of it was broken, so there was no way to know whether, in ages past, it had stretched up any higher. At any rate, the sound of Drew's knocking certainly would have reverberated throughout what remained.

"Cerberus, it seems, is not at home to visitors."

"One way to find out for certain," Nick said. He put his pinkies at the corners of his mouth and drew a deep breath. Drew winced at the long, high, piercing whistle that, in the city, would have had every dog for a mile round barking. But no bark came. "If anything's in there," Nick said, "it isn't a dog."

Drew nodded, his attention once more on the scratches around

157

the keyhole, which seemed to have been made by someone with an unsteady hand trying to put the key into the lock.

"A dog's not in there now, but that doesn't mean there hasn't been." Drew looked over at the print in the dirt. "Or that there won't be again. We'll have to keep an eye on the place."

— Eleven —

W e probably shouldn't be in here."

Sabrina's quiet voice sounded louder than it was in the abandoned north wing, and Madeline instinctively shushed her.

"Of course we shouldn't be in here. Our husbands will both be very put out with us if they find out, but Drew's being awfully stubborn about even looking. Besides, if there's nothing to see in here, as they keep telling us, then we just won't tell them about it. And if there is something to see, they'll be glad we found it."

"And if we fall through the floorboards or the staircase, as Beaky tells me we shall?"

"Then they'll get to say 'I told you so.' Now come on."

Madeline glanced around at the once-opulent moth-eaten curtains and the dust-coated furniture as they passed from what might have been a drawing room into the library. There were still some books on the shelves, but they were shrouded with spider webs, and more than one had had its pages shredded, no doubt to serve as nesting for mice or rats. It all seemed so gloomy and sad.

"How long ago was this wing last lived in?"

"Oh, ages," Sabrina said. "I can't remember exactly when Beaky said it was closed up. Back in the eighties, I think." She shivered, hunching her shoulders. "It's positively creepy in here. I'm glad it's daytime, though it would be nice to have some lights on. Of course, they never put electricity in here. It's only the old gaslights, and Beaky says it's been so long since they've been lit, that's not safe either."

Madeline shone the flashlight around the library, stopping when the light glinted off of something on the window seat. "What's that?"

She went over to it and found a few slivers of broken glass had fallen from the boarded-up window and onto the torn velvet cushion.

"When did this happen?"

Sabrina shrugged. "I don't know. Months ago. One of the times Beaky had some men look it over to make sure we hadn't had intruders. They found that window broken, but only part of one of the panes. He said nothing bigger than a squirrel could have gotten in that way, but they boarded up all the windows just to make sure they were closed off."

The glass was nearly as dusty as the cushion itself. It seemed unlikely it had fallen there recently.

"Did he tell you about anything else they found the last time the men were in here?" Madeline asked, shining the light along the baseboards and then over the time-ravaged carpet. "I suppose all of these footprints are theirs."

"I think they must be. Beaky told me there wasn't any sign of anyone being here, but I know the kinds of sounds mice and squirrels make. That's not what I've heard in the night."

Sabrina's voice quavered, and her hands fluttered, no doubt reaching by force of habit for the cigarettes she hadn't brought with her. But there was determination, even defiance, in her pale face.

Madeline shone the light around the library once more and then took her arm. "Why don't you show me where your bedroom wall meets up with this wing?"

Sabrina nodded. "If you think the stairs are safe. And the upper floors."

"We'll be careful."

The front stairs, the grand entrance from the main hall that led to this wing, merely ended at locked double doors, so they took the back stairs, narrow and steep, up to the second floor, holding tightly to the rail and testing each step before putting their full weight on it.

There were more footmarks up here, where Beaky's men had searched, and even more abundant, the signs of small animals, torn curtains, and unstuffed upholstery. It would be a nasty place to clean out when it was time to refurbish the place.

"This way."

The floor creaking beneath them, Sabrina led her down a wide corridor with faded wallpaper marred with nails and picture wires and less-faded rectangles where paintings must have once hung. A large spider web covered the upper part of the mullioned window at the very end.

"In there," Sabrina said when they reached the last door on the left. "Those double doors go out to the upper floor of the main wing, but I'm fairly sure they're locked. Even if they aren't, we don't want to pop out of them and have Halford or someone see us and report us to the master. But I don't think this room is locked."

She reached for the knob on the single door and then faltered.

Reminding herself it was likely just an empty room, Madeline put a steadying hand on her shoulder. "Do you want me to—"

"No." Sabrina squared her shoulders and took the flashlight from her. "No, I'm not so great a ninny as that. Come on."

She grasped the doorknob, turned it, and flung open the door. This had clearly been a bedroom, though there was nothing left of the bed but the heavy frame and the canopy with rotting shreds of brownish ivory brocade still hanging from it. The upper windows hadn't been boarded up, though what remained of the curtains was closed. The mild sunlight shone through a number of tears, but it was still dim enough in the room to make the flashlight useful.

Sabrina shone it toward the curtained back wall. "I'm sure that's the one that backs up to my room. Well, my dressing room. That was probably a dressing room, too."

That curtain looked to be made of the same stuff as the window curtains, a heavy brocade like the bed hangings, though this was pale blue, faded but less so than the others. Sabrina whisked it back, making the rings whir against the rod, and then shone the light around the shallow area.

"The last time I heard anything from here it was—"

With a muffled shriek she let the flashlight fall to the floor with a hollow thud.

Madeline snatched it up. "What is it? What—?"

Her own eyes widened as she focused the light down at their feet. There in the thick dust, more recent than and well away from the footmarks of Beaky's men, were the paw prints of an enormous hound.

When they reached the crossroads, Nick took the path toward the village. Drew went north to the Lodge. Before he was halfway there, he noticed a man a few hundred yards ahead of him carrying a muddy sheep across his shoulders.

"Good afternoon," he called, quickening his pace, certain it was the gamekeeper.

Delwyn turned, and Drew wasn't sure if his taut expression was an indication of annoyance or anger.

"Mr. Farthering, sir. I hadn't expected to see you out on the moor."

"Just having a look about. The stone church . . ." Drew watched the Welshman's dark eyes as they walked along. "The old kiln out past Midgley's."

The eyes flashed and then narrowed. "What do you want to be going out to those places for? There's nothing for you there."

"No?" Drew asked pleasantly.

"Just a waste of your time, sir."

"Not at all. I came up here to look into things. It seems a very good use of my time."

Delwyn's mouth tightened. "Those murders are a village matter, if you'll pardon my saying. Nothing to do with the mischief out here on the moor."

"Any particular reason you'd rather I not look into those places?"

For a moment there was only the sound of the gamekeeper's heavy boots on the footpath, and then he slowed to a stop and gave Drew a hard look. "It's not my usual job to tend the sheep, but I found this one caught up where she oughtn't to have been. Leg's broken." He shifted the animal to get a better hold, and she let out a piteous bleat. "But then she's just a poor, dumb beast. A smarter creature would keep out of places that aren't safe."

He held Drew's gaze for a moment more and then started walking again, saying nothing else until they reached one of the pens.

"If you'll pardon me, sir, I'd better get Johnson to tend to her." He ducked his head, unable with his hands full to give the customary touch to the brim of his hat. "You know your way back to the Lodge from here, do you?"

The Lodge was plainly visible from where they stood.

"I think I can manage," Drew said coolly. "Oh, one question, Delwyn, if you don't mind."

"Sir?"

"You said old Mr. Bloodworth's dog is very large."

"He was, sir."

"Any idea how big his paw prints might be?"

"His . . ." Delwyn knit his dark brows. "I dunno. Might be the size of my clenched fist. A bit smaller."

Drew held up his hand, fingers spread. "Not as big as this?"

The gamekeeper quickly shook his head. "Why?"

Drew passed over the question. "Have you seen him lately?"

"Not for some while. This past March or April. Maybe it was before that. He's getting on a bit. I'm wondering if he might not have laid himself down somewhere out on the moor and never gotten up again."

"I thought he was your explanation for some of the incidents out there."

There was a wicked touch of humor now in Delwyn's expression. "Better than blaming the barghest, eh?"

Drew only looked at him. The sheep squirmed again, bleating loudly.

"I'd best get her seen to then, sir." Again Delwyn ducked his head. "Mind how you go."

164

Calling for Johnson, he carried the sheep around one of the sheds and out of sight.

"You do the same, Delwyn," Drew said before he turned again toward the Lodge. "If you're wise."

Drew had barely stepped inside the front door when Madeline rushed up to him, a pretty flush in her cheeks and her eyes bright with excitement.

"You won't believe what we found."

"What have you done now?" he asked, trying to be stern and failing miserably. "You didn't go back out on the moor, did you?" He gave his hat to the young maid who made a sudden appearance.

"No, we did not go back out on the moor," Madeline said. "We didn't even leave the house."

"Yes, well, I don't have to remind you of the trouble you get into when you don't even leave the house." Drew gave the maid his overcoat and thanked her as she scurried away.

Madeline huffed. "Fine. I just won't tell you what we found."

He caught her hand before she could flounce off and pulled her near. "Tell me."

She shrugged one shoulder and turned her face disdainfully away.

"Tell me," he breathed into her ear, "or I won't tell you what Nick and I found out at the stone church."

Her breathing quickened, though whether that was from how close he was holding her or from excitement over the case, he wasn't entirely sure.

"What?" she whispered.

He looked around, making sure they weren't overheard,

and kept his voice low. "That tower has been opened recently, though it's locked now, but outside it we saw the paw print of an enormous—"

"An enormous hound!" she finished for him, her eyes shining.

"Shh!" He glanced around again. "How did you know?"

"Because that's what we saw, Sabrina and I. In the north wing." She wrinkled her nose at him. "You're not the only one who can do some investigating."

He stepped back from her. "I gather neither of you ended up with a broken neck, so we won't discuss the wisdom of your going up there alone." Unable to help the little surge in his own heartbeat, he allowed the tiniest flicker of a smile to touch his lips. "You'd better show me."

"I'd have to get the key from Sabrina again, and she says she won't go back up there. Not until we figure out what's been going on."

Drew frowned. "I'll just get it from Beaky. He'll want to see, as well."

"Wait," she said as he strode toward the corridor that led to Beaky's study. "She doesn't want him to—"

"I already know," Beaky said, coming from the opposite way and obviously trying to lighten his annoyance with good humor. "Seems I can't even go look at Mr. Hanover's new generator without there being mischief done."

Madeline went to him, looking contrite and very charming. "I hope you're not upset with Sabrina. It really was all my idea."

"I suppose no harm done, eh?" He turned faintly red. "Though you really ought to be careful." He looked at Drew. "What do you say? Shall we have a look ourselves?"

Drew didn't have to be asked twice, and a few minutes later

the three of them were in the north wing, an electric torch shining on the undeniable print of a large hound.

Drew held his hand over it, fingers spread. "I would say that's the same print I saw." He turned the light on the dusty floor, but it showed him only the marks of workmen's boots. "But I would like to know how they got up here."

The shredded curtains still let in pale strips of light from the window. Nothing had disturbed the dust from that quarter of the room. The animal's prints were not mixed in with the others coming from the door. They were only there in the curtained dressing room that was on the other side of the Bloodworths' bedroom.

"You didn't see prints anywhere else?" he asked Madeline.

"Sabrina practically dragged me back to the main part of the house once we saw these, so I didn't have much time to look, but we certainly didn't notice anything like that on our way up here, and we saw pretty much everything downstairs."

"Might someone have come in from the upper floor?" he asked Beaky.

"I don't think so. Those doors are kept locked, and even if someone had, there would be prints coming from that way, wouldn't there? And it's a good way down to the ground from that window. I don't see how a dog could have gotten in. Not an ordinary dog at any rate."

"Well, I promise you it's not a demon hound with huge claws and teeth and red glowing eyes," Drew said, examining the prints again. "Though how these came to be here is certainly a puzzling question. And you're sure no one in the house would have reason to let one of your dogs in? One of the sheepdogs or something? I mean, besides Raphael, and he certainly didn't make a print that size."

167

Gloucester Library
P.O. Box 2380
Gloucester, VA 23061

"None of our other dogs are that big either," Beaky said, his forehead wrinkling. "Uncle Hubert used to have a large dog, but I expect you know that already. He's been gone for months now. Well before these prints were made. And he never would have come in here anyway. Uncle was very strict about leaving the north wing locked up. Didn't want to heat it or run the gaslights or make it safe enough for people to come into, I expect."

"And none of your people have heard or seen anything either?" Drew asked. "Besides what you've already told me?"

"No. And they are under strict orders to come to me at once if they see or hear anything out of the ordinary. No stray animals. No strangers. Nothing at all. But clearly . . ." Beaky looked at Drew rather helplessly. "I just don't know what to make of any of it."

Drew clasped his shoulder, turning toward the door, shining the torch to illuminate the way. "That's what Madeline and I are here to find out. It's not very clear so far, but as our dear chief inspector likes to tell me, it's early days yet. Early days."

Sabrina was waiting for them at the door to the north wing, a burning cigarette in her trembling fingers. "Did you find anything else?"

"Nothing more than what you saw, my dear." Beaky locked the door to that part of the house and put the key in his pocket. "And whoever or whatever has been over there, he won't come in here."

She took a deep puff and blew out the smoke in a sullen stream. "You don't know that."

He glanced at Drew, an obvious plea for support, and, seeing the subtle urging in Madeline's expression, Drew turned to Sabrina, assuming his most confident demeanor.

"I'm sure we'll get it all sorted soon. Meanwhile, I trust you'll be well-protected here, won't she, Beaky, old man?"

"Oh, good. Beaky." Sabrina's smoldering cigarette bobbed with the negligent motion of her hand. "Very good. I suppose you'll throw yourself courageously into the path of the beast so that I might be spared."

Her rouged lips twisted into a sneer, but Beaky did not look away.

"I would," he said, his voice soft. "I would."

For an instant she didn't move. Then with a glance at Drew and Madeline, she laughed. "I might as well have Raphael to protect me." She turned a bright smile on her guests. "Beaky's always making jokes, isn't he? Even in a serious moment. Ah, well."

Beaky always reddened at the slightest provocation. Now his face was like fire. "Have . . . have you told the Fartherings about our dinner invitation, Sabrina, dear?"

Sabrina's smile vanished. "That. I suppose there's no way we can decline, is there?"

"It wouldn't be very polite, dear."

"The Grays?" Drew asked, and Sabrina's expression grew more dour.

"Yes, though I didn't think they had such a wonderful time here that they would want to repeat it anytime soon."

"They want to be polite, I'm sure," Beaky said. "We didn't have so awful an evening, did we?"

Sabrina merely puffed on her cigarette.

"Well, I want to go," Madeline said, taking Drew's arm. "Don't you?"

"Whatever for?" Sabrina grumbled. "It can't be to become fast friends with the delightful Mrs. Gray."

"Are you sure old Mr. Gray will have us in the house?" Beaky asked.

"Her note says he has agreed to behave himself. If so, I expect it will be a first."

"Now, Sabrina, we have to mend things somehow. Perhaps he's as tired of this nonsense as everyone else."

"I think it's the perfect opportunity," Drew said. "The more people we can talk to, the more likely it is that someone will say something or do something that will help us. If you'd like to know what's going on here, don't you think we ought to see what the Grays know?"

Sabrina's mouth opened just slightly, but for a moment no sound came from it. Then she merely looked annoyed. "Oh, I suppose you're right. I'll send our acceptance round to Westings. And, yes, I will mind my manners when I'm there. I'll be absolutely dripping with charm."

Drew hadn't been entirely sure what to make of Morris and Frances Gray, and under no circumstances was he going to miss an opportunity to meet Carter Gray. If nothing more, the old fellow was sure to know more about earlier times here in Bunting's Nest, perhaps even unknowingly reveal some connection between the two murder victims that hadn't before come to light.

He gave Sabrina an approving nod. "Excellent."

— Twelve —

Westings was a red-brick Georgian affair, not as old or as large as Bloodworth Park Lodge, but grand enough in its own right. The chauffeur turned the Bentley into the drive and through the open gates.

"There she is," Beaky said, "and without a whole wing that needs remodeling."

"Nice," Drew said. "Very nice."

Madeline gave him a knowing grin. "The house or the cars?"

"Wouldn't say no to that Jaguar SS2 Saloon there. And that *is* a nice little Alfa Romeo," he said with a longing look at the one parked in the drive, "you have to admit."

"Red's not your color, dear."

He gave her a cheeky grin. "Wouldn't have to be red."

"There's nothing like it on a night with only the moon and stars and miles of empty road," Sabrina said, eyes alight. "And with the cold wind making your face tingle and your blood run fast."

"You've ridden in it then, have you?" Drew asked.

"Oh, not his." She hurried out of the car when the chauffeur opened the door. "I meant my little Austin. You've seen it in our drive, haven't you? Come along, Beaky."

Drew narrowed his eyes, watching her walk up to the house on Beaky's arm until Madeline came up beside him and elbowed him subtly in the ribs.

"What sort of mischief are you imagining she's up to now? As far as I've heard, it's not a crime in this country to drive a little sports car in the moonlight."

"It depends, darling, on whether the car belongs to you or to someone else."

Before she could demand an explanation, he slipped her arm through his and escorted her up the steps to join Beaky and Sabrina in Westings' foyer. The maid took their coats, and an ancient butler tottered ahead of them to the sitting room.

"Mr. and Mrs. Bloodworth," he announced in a quavering voice. "And Mr. and Mrs. Farthering."

Morris and Frances Gray, and an elderly man with a cane who must be Carter Gray himself, were waiting to receive them.

"Good to have you," Morris said, shaking Drew's hand and bowing graciously over Madeline's. "I daresay, seeing how lovely you and Mrs. Bloodworth look this evening, even Lord Byron would have been—"

"Stop that blathering, Morris, and introduce us." The elderly man peered at Drew from under heavy white brows. "You're young Bloodworth's detective, are you?"

Morris glanced at Drew, looking embarrassed and apologetic all at once, but Drew only smiled at the elder Gray and escorted Madeline over to him. She would be just the tonic for the old man's irascibility.

"Drew Farthering, sir, and this is my wife, Madeline."

"My father, Carter Gray," Morris said rather lamely.

"Good evening, Mr. Gray," Madeline said, giving him her prettiest smile. "It's so nice of you to have us to dinner."

"American, eh?" Gray looked her up and down and then turned to Drew. "One of our English girls not good enough for you, boy?"

"Not after I met my Madeline," Drew said good-humoredly. "And I daresay you don't blame me, sir."

The old man snorted, but there was a sly smile playing at his thin lips.

"And Mr. and Mrs. Bloodworth are here as well, Father," Morris said. "You remember Mr. Bloodworth, don't you?"

"Remember him?" the elder Gray barked. "Of course I remember him. He came to see me about some nonsense between Westings and the Park Lodge some months back, and I was going to set my hounds on him. Well, young man, are you keeping your end of the bargain and not doing any mischief?"

Beaky turned slightly pink. "Yes, sir. Of course. In fact, I was going to ask you about—"

"How'd you end up with so handsome a wife, eh?" the old man interrupted. "And from London, I'll be bound. One of these modern creatures who don't mind what they do, eh?"

Beaky's face was flaming now. "I wouldn't exactly say—"

"London is *such* a wicked place," Sabrina purred, sweeping up to Beaky's side and taking his arm. "Though not nearly as decadent as I hear it was back in the eighties." She put one graceful hand up to her cheek. "I understand you young blades got up to the most shocking escapades."

He gaped as she batted her long lashes at him. Then he burst into laughter.

173

"Hang me if you're not right about that. The girl has spirit, Bloodworth. You could have done worse."

"Now, Papa Gray, you mustn't tease." Frances put herself between him and Sabrina. "People will think you're serious, and you wouldn't want to embarrass Mr. Bloodworth." Her mouth was suddenly very prim. "Not about his wife."

"What? Oh. No harm, young Bloodworth. No harm. We're all friends these days, eh?"

Beaky glanced at Sabrina, saw she was smiling, and smiled, too. "Of course we are." He patted the white hand that clung to his arm. "In fact, when Drew and Morris and I were at the Hound and Hart the other day—"

"Just for a bite of lunch, my dear," Morris said as Frances shot him a poisonous glare. "Mr. Farthering had stopped to have a look at the Alfa Romeo and we got talking and—"

"Oh, don't go on about that silly car." She gave Drew a saccharine smile. "It's perfectly all right for you young fellows, of course, but Morris ought to have outgrown that sort of thing ages ago, don't you think?"

"It's a boy's car," the old man growled. "Something some scapegrace from university ought to be driving, not a man well into middle age."

"It doesn't do any harm, Father," Morris said, his voice scarcely audible.

"Quite right, Papa Gray," Frances said. "I've told him time and again—"

"I love sports cars," Sabrina said brightly. "They're so much fun." She edged past Frances and perched herself on the arm of Mr. Gray's chair. "You should come riding in my little Austin someday. You'd love it."

He chuckled. "Would I now? Well, well. Perhaps I should."

"Now, you know that would be very bad for your lungs," Frances said, tugging solicitously at the afghan over his lap. "Dr. Pine says you must stay warm."

"Pine's a quack," Mr. Gray muttered, but he patted her hand. "Don't fret now. There's life in the old man yet." He turned again to Sabrina. "Wouldn't know what to do without her, you know. It was the only worthwhile thing my son ever did, marrying her. I don't know how Westings would have gotten along if she hadn't taken charge of it. You'd think she had the blood of the Grays running in her veins and he the one who had only married in."

"We can't all be so practical," Sabrina said, and she turned her smile on Morris. "How dull it would be to think about sheep and generators and fencing all the time, don't you think?"

Before he could do more than give her a grateful nod, the butler returned and announced that dinner was served.

Sabrina hopped up from the arm of Mr. Gray's chair and, with a sly look at Frances, held out her hand to Morris. "You will take me in to dinner, won't you?"

"It would be my pleasure," he said, suddenly looking more suave and composed than Drew had ever seen him.

The elder Gray struggled to his feet with the aid of his cane and his daughter-in-law. "Mrs. Farthering, would you do me the honor?"

Madeline took his arm. "You must tell me all about Westings, Mr. Gray. It's such a lovely place."

He beamed at her, and Drew knew the old man was in safe hands for the time being. That left only Frances.

Drew made his most elegant bow and then offered her his arm. "May I, Mrs. Gray?"

With a baleful glance toward her husband, she accepted, and then she turned hospitably to Beaky.

"Don't be left out, Mr. Bloodworth. You must come along with us." She laid her hand on his arm, allowing him to escort her, too. "It's terribly awkward having odd numbers, isn't it? But, well, we couldn't leave out Papa Gray, could we?"

"Of course not," Beaky said, looking past her to where Morris was pulling out a chair for Sabrina at his father's left.

Frances followed his gaze, and her expression turned arch. "Poor Morris. Always in his little dream world, even if he knows it can't last long. But who am I to complain? I have Westings to look after, and of course, you have the Lodge. They are always there no matter who comes and goes."

She stopped at the opposite end of the long table from Mr. Gray, and Drew pulled out the chair for her. He took the seat to her right, across from a bemused-looking Beaky, unable to keep from wondering precisely what, or who, was in Morris's little dream world.

Morris sat himself between Drew and Sabrina. "I'm sure one of you can tell me something about what's going on in the civilized world. London and all that. I believe you lived there before you came up to the Lodge, Mrs. Bloodworth."

"Oh, yes," she said, leaning back slightly as the maid served the watercress soup. "All my life. Not that Yorkshire's not entirely charming, of course, but I am still very fond of London. I think I miss the theatre most."

"And well you might," Morris said with a sigh. "It's like visiting a new world every night. I did manage to get down to see *Richard of Bordeaux* last year, starring the magnificent Gielgud."

"Wasn't he wonderful?" Sabrina said. "King Richard was

certainly presented in a better light than he was in Shakespeare's version. Not so entitled and full of himself."

"But even in that, one feels rather sorry for him by the end. Shakespeare had the remarkable ability to evoke sympathy for even—"

"Really, Morris." Frances peppered her soup and then ate a spoonful. "I'm sure these young people don't want to hear about stuffy plays all night."

"No, my dear," Morris whispered, and he looked down into his soup.

"I enjoyed *Richard of Bordeaux* when Drew and I went to see it," Madeline said.

"Well, of course you would," Frances said. "You newlyweds don't even know where you are or what you're seeing half the time. Not that it isn't entirely sweet, of course."

She ended with an indulgent little smirk, and Mr. Gray peered at Madeline over his spoon.

"Newlyweds, are you? Ha. Doesn't surprise me. The two of you look as if you stepped out of one of those new talking pictures they have on in the city."

Drew didn't dare smile, even though talking pictures had been out for some years now and silents were quickly becoming a thing of the past.

"Not quite newlyweds anymore, sir. We'll be celebrating our second anniversary come December." He raised his glass to Madeline, meeting her eyes with a look meant for her alone and receiving such a look in return. "And I couldn't ask for anyone so perfectly suited to me. She even likes a good mystery as much as I do."

"'Let me not to the marriage of true minds admit impediments,'" Morris quoted, raising his glass as well. "You're a fortunate man, Farthering."

"I am a blessed one," Drew said, "in spite of myself."

"Balderdash," the old man sputtered. "It would be more of a miracle if a personable young man of intelligence, wealth, and family *didn't* end up with a fine-looking wife."

"That may be so, sir, though I know what a hash I've made of things choosing without God's blessing."

"Poppycock!"

"Father, please," Morris said.

"It's poppycock, and I shall say it's poppycock. Next thing this young gull will tell us is that he expects to find the great hound leering at him at the next crossroads."

Sabrina's spoon rattled into her bowl to break the sudden silence, but Drew only chuckled. "I daresay someone would like me to think so, but barghests hardly fall under my idea of Christian orthodoxy."

Mr. Gray drew his heavy brows together and then gave a low growl of a laugh. "Hang me if you don't remind me of that fool Miles. I never could get him to lose his temper either. Vicar or not, it's an outrage what happened to him. If Trenton and his imbeciles can't find the killer, I expect you to, am I understood, boy?"

"I shall certainly do my best, sir," Drew said, sobering. "If it wouldn't trouble the ladies too much, I should like to know your opinion of the whole situation. You've been here all your life and know everyone. Do you have any theories?"

"I'm afraid I'm the only one who ever had a cross word with him, and he never would answer me back." The old man's expression was tinged with regret. "He said he rather liked talking to me. It made him have to think about what he believed and why. Now, don't give me that sort of look. It's still nonsense, but he was sincere about it." He considered for a moment more, and his expression turned hard. "There'd be few tears shed if our local poacher swung for the murder, I can tell you that, but I can't think of why he would have done it in the first place. He's not one to lift a finger without there's profit in it. I know."

Drew hesitated, wondering if he ought to risk being asked to leave. Still, the opportunity might never again appear. He glanced at Madeline and then plunged ahead. "No disrespect, sir, but might I assume you've . . . had dealings with Midgley before?"

Mr. Gray frowned. "I can't say he hasn't done a job for me now and again. Years ago now, mind you, when Bloodworth was alive and really deviling me." He narrowed his jaundiced eyes. "I always suspected Midgley wasn't above taking money from him as well, laughing up his sleeve at us both."

Morris looked faintly disgusted but unsurprised.

Frances put her hand up to her open mouth. "Papa Gray! How could you!"

"Oh, don't look so shocked, girl." He held up his gnarled hands. "Did you think I was going to go out and cut fences with these? And Bloodworth was no better. I daresay even his nephew there would agree."

Beaky blinked. "Yes, sir, I would. And it doesn't surprise me in the least to hear he had Midgley do some of his dirty work. I'd like to apologize on his behalf, sir."

Mr. Gray scowled. "Oh, don't go on about that again. I'm too old and tired to worry over it anymore." He leaned over toward Beaky, more forbidding than ever. "I don't wish to discuss it ever again."

"Right." Beaky nodded, looking relieved. "We will consider the subject closed."

"About time," Sabrina said, giving her sweetest smile to her hostess. "It will be ever so much more neighborly."

She smiled at Morris, too.

The watercress soup was followed by poached salmon with cucumber, boeuf bourguignon, and some rather overcooked green beans. That one flaw in the meal was well compensated for by a divine raspberry meringue pudding and some of the best coffee Drew had ever tasted.

They retired to the drawing room for a glass of port and more conversation until the elder Gray began to nod off. Beaky quietly suggested it would be an opportune time to end the evening, and with thanks and compliments to the hostess, they all made their way to the car. Rather than waiting at the open door of the Bentley, the chauffeur was bent over the engine, electric torch in hand.

"What's the trouble, Basset?" Beaky asked, coming up to him.

"Beg pardon, sir, but she didn't sound right when I started her up. I just wanted to give her a look."

Beaky looked under the bonnet himself. "Anything?"

"Nothing I could tell in the dark here, sir. But I may have to tinker with her a bit in the morning."

"Will she get us home?" Sabrina asked, pulling her fur wrap closer as she, too, leaned in for a look.

The chauffeur touched his gray cap, his earnest young face looking younger and more earnest under the stylishly thin mustache he was attempting to sprout. "I believe so, madam. I don't think it's much of anything."

He shut the bonnet and then opened the door for her. Beaky handed her in and then Madeline, and then he and Drew took their places beside them.

"Old Gray wasn't such a bear as I'd expected," Drew said once they were under way.

Beaky shrugged. "He's a brassy old cove, there's no denying, though he seems to have taken to the two of you well enough."

"He and Frances oughtn't to bully Morris the way they do," Sabrina said, and then she made a dismissive gesture with one graceful hand, hardly more than a glitter of her diamond bracelet in the dimness of the car. "Not that it's any of my business if he won't stand up for himself."

"It's very kind of you to try to stand up for him, my dear," Beaky said, patting the hand in her lap.

At this, Drew glanced over at Madeline, but she was looking out the window and didn't, or wouldn't, see.

"Stop it," Madeline said once they were alone in their room that evening.

He turned to her, his dinner jacket only halfway off and one eyebrow raised.

"You've been smirking at me all night. Stop it."

"Smirking? Me? I never smirk."

"You always smirk." She put her hands on her hips. "You're doing it now. You always do when you think you're being clever. Stop it."

He chuckled and finished extricating himself from his jacket. "Well, don't pretend you didn't notice."

"She was just being nice." Madeline sat at the dressing table and began removing her jewelry. "Mr. Gray and Frances *are* awful bullies. Even you must have pitied poor Morris."

"I did and I do. I don't believe I've ever seen a man more unhappy with the realities of his life. He and Frances seem entirely unsuited for each other."

"That doesn't mean he and Sabrina are involved."

"No," Drew said, standing behind her so he could see into the mirror as he unknotted his tie. "But I've been thinking about that old kiln out on the moor. I thought it was odd finding those books there and that bottle of expensive wine. What if that's not the hiding place of our murderer but something a little more mundane?"

Madeline wrinkled her nose. "Nasty place for a lovers' meeting, isn't it?"

"Not exactly the Ritz, I'll grant you, but there's an awfully slim chance of being caught there. And Sabrina does enjoy her solitary walks out on the moor."

Madeline pursed her lips as she reached back to unfasten her necklace. She swatted Drew's hand when he tried to help her.

"I went out walking with her every time she's gone since we got here. She never once went that way."

"Exactly."

"And what does that mean?"

"She made sure to take you along, proving she does nothing but walk her dog, well away from the kiln."

She turned to him, eyes flashing. "And if she had gone that way, you would have seen that as proof, too."

He narrowed his eyes at her, determined to be offended, but he couldn't quite manage it and laughed instead. "You know, I expect I would have." He sighed and slouched against the corner of the dressing table. "Whatever are you going to do with so hopeless a wretch?"

She tugged the loose ends of his tie to pull him down to her for a brief kiss. "I think you're mistaken about Sabrina, but I'm not absolutely sure. If you hadn't been so determined Beaky was being wronged before we even came up here, I might have agreed with you by now. But I just don't see it. Delwyn, perhaps."

He pulled her up into his arms. "So you like the rugged type, eh? All that hair and dark mystery?"

"He could be attractive," she said, just to pique him. "To some women."

"I see."

She kissed his nose. "That's Delwyn, though. Morris? I just can't see it."

"I don't know." He thought for a moment. "It was rather telling when he mentioned the marriage of true minds. He certainly hasn't got that with Frances."

"No. However did they end up together?"

"But he and Sabrina did seem to enjoy talking about plays and the arts in general. It was all a bit too chummy, don't you think?"

"I do not think." She wriggled away from him and went into the bathroom to turn on the water in the sink. "It means only that she's a good conversationalist. Isn't that what we're all taught to do? Find something that interests the other person and then let him talk about it?"

She had him there. It was one of the most basic tenets of social grace.

He sat on the bed and removed his shoes. "True, darling, true. I promise you, I am trying my best not to leap to any disastrous conclusions. But I mustn't discount any possibilities either."

He heard nothing in response but the rustle of silk and then a bit of splashing, but soon she came out of the bathroom in just her slip, carrying her dress over one arm. She hung the dress in the armoire and then sat herself on the bed beside him, her arms around his waist.

"I guess it wouldn't hurt for me to keep an open mind, too. I don't really know Sabrina well enough to say what she might or might not do. I just wish we had more to go on."

He squeezed her close and kissed her fragrant hair. "We will, darling. We will."

— Thirteen —

After breakfast the next morning, Drew tapped on the open door to Beaky's study. Beaky sat at his desk, his brow furrowed in concentration over the letter he was reading, but it smoothed when he looked up and saw Drew.

"Oh, come in. Come in. I was hoping you'd pop by."

Drew came to the desk, taking a quick glance at the variety of envelopes scattered there, most of them still unopened. "Something about the case?"

Beaky shook his head. "Nothing about that, I'm afraid. But I did get an answer from the asylum, and now I'm more puzzled than ever."

"Oh, yes?"

Beaky handed him the letter. The letterhead gave an address in Norfolk.

My dear Mr. Bloodworth,

Thank you for your kind inquiry regarding support of St. Anthony's Mental Hospital. As I mentioned in my earlier letter, until the time of his death your uncle had been a great patron of ours, his generosity easing the suffering of many of our unfortunate residents for well over fifteen years. However, to answer your specific question, his contributions have chiefly been for the benefit of one Mr. Reginald Faber, who came to us in 1918 after serving in the late war. It was the elder Mr. Bloodworth's request that Mr. Faber should be cared for by every means at our disposal.

It is a sad reality that many of His Majesty's most valiant fighting men came back from the war not with victory, but with wounds, physical and mental, that are not easily healed. Here at St. Anthony's, we strive to give these men the treatment, shelter, and comfort that is no less than their due for the immense sacrifice they have made for king and country. Sadly, though, our resources are limited, and to many of our countrymen, the war and those who served in it are something long past and easily forgotten. It is only through the generosity of men such as your uncle and yourself, I have no doubt, that we are able to help those who have nowhere else to turn.

In hope that you will carry on your uncle's generous good work and continue to help those who cannot help themselves, I remain

> *Your obedient servant,*
> *Chesterton A. Grant,*
> *Superintendent*

Drew read the letter over twice and then handed it back. "Who's this Reginald Faber?"

"That's the puzzler," Beaky said. "I don't recall having heard the name before. I know Uncle never mentioned it to me."

"Perhaps someone in your family?" Drew suggested.

"I haven't heard of anyone called Faber among our relations. Perhaps Halford would know. He's been here longer than anyone. Well, except Cook. I ought to ask them both."

"Excellent idea. I've been wanting to talk to them anyway."

"You have?"

"If they've been here the longest, maybe they know something about the vicar that everyone else has forgotten. I haven't found anything to link him with Miss Patterson except that they were both elderly. It might be that your butler and your cook can think of something more significant. Something that actually makes sense."

Beaky nodded. "No harm trying, I expect. Shall we have them in separately or both at once?"

"Both, I think," Drew said after a moment's thought. "They may well think of something between the two of them that they wouldn't have lighted on individually."

"Right."

Beaky rang the bell, and Halford soon appeared, his dignified and carefully schooled expression unchanging when Beaky asked him to fetch the cook. He returned shortly thereafter with a tall, sallow-faced woman with hair too black to be natural.

"Good morning, Mrs. Norris," Beaky said. "Won't you sit down?"

She glanced warily at the chair he indicated.

"Please," he urged.

She finally sat, hands folded in her lap, legs crossed at the ankles, back ramrod straight and not touching the back of the chair. Halford, after some prompting, took the chair next to her.

"How are you this morning, Mrs. Norris?" Drew asked, taking a seat on the corner of Beaky's desk. "I must say the eggs at breakfast were a delight. I know they don't come out just right like that unless they're babied the whole time they're being cooked."

Mrs. Norris's sallow face colored faintly. "Very kind of you, sir. I do take as much care of them as I'm able. And I'm very well, thank you."

She didn't look very well. It might have been that she was just nervous about being called into Beaky's study, but somehow she seemed more unsettled than that.

"I won't keep you from your work more than a moment," Beaky said. "But since you and Halford have been at the Lodge longer than any of our people, I thought you might be able to answer some questions. Have either of you ever heard of a Reginald Faber?"

Mrs. Norris glanced at Halford, looking surprised by the question. "Faber? Yes, sir, I remember Faber. He was Mr. Sylvester's valet before they both went off to war. I don't know what happened to him after that. I always supposed he was killed when Mr. Sylvester was."

"Oh, no," Halford said decidedly. "Mr. Bloodworth, I mean your uncle, sir, told me years ago that Faber was in some sort of hospital on account of shell shock."

The cook covered her mouth with one sturdy hand. "A madhouse?"

"A hospital, Mrs. Norris," Beaky said firmly. "Halford, do you know if he and my uncle Sylvester served in the same unit?"

"I believe Faber was Mr. Sylvester's batman at the time of

his death, sir, and the only one in his unit to survive that particular battle."

Drew looked to Beaky for an explanation.

"He led his men straight into an ambush, forcing the Huns to spring their trap before the main force reached them," Beaky said. "My father said that saved hundreds of lives, even though Uncle Sylvester and all his men were lost. They gave him the Victoria Cross for it."

"A true hero," Drew said, and Beaky nodded, a wistful pride in his pale eyes.

"I wish I had known him longer. But at least we know now why Uncle Hubert was sending money to this St. Anthony's. I'll tell Rogers to carry on with whatever he was sending before. Poor Faber, he deserves at least that, wouldn't you say?"

"If he served your uncle in war as well as he had in peace, I'd say so, yes. I'd have thought you'd remember the name, though—if he was your uncle's valet."

"I suppose I must have heard it a time or two, but I wasn't here all that often before the war, and neither was Uncle Vester."

Drew thought for a moment. "I wonder how badly off the poor chap is."

Beaky shrugged. "Bad enough to be in an asylum all this time. Why?"

"How long was Faber at the Lodge?" Drew asked Halford. "Before he went to war."

"He came to us when Mr. Sylvester returned home from university, sir."

"So, besides yourself and Mrs. Norris here, he would have come before anyone else in service here now, yes?"

"Excepting Miss Patterson, of course," Mrs. Norris put in, "begging your pardon. She was before any of us."

Drew gaped at her. "What?"

"Oh, yes, sir. Miss Patterson was here until all the young gentlemen went off to school. Mr. Hubert, Mr. Marcus, and Mr. Sylvester. It was then she took a position in London, and we didn't hear from her again. You remember, Mr. Halford."

Halford nodded. "Indeed."

Miss Patterson had been here at the Lodge? How had no one mentioned this before?

"Did you know this, Beaky?" Drew asked.

"No. I knew they'd had a governess, but I had no idea it was the same Miss Patterson whom Sabrina had when she was a girl. I don't suppose I'd ever heard her name before Sabrina's father died, her time at the Lodge being well before mine." Beaky blinked rapidly. "Still, she would have left the Lodge years before Faber came. I don't know what they could possibly have to do with each other."

"No, obviously," Drew said. "I was just thinking, if he had times when he was thinking clearly, he might remember something about the old days here, something about the vicar perhaps that could help us with the investigation. I didn't expect this new twist."

"Nor I," Beaky admitted.

"Are there any other bits of information you haven't yet brought up, Mrs. Norris?" Drew asked with a wry smile.

The cook winced slightly. "No, sir. Mr. Halford and I have spoken of it. I hope we didn't do wrong, but we thought we might be of help. The only thing we see to link Miss Patterson and the vicar is that they were both old." She gave a nervous little laugh. "Made us wonder wouldn't we be next, if that's the case." At a reproving glance from the butler, she sobered. "I hadn't thought to say anything about Miss Patterson being here.

I hadn't thought it was important. I reckoned the police would know just in their regular investigations and all. It wasn't as if Miss Patterson was killed here or anything." She shuddered. "Not that we need more reminders of death."

Halford cleared his throat and gave her a withering glare.

She ducked her head. "Beg pardon, sir. My nerves are just a bit on edge this morning."

"Has something happened?" Beaky asked.

Mrs. Norris glanced at Halford and then quickly shook her head. "No, sir. I just—I'm sure it's nothing that ought to worry you, sir. Just foolishness, and I won't have it in my kitchen."

"Foolishness indeed," Halford said, his face a picture of grave disdain. "And in this day and age."

"What happened?" Drew pressed, intrigued now.

"Well, sir," the cook said, "it was Sigrid, the scullery girl. She went to the back door to bring in the milk first thing this morning like always and then came running back to me, her face as white as the milk she was holding. 'Look, Mrs. Norris,' she says. 'There over the threshold. The barghest!'"

"She saw it?" Drew asked, his pulse beating just the tiniest bit faster. "The hound?"

"Oh, no, sir. Nothing as daft as that. But there were some dirty marks on the floor. A floor that was clean enough to eat off last night, mind you. I think it was her imagination like as not and not truly a dog's paw marks. How would a dog have got in there, I'd like to know? That door is locked last thing every night, I can vouch for that myself. Besides, those marks were far too big to be paw prints. Why, they were nearly the size of my sauté pan."

"You should have told me, Mrs. Norris," Beaky said.

"I'm sorry, sir. I didn't like to disturb you with superstitions and such. Sigrid is a gullible little thing and believes anything she's told."

Drew got to his feet, releasing the tight grip he'd had on the edge of the desk. "I'd like to see the marks if I might, Mrs. Norris. Whatever made them."

"Oh, I'm sorry, Mr. Farthering, but I had Sigrid scrub them off. The whole floor, as a matter of fact. I didn't want her repeating that nonsense to the other girls and spooking the lot of them before breakfast was got on."

Drew pressed his lips together, fighting to keep nothing but mild disappointment in his expression. "Bad luck that, eh? I would count it as a great favor, however, Mrs. Norris, if you would leave anything of that sort as it's found, if anything should again be found, until either I or Mr. Bloodworth have had a chance to give it a look. Fair enough?"

"Yes, sir. I didn't mean . . ."

"We understand," Beaky said. "Just be careful to let one of us know if you see anything or remember anything, no matter how small you think it might be. You as well, Halford."

"Just as you say, Mr. Bloodworth."

Mrs. Norris ducked her head. "I'm very sorry, sir. I hadn't thought it would be important to the case, not something as silly as the barghest."

"One never knows what might be the key to an entire investigation," Drew said, and then he added, "I don't suppose there's any use looking at your floor now, is there?"

Mrs. Norris looked genuinely distressed. "I'm sorry, sir, but no. My girls know when I say scrub, I mean scrub. I wish I had thought better than I did when I had those marks cleaned up, but I can't tell you any more about them now than I have done already. Not that you're not more than welcome to come and have a look anytime you like."

"I don't suppose that will be necessary. Anything you'd like to ask, Beaky, old man?"

Beaky looked faintly befuddled. "I expect we ought to let them get back to their work."

"Not yet." Sabrina was suddenly there at the study door, her mouth defiantly firm despite the hint of a quaver in her voice. "I want to know what it was. What was lying over the threshold in the kitchen?"

Beaky leapt up from the desk and went to her. "Don't be silly, dear. There was only some dirt tracked in, I imagine. Mrs. Norris says it was nothing."

"That's not what Sigrid told Louise."

"Now, you know Sigrid is a very silly girl," Beaky soothed, ushering her over to the chair the cook had vacated at her mistress's arrival. "And Louise may be a very fine lady's maid, but she's a terrible talebearer, and most of what she says isn't the least bit true."

"I'm very sorry, madam," Mrs. Norris said. "I told Sigrid not to be spreading fables among the girls. I see I shall have to speak to her about it."

"No," Sabrina said, now looking more angry than frightened. "Don't scold her. I'm glad I heard about it. You should have told me, Beaky. It's only right I should know."

"I only just heard it myself. And really, it's nothing." He shook his head at her just the slightest bit and then turned to the butler, who was looking as distressed as the cook over the unseemly display. "Halford, you and Mrs. Norris had best get back to your work. We'll ring if you are needed."

"Very good, sir."

The two of them made a hasty retreat, and Beaky shut the study door after them.

"You don't believe that nonsense, Sabrina," he said, and while his tone was mild, he looked more vexed with her than Drew had seen before.

She lifted her chin, her mouth firmly set. "But it was in the north wing. I saw the paw prints. And now it's been in the kitchen."

"Nonsense. The kitchen door is kept locked at night. How could it have gotten in?"

"How could it have gotten upstairs in the north wing?" she demanded. "And with no prints coming and going?"

"Sabrina—"

She shoved his hands away from her. "It was over the threshold. You know what that means."

"Sabrina, dear—"

"It means someone in the house is going to die!" There was a moment of utter silence, and then she drew a sobbing breath.

"It's nothing but a story," Beaky said gently. "You know that."

She turned to Drew, a glitter of frustrated tears in her eyes. "I told myself it was foolishness and I wasn't going to listen to it. I'm from London, not one of these backward villages on the moor. But now . . . Oh, I just don't know what to think."

"We don't know exactly what Mrs. Norris saw," Drew said quietly. "Or the scullery girl. Perhaps it was paw prints. Perhaps it was something else. I'm fairly sure that whatever it was, it was not caused by a spectral hound seeking to avenge itself on unpunished wrongdoers."

She gave him a defiant glare, yet she seemed to calm somewhat. "There were paw prints up in the north wing. You can't deny those."

"No," Drew admitted. "But we can find out what made them

and why." He leaned down just a bit, looking steadily into her eyes. "We will find out, I promise you that. For now, try not to worry about what these superstitions say."

"But—"

"I'm not saying there's no danger. That, I believe, is very real. Like the perpetrator. We just don't know what all of this means yet."

She didn't say anything more, but only looked back at him, her dark eyes wide and as vulnerable as a child's. Then she pursed her lips and flipped open the carved box on Beaky's desk and extracted a cigarette. Beaky immediately lit it for her.

"He's right, my dear. I don't want you to worry. Drew here's the expert. We just have to give him time enough to solve the case."

She exhaled, the smoke coming out in jerky puffs rather than a smooth stream. "Yes, of course." She forced a smile. "It works on one, you know. The moor. Miles and miles of emptiness, and the wind. Oh, the ceaseless wind." Her voice shook, and she took another deep drag on her cigarette.

Beaky looked at Drew, clearly distressed, and then he turned again to his wife. "You know I'm supposed to go to Harrogate about the loan for the remodeling this afternoon. Would you rather I put it off?"

"Don't be silly, Beaky. I'm not going to have a hysterical fit. Go do whatever it is you need to do."

"Perhaps you and Madeline could go shopping in the village or go out for tea or something nice."

Sabrina rolled her eyes and stood. "I'm not so badly off that I need minding. I'll find something to do. Don't you worry about me." She crushed out her cigarette and let herself out of the room.

Drew watched her go, taking particular care to keep his thoughts out of his expression. The hound's prints had been seen in the upstairs of the north wing and, perhaps, near the kitchen door. Both places had been locked, inaccessible to anyone or anything from the outside. But what about the inside? Someone who would have been locked in rather than out? For someone who seemed so practical and cynical, Sabrina had seemed awfully shaken by a creature formed wholly out of superstition.

"Are you certain you ought to go just now, old man?" Drew asked.

Beaky frowned. "I can't say it's the best of times, but Treadwell at the bank there has offered me an excellent rate, and I'd very much like to get that settled while it's available. We can't start the work until winter is over, of course, but I'm also supposed to meet with the architect while I'm there. I'd like to get him working on plans and get things like furnishings and draperies and such started. There's a man in York who does lovely carved furniture pieces and even moldings and such for the house itself. I'd like to be able to get him going as quickly as possible, too."

"Very nice."

"And just between ourselves, I think it would do Sabrina a world of good to have something to occupy her time for a few months. She's seemed a bit moody the last little while. I know the moor is not what she's used to."

"Perhaps brightening up the old place, making it more her own, would be just the thing." Drew hesitated. "Do you think your car's in the sort of shape she ought to be to make the drive? I thought she sounded as though she was struggling a bit on the way back last night."

"It seems everything happens at once," Beaky said, looking

resigned to his fate. "There's nothing for it, but I must take Sabrina's little Austin."

Drew chuckled. "I'm sure you'll be positively fetching in it."

Beaky made a face. "Well, besides it being that hideous shade of yellow, I always look rather the fool driving it. I always end up with my knees up around my ears trying to accordion myself behind the wheel."

Drew swatted his shoulder. "You'll survive, I'm sure. Oh, what do you think about me sending someone along to St. Anthony's to ask after this Faber chap? Some of these fellows who can't remember yesterday can talk in great detail about what happened twenty years ago."

"Yes, I've seen that before. Very well, if it's not too large an imposition, I'd appreciate your seeing to that. Let me know what you find out. But really, Drew, mind who you send. Don't have some ninny blunder down there and badger the poor fellow. He's clearly been through enough already."

"Not to worry," Drew assured him. "I have just the man for the job."

Once more, Mr. Stapleton requested the honor of Mr. Selden's presence. Nick looked even scruffier and more disreputable than ever.

"I've had more time with Midgley," he said by way of explanation.

"'Bad company corrupts good morals,'" Drew said piously. "I think you shall have to be sent away for the sake of your own soul. If it's not already too late."

Nick made a great show of remorse.

"Seriously," Drew said, "I need you to go down to Norfolk

for me and speak to this chap Faber. Or if he's not in a position to see you, find out more about him."

He gave Nick a card with St. Anthony's address on it and the name of the superintendent.

Nick looked at him, eyebrows raised. "An asylum?"

"He was employed at the Lodge before the war." Drew gave him the details. "I'm hoping he might know something about those days that might tell us a bit about the vicar or even Miss Patterson. It's a long shot, I grant you. He may not be able to speak to you, or make much sense if he does, but I'd like you to go down all the same. If you would."

"I'll do my best."

"And do be very gentle with him, eh?"

"Naturally," Nick said. "It can't be easy for him, no matter how well he's treated there."

"One last thing. I called down to Farthering Place this morning, just to see how things were getting along and all. Denny wanted me to give you a message."

"Good old Dad. How's the buttling coming on? I expect he's perishing to see me."

"He did mention a shocking lack of tomfoolery about the place without you there."

"I promise I'll make it up to him when I get back. And what was it he wanted you to tell me?"

"He says he's sent an envelope with no return address to one Tom Selden, care of General Delivery here in Bunting's Nest. He thought you wouldn't want to wait to see the contents until after you returned home."

"The contents being?"

"A letter from a Miss Holland, Charleston, South Carolina, United States of America."

Nick's face lit. "Carrie. I was hoping to have something from her before too much longer." Concern darkened his expression. "Poor girl. I wish I could be there with her."

"How is Mr. Holland?" Drew asked. "Still the same?"

"Carrie says he's been declining since last year. She hasn't come out and said it, but I think she fears the worst is coming."

Drew felt a sudden heaviness in his heart. He had liked Carrie's father. Madeline had been close to him, so close that she had asked him to give her away at their wedding. And poor Carrie, she was clearly her daddy's girl. *Dear God, if it is his time, comfort them both.*

"If you want to go to her, Nick, you know you need only say so."

The concern in Nick's eyes was overshadowed by pain. "I've begged her to let me come. I told her I didn't want her to go through this by herself, but she said it would be better if I left things as they are. She said she needs to be with her father if . . . if this is to be the last. I suppose she's right." He drew in a hard breath and then squared his shoulders and lifted his chin. "She knows she can call on me if she needs me. For now, though, I have a job to see to. Anything you need while I'm out? Milk? Bread? Some of that fishy sandwich paste they serve at the pub?"

Drew chuckled softly. Nick was never one to stay down long. "I think we're well stocked at the Lodge. How are things at Mrs. Denton's? Anything you need?"

"Apart from at least one morning when I'm not jarred from sleep before six? No, can't think of anything."

"Well, buck up, old man. You'll have a night or two in Norfolk to catch up on your rest."

"Right. I'll let you know what I find out from Faber."

With a nod, Nick strode back toward Partridge Row.

"Oh, Nick," Drew called after him, and he turned. "Do stop by the post office before you go."

Nick grinned. "Wouldn't miss it."

— Fourteen —

Drew returned to the Lodge just before teatime, happy to see that Madeline hadn't gone into the village with Sabrina after all. The three of them sat down to cucumber and prawn and egg and watercress sandwiches, petit fours, and the promised tea cakes and jam. Their hostess ate very little, and no matter how much Drew and Madeline tried to engage her in conversation, she responded only minimally. It was already growing dark when the maid took the tea things away. Soon the footman came to replenish the fire and turn on more lights.

"I suppose we'd all better go dress for dinner," Sabrina said, startling the dog dozing at her feet. "Of all the nights in the year, Beaky would be late tonight."

Without another word, she tossed her ever-present cigarette into the fireplace and stalked out of the room. Still dazed from sleep, Raphael trotted after her.

Drew looked at his wife, one eyebrow raised.

"I think that paw print at the threshold bothers her more than she admits," Madeline said, her voice low.

"She does seem rather unsettled," he mused, "but is it over something that's happened or something she thinks will happen?"

"The barghest?" Madeline glanced toward the door, lowering her voice even more. "Do you think she truly believes all that?"

"Or wants us to believe she does."

Madeline put one finger to her lips and then hurried upstairs to dress. Soon Drew found himself admiring her reflection in the tall looking glass. Her simple gown of draped rose-colored silk made her skin look as fine as porcelain with just a hint of a blush, and the Farthering pearls complimented it admirably, but she frowned as she touched her chignoned hair.

"I wish I had Beryl here. Just for twenty minutes or so."

"Nonsense. You've done it beautifully." He kissed the one shoulder the gown left tantalizingly bare. "Besides, we haven't got twenty minutes. I'm sure they'll sound the gong for dinner any time now."

But they heard nothing. They found Sabrina precisely where she had been earlier, sitting before the fire in the drawing room, puffing away on a cigarette with Raphael at her feet. The only difference was that there was a diamond clip pulling back her golden hair at one side and she had on an ice-blue beaded gown that gave her blue eyes a spark of cold fire.

"No gong?" Drew asked, checking the time on the mantel clock. It was three minutes past eight.

"No Beaky," Sabrina said, her mouth turned down in annoyance. "He might at the least have rung up to say he'd be late."

Just then the telephone did ring. There was a moment's delay, and then Halford appeared in the drawing room doorway.

"The telephone for you, madam."

"At last." Sabrina put out her cigarette and snatched up the receiver from the telephone at the end of the sofa. "Really, Beaky, if you're going to be as late as—oh."

As she listened to whoever was on the other end of the line, her expression changed from annoyance to bewilderment and then was suddenly without emotion at all.

"How bad? He's not—"

She listened again, and then exhaled, a touch of color returning to her face.

"Yes. Of course. Right away. Thank you."

She rang off and stood looking as if she didn't know which way to run.

Drew took her arm, steadying her. "What is it?"

She pressed her clasped hands to her mouth for the briefest of moments, and then she pulled away from him, giving him her usual hard smile. "Beaky's gone and cracked up my car coming back from Harrogate. No, no, don't look like that, he's all right. He's at a house in Ripley, where the police took him after the accident, and he's had a doctor look at him and everything. Would you mind terribly driving with me over to collect him? Has the Bentley been seen to, Halford?"

"Basset told me earlier this evening that he had found the problem and had mended it, madam. I should think it would handle the drive nicely now."

"Good. Very good." Sabrina turned again to Drew. "Will you go with me?"

"Right away," Drew said. "Would you like to come along, Madeline, or had you rather stay here?"

"I could do with just Basset, if you two had rather not," Sabrina began, but Madeline was already telling Halford to get their things.

"We couldn't let you go by yourself."

"Wouldn't dream of it." Drew took Sabrina's coat when the maid brought it and politely helped her into it. "We'll get over to where they've got Beaky and bring him right home. No need to worry."

Ripley lay just north of Harrogate. Sabrina smoked the entire length of the drive from Bunting's Nest, leaving Drew and Madeline no choice but to leave the windows down despite the frigid night. They talked hardly at all. Sabrina knew little more about what had happened than what Drew had overheard of her conversation, and it was only natural for her to be preoccupied and upset just now.

The trip was not a long one, and soon they were pulling up at the end of a row of houses at the west end of the village. Drew peered up at the last one.

"I think this is Greengate, Basset. I can't tell if the gate is green or blue or lavender, but it's the only one with a light on. I think it's worth a try. Stay here until I find out for certain."

The chauffeur pulled over. Drew went up to the house and was quickly back again.

"He's here all right."

He opened the rear door of Beaky's car to hand the ladies out, but Sabrina was too quick for him. She was nearly at the door before Drew and Madeline caught up to her, but the three of them went in together.

The house belonged to an elderly couple called Blankensop, and it seemed unlikely that either of them had stayed up at such a scandalous hour since Armistice Day. They both sat owl-eyed on the sofa staring at Beaky, who was bundled up in an easy chair with his clothing torn and bloodied and one bandaged leg propped up on an ottoman.

"There you are, my dear," he said when he saw Sabrina,

trying to smile and then thinking better of it when it tugged at his split lip.

She merely stood there, hands on hips, mouth in a tight line. "What in the world were you thinking, Beaky? And what have you done to the Austin? You know how much I love that one. How could you?"

Beaky winced and smiled anyway. "Sorry, darling. It couldn't be helped. The brakes just went on me all of a sudden."

"How bad is it?" Drew asked, and Beaky shrugged, wincing again.

"She's a goner, I'm afraid. I hit that stone wall and then—"

"No, not the car, old man. How are you?"

"Oh, right." He glanced at his wife. "It's not so bad. Bumps and bruises mostly. I'll likely have a few scars as souvenirs. There's the leg and this wrist." He held up his left arm, showing the hand and forearm tightly bandaged. "And my head is going something awful."

"What did the doctor say?" Madeline asked.

"Looks worse than it is," he said, again glancing at Sabrina. "I bashed my wrist and my head when I crashed. The leg I bunged up trying to get out of the ditch. The trousers wouldn't be so bad if the doctor hadn't had to cut one side open to the knee."

"So you were coming back from Harrogate when you—"

"Oh, no," Beaky said. "Hadn't got there actually. I was headed that way at a pretty good clip and came to a rather sharp bend in the road. Well, the road bent but the car didn't. I couldn't slow her down enough to take the turn without flying into that wall. I think I must have sat there some while before I came round again. Then I had to work my way out of the car. The front's sort of mashed to one side, a bit like an accordion." He looked again at his wife. "Sorry, darling. Anyway, once I got myself out, I fell into the ditch at the bottom of the wall. It was full of slush and I don't know what. Nasty. Gave myself a fairly good cut on the shin—nearly to the bone, the doctor said."

Sabrina shook her head, lips pursed. "You've got to be more careful, Beaky. Really."

"The doctor did clean it up well, didn't he?" Madeline asked.

Beaky chuckled. "I don't know how even one germ could have survived, judging by whatever he poured into the cut. It stung like blue blazes."

"Good old Beaky," Drew said, giving him a gentle shake of the shoulder. "Do you think you can manage getting out to your car?"

"If you'll lend a hand. I'd rather like to get out of these folks' way as quickly as I can."

"It's no trouble, I'm sure," said Mrs. Blankensop, though it seemed from her tone that it was a great deal of trouble indeed. "It was rather a surprise when young Mr. Clopton brought him in here, wasn't it, Father?"

"Eh, Mother?" said her husband, cupping one hand to his ear.

"I said it was a surprise when the gentleman was brought in!"

Drew smiled and nodded at the old man, trying not to cringe at the near shout. "Yes, it must have been. Well, we'll just take him on home and be out from underfoot."

He managed to get Beaky to his feet. Madeline took his battered hat and put it firmly on his head, and between the two of them they got him into his coat and gloves. Sabrina stood to one side, watching the whole process, and Drew couldn't decide quite how to read her expression. Fearful? Bewildered? As usual, she didn't give away much, but there was something there.

Beaky leaned heavily on Drew's shoulder and, hopping on his good leg, got down the walkway without much trouble. He got a shoe full of slush at the curb and twisted his bad wrist trying to lower himself into the back seat, but otherwise the operation was a success, and they were all soon back at the Lodge.

"I'd better get Anderson to help him to bed," Sabrina said once they were inside.

"We can manage," Drew told her. "Don't you think so, old man?"

Beaky looked at the curved stairway that led to the upper floor. "I think so. Don't you worry, Sabrina, darling. I'll be right as rain before long."

"I wonder you didn't kill yourself," she said. "I told you to be careful in this weather."

"I was," he said, leaning more heavily on Drew. "It was just an awful time for the brakes to go, and there's not a lot I can do about that."

"Had you been having trouble with them?" Drew asked.

"I didn't usually drive the Austin. I don't know. Had you noticed anything wrong, Sabrina?"

She shrugged. "No. But you know I don't know anything about cars beyond driving them."

"I'm glad you weren't driving tonight. You drive much too fast as it is, and you might have gotten into a worse crack-up than I did."

"I drive fast because I'm a better driver than you are. More than likely, I would have made the turn and not wrecked the car." She sighed. "I did rather like that one."

"And you shall have a new one, my sweet," Beaky promised. "The very moment I'm back on my feet."

"I don't think you ought to still be on your feet right now," Madeline said. "Shouldn't you get him up to his room, Drew?"

"Right away, darling."

They all trooped upstairs to find Miss Windham and a pair of maids in the master's room, stoking the fire and warming the sheets and generally making things cozy. Beaky's valet had laid out his night gear and was waiting to help him into it. Seeing they were no longer needed, Drew and Madeline went back down to the drawing room, where Miss Windham had said that sandwiches and tea would be waiting. Sabrina followed them down.

"I was afraid something was wrong," Sabrina said, her mouth tight. "I could just feel it."

Madeline took her arm and sat her on the sofa and then poured her some tea. "I'm glad it wasn't any worse. Too bad about your car, though."

Drew took a cup for himself. "I don't much care for what Beaky said about the brakes. About their going all of a sudden. That'll have to be looked at."

"I don't think it's any use." Sabrina set down her cup and lit a cigarette. "From what he said, the thing's a complete loss, even if the brakes could be repaired. I'm sure it'll have to be hauled away."

"I'm not worried about repairs," Drew said. "I'm wondering if someone didn't mean for there to be an accident tonight."

She laughed, but there was no humor in the sound. "Don't be absurd. Who in the world would want to kill Beaky?"

"Who wanted to kill the vicar? And Miss Patterson?"

Sabrina picked up her cup. "But he almost never drove that car. Who would have known he would take it this time? Usually I—" The cup made a faint rattling noise against the saucer, and she set it down swiftly. "Usually I drive it."

He said nothing in response.

Madeline's eyes were round. "Drew, you don't think . . . ?"

"I don't think anything just yet. We'll have to have the car looked at before we can even begin to consider it wasn't just a breakdown."

Sabrina shoved her teacup away and picked up her cigarette. "It doesn't make sense," she muttered, almost to herself. "None of it makes sense."

"Do you know of anyone who might want you out of the way?" Drew asked.

She shook her head, making the perfect curl of fair hair against her cheek tremble.

"Don't worry about it tonight," Madeline said, giving Drew a reproving glance. "It was probably just an accident."

"Right," Sabrina said, a little tremor in her voice. "Right. Of course."

"Come on," Madeline said, holding out her hand. "Why don't you go on up to bed, too? You'll feel better out of those fussy clothes and into a hot bath. Things always look brighter in the morning."

Sabrina rubbed one eye with her fist, smearing her mascara. She nodded and followed Madeline away like a child.

"Is she settled in?" Drew asked when Madeline returned several minutes later.

"Louise was seeing to her. I'm sure she will be fine. Thank God, Beaky wasn't seriously hurt."

"Yes," Drew said. "Funny, don't you think, that Beaky just happened to be driving her car today?"

Madeline nodded. "No matter what she says, it's a good thing he was driving and not she. She would have been in a much worse fix, especially trying to climb out of that ditch."

"Or there might not have been a fix at all."

For a moment she looked puzzled. Then she looked cross. "Exactly what are you trying to say? You saw how upset she was."

209

"Upset because he was in an accident? Or because it wasn't fatal?"

She gave him a cool glance. "That's a rather horrible thing to say, don't you think?"

"It's a rather horrible thing to *do*." He glanced toward the door, only then noticing she hadn't shut it behind her. "If you want to hear me out, perhaps we'd best talk in our room."

He offered her his arm, but she merely swept out ahead of him and hurried up the stairs. He followed her up and, making sure their bedroom door was firmly shut, sat beside her on the divan in front of the window.

"Just exactly what are you accusing her of?" Madeline asked when he didn't immediately speak.

"Nothing. Yet."

"But what are you thinking?"

"It just seems quite the coincidence that those brakes should fail on one of the rare times he's driving her car, and at the same time his car happens to be out of service."

"I agree," she said. "It seems like a very sloppy way to get rid of Beaky, if that was the plan. Why not just fix the brakes on his car?"

"That wouldn't do. Not if one wanted to give the impression that Sabrina was the intended victim and Beaky had just been in the wrong place at the wrong moment."

"And if that really is the case?"

"It would be quite the coincidence." He gave her a look that plainly said he thought she knew better. "Do you genuinely believe it was? Just that?"

She sighed and began unpinning her hair. "It does seem awfully convenient. But it *could* have happened that way."

"Yes, I grant you, it could."

"But if it was all planned, as you say, someone had to have tampered with Beaky's car before Sabrina's. You don't suspect their chauffeur, do you?"

Drew frowned. "I'll talk to him, of course, but from what I've seen of him, he seems rather stolid and loyal."

"Anyone might be paid off, you know." Madeline undid her bracelet and then slipped off her rings, apart from her wedding band and engagement ring. "And who else would have had the opportunity or the means?"

"Think back, darling. When did the Bentley start having trouble?"

"After dinner. At Westings."

"Precisely. And no doubt our stolid and loyal chauffeur was in the Grays' kitchen all night with his feet up by the fire, having a mug of cider and whatever was left of our boeuf bourguignon and chatting up the parlormaid. Anyone could have gone out to the drive and done a bit of mischief. Anyone who's familiar with engines."

"Drew," she breathed, "you don't mean—?"

"Morris likes cars. Very much."

"So you think Morris wanted to kill Beaky? Over Sabrina?" she demanded.

"Morris also likes art. And literature. And romantic foreign places."

She wrinkled her brow, clearly not following him now.

"Think of what Nick and I saw in the lime kiln. Novels about stormy romances and forbidden loves, fine wine." He raised an eyebrow. "Sonnets."

"I'll admit it does seem more like a trysting place than a murderer's lair, but Morris Gray is certainly not the only man in the world to use a poem or a love story to seduce a woman."

She looked rather disgusted. "You've certainly dropped Delwyn as a suspect awfully suddenly."

"Oh, no," he said. "It's decidedly not Delwyn. Not there anyway."

"How can you be so sure?"

He stepped on the back of his left heel with his right foot, pulling off his shoe in a way that would have made his valet, Plumfield, come near tears. "Opportunity, my love. Delwyn lives in his own cottage away from everyone else. Alone. If he wanted to entertain a visitor, no one need ever know it." He pulled off his right shoe just as he had done the left. "Morris Gray lives with his wife and father and a houseful of servants. For him, a trysting place, no matter how miserably tawdry, would be a necessity."

She removed her necklace and put it with the rest of her jewelry in the velvet-lined case she had brought along with her. Then she slipped off her satin slippers and set them neatly in the bottom of the armoire with the others she had brought. Finally she came to stand before him again.

"You know you haven't the slightest proof of anything."

He shrugged. "I rarely do. But now it's you who must be fair. It makes a bit of sense, doesn't it?"

Her mouth tightened. She wasn't going to admit it.

"Why do you feel you must defend her?" he pressed. "You barely know her."

"I know she's been hurt."

He sat forward a little more. "She's told you something."

"No, not specifically, so don't get that bloodhound look. I just . . . can tell."

He leaned back again, disappointed. Madeline was a perceptive woman, often picking up on nuances of emotion that he himself missed. There was certainly more to Sabrina than her sophisticated and often-hard exterior, but what was it? Neither of them really knew. Not yet.

"So you haven't the slightest proof of anything either."

"No," she admitted, and then her cold expression softened into regret. "Oh, I don't know what to think. Of course I don't know. And you don't know. Everything you said about her and Morris is perfectly possible." She sat next to him again, clinging to his arm. "I just don't believe it. If you think Beaky is too dull and unattractive to suit her, how can you think poky old Morris would be? And enough to commit not one but ultimately three murders over?"

He gave her a sly little grin. "It's hard to say what makes someone attracted to someone else. It's not always what you'd think."

Her lips twitched. "That's my line."

"It does seem a rather odd pairing. Perhaps, deep down, Sabrina is a romantic. Shall I woo you with poetry and romantic prose?"

That made her giggle. "You already do, and it's terribly irresistible, but . . ."

"But?"

She considered for a moment, sobering once more. "I don't know if it would be the least bit effective if I didn't already love you. It certainly wouldn't make me want to meet you out in some nasty hole in the ground or become a murderer."

"But if someone else had found you out? The vicar? Your old nursemaid? If they knew and were going to spoil your comfortable and privileged situation by telling it to just the wrong person, mightn't you? Perhaps the thing with Morris wasn't anything like a grand passion. At least not on her part. She seems the type who might amuse herself with someone merely because she could. Perhaps even just to get one over on Frances. I hadn't thought of that before. But Frances seems oddly unmoved by the idea of her husband making temporary liaisons. Westings will continue on."

"But why kill Beaky, then?" Madeline asked. "If the two people who knew your secret were already dead and you didn't actually want to be free to marry your lover, the man you were merely toying with, why go to the trouble of killing your husband?"

"So you could be free to marry the gamekeeper?"

"Ugh." She poked his shoulder with one finger. "You're incorrigible."

"What? Didn't you say Delwyn was the sort of fellow a woman might have a grand passion for?"

"Now you're just running in circles." She pushed away from him. "I'm going to wash my face and go to bed."

She stood, but he caught her hand before she could take even one step. "I've thought of something to do for Iris."

"Iris?"

"Midgley's girl. You remember."

Madeline thought for a moment. "I'm not sure you ever told me her name."

"Didn't I? Anyway, I thought we might go into the village in the morning and then go out and see her."

Madeline looked faintly suspicious. "You want me to go with you this time? What if he's there?"

"I happen to know he and Mr. Selden have a job of some sort tomorrow. Nick assures me that it's nothing very illegal."

"And meanwhile . . . ?"

He tugged her hand, urging her toward him so he could

touch his lips to it. "Meanwhile you and I go out to visit Iris. You can tell her how much you admire her spinning, and at the same time look her over, and the cottage as well, and tell me if there's anything I've missed." Again he kissed her hand. "Even if I do bicker with you from time to time over it, I know I don't always notice everything I ought. Especially about ladies and their particular ways."

She tried to look annoyed. "You were going to say 'peculiar,' weren't you?"

He grinned. "Either way. The point is that I wouldn't be nearly so well off without your help. What do you say?"

"I still say you're incorrigible, but I must be just as bad. What are we going to do for her?"

"We will, I hope, give her a passport to anywhere in the world she would care to go."

— Fifteen —

The next day, as advertised, Drew and Madeline walked into Bunting's Nest and made their way over to the Midgley cottage, Drew with a box under one arm.

She looked the place over when they approached it. "Not very nice, is it?"

"Not Buckingham Palace, for certain," he said, "but it's sound enough."

He knocked on the door and immediately heard the scrape of the Midgley girl's gun.

"Who's there, please?" she asked, again with that forced calm that didn't quite cover her wariness.

"Miss Midgley? It's Drew Farthering here, and I've brought along Mrs. Farthering. I hope we haven't come at an inconvenient time."

She opened the door, her pale face puzzled. "I—I didn't think you would come back." She wiped her hands on her apron and gestured for Drew and Madeline to come inside. "I haven't gotten to my tidying yet. I do hope things don't look too very bad. My father—" she faltered—"if you've come to ask me about my father, I'm afraid I can't tell you any more than I already have. He's in and out of the house to the Lord knows where, and I certainly don't."

Madeline looked questioningly at Drew. He couldn't keep the disappointment out of his expression.

"I would be remiss, Miss Midgley, if I hadn't asked about him, but that isn't what we've come for."

Iris made her way to one of the ladder-back chairs. "Please sit down."

"We won't stay but a moment." Drew put the box down on the table. "If you would, Miss Midgley, allow me to present my wife."

Again Iris wiped her hands on her apron and then dropped just a hint of a curtsey. "Good morning, Mrs. Farthering. I'm very pleased, I'm sure."

"I'm the one who's pleased." Madeline took the girl's outstretched hand. "I must tell you how much I enjoy knitting with your yarn. I've never had any that was so soft and smoothly spun."

"You've come about my spinning?" The girl turned faintly pink. "You're too kind, ma'am."

"I don't know how you manage it, not being able to see." Madeline was somehow able to sound admiring and not patronizing and not the least bit awkward. "I don't think I could do it."

"Oh, I wasn't born blind," Iris told her placidly. "I had scarlet fever when I was twelve. My mother said they should have had the doctor come sooner, but it's just as likely it wouldn't have made any difference."

"I'm so very sorry," Madeline said.

"I can be sorry for myself or I can get on with things. That's what Mum always told me." A smile touched Iris's pale lips. "And what I can't see, I can imagine."

Madeline went over to the spinning wheel, admiring the wool Iris had been working with, a soft shade of lavender that perfectly suited her coloring. Her eyes lit. "This is lovely, what you're working on now. Is it promised to anyone?"

Drew made a note to himself to make sure they came away with some yarn that color.

"No." Iris reached out to stroke the cloud of wool on the distaff. "Except I generally take most of it to Mrs. Preston to sell in Bunting's Nest."

"She wouldn't mind if you sold us this now, would she?" Drew asked, and the girl gave a shy shrug.

"I don't suppose. I could always spin some of the other colors I have waiting."

"Excellent." Drew pressed some money into her hand. "Will that be enough?"

She took it, feeling the coins, and her sightless eyes widened. "That's far too much, sir. And I haven't any change. I'm afraid I—"

"Well, bad luck me then, eh?" he said with a chuckle, pressing her hand around the coins. "I suppose I shall have to be a bit better prepared the next time."

"I would probably pay that much in London for yarn of this quality," Madeline assured her. "And you've saved us the expense of a trip."

The girl reddened even more but smiled. "You're too kind, ma'am. Sir. Is there something more I might do for you?"

He glanced at Madeline and she nodded in response.

"My husband was telling me how helpful you were, answering his questions the other day and everything, and we were wondering if you might not do us another favor."

Iris looked slightly puzzled. "If I can, yes."

"It's sort of a long story," Madeline began, "but we're very fond of our housekeeper, Mrs. Devon. She's made me feel so welcome at Farthering Place. Anyway, she enjoys listening to the radio when she can, so when he was in the village here, Drew bought her one."

"I thought she could have it in her room to listen to whenever she likes," Drew put in. "And I thought this would be a fine opportunity to get one for her without her knowing. If I had bought it in our own village, someone there would surely let out the secret."

"I wish he'd asked me about it first, though," Madeline said, "because I know Mrs. Devon's son, he lives in Aberdeen, is planning to give her one for Christmas. He telephoned and asked whether she already had one, and I told him no."

"But she didn't tell me about it," Drew said in an indulgently scolding voice, "so here I am with an extra wireless and nowhere to park it."

"You could return it to the shop," Iris said wistfully. "I'm sure if you explained . . ."

"Oh, but the man there seemed so grateful to make a sale. And as it really wasn't that much of a sale, I hate to take it back. Long and short of it is, we thought you might like to have it." He took her hand and put it on top of the box. "It's nothing grand, mind you, but I'm told it gets broadcasts from all over. What do you say?"

She pulled her hand back. "I really couldn't. It's too much."

"Nonsense."

Drew opened the box and took out the wireless. It was small, as he had said, perhaps eight inches high and twelve wide, and made of a rich satin-finished mahogany. The dial was pale yellow, a warm compliment to the wood. It wasn't a grand console by any means, but it was quality. He took her hand again, letting her feel for herself. This time she didn't pull away.

He switched the wireless on. "It's got batteries in it already, and there are extras in the box. For when you need them."

It took a moment or two to warm up, and then, after a little fiddling, the music of a dance band filled the little room. Madeline beamed at him, and Iris was smiling in spite of herself, her hand still atop the wireless.

"Ah, lovely," Drew said as Al Bowlly began singing "The Very Thought of You."

Madeline slipped her arm around Drew's waist as they both watched Iris's dreamy expression.

She blushed when the song ended and she became aware of them again. "You know, I'm not really sure there is a Mrs. Devon."

"Of course there is," Drew sputtered. "She's been at Farthering Place since before I was born."

"Or that she has a son," Iris continued.

"She does," Madeline assured her. "His name is Lewis, and he lives in Aberdeen."

"Or," Iris said, "that he plans to buy his mother a wireless for Christmas."

Madeline glanced at Drew. "Well . . ."

A hint of a dimple appeared in the girl's cheek, making her look entirely charming. "But it would be rude of me to say so after you've both been so kind."

She still had her hand on the wireless.

Drew gave that hand a gentle pat. "It definitely would be, so we'll hear no more of it, eh?"

There was a glimmer of tears now in her eyes. "Mr. Farthering—"

"I said we'll hear no more of it."

"We're very glad to know you'll enjoy the radio," Madeline said, giving the girl's arm a squeeze. "And if there's ever anything we can do to help you, do let us know. Mr. Bloodworth at the Lodge knows how to get in touch with us."

While Madeline was close to her, Drew caught her eye and then touched his ear, looking pointedly at Iris. Madeline merely gave him a serene nod. He made a quick gesture around the little room, a silent request for her to take a good look around. Again she nodded. She had seen what she needed to see.

"I suppose we'd best toddle along then," Drew said. "Thank you, Miss Midgley, for permitting us to call."

"I'm sorry I don't have anything else to tell you about your investigation. My father really doesn't tell me anything."

"Do you think he'd go as far as murder?" Drew asked quietly.

She started, and the wheel lurched to a stop. "Why—why do you ask that?"

"You've . . . heard something." He'd almost said *seen*. "Be honest."

Again she lifted her determined chin. "You tell me first. Why do you ask that? About murder in particular?"

"Someone tampered with the brakes on Mrs. Bloodworth's car. Mr. Bloodworth ran into a stone wall out on the road last night. He could quite easily have been killed."

"And what has that to do with my father?"

"He was seen loitering by Mrs. Bloodworth's car when she had it in the village day before yesterday."

That was hardly proof of anything, of course, but then again, a hot denial did not immediately leap to her tongue.

"Why would he want to kill Mrs. Bloodworth?" The question

came out thin and bewildered. "Or Mr. Bloodworth? We—we hardly know them."

Madeline touched his arm, a plea for gentleness, and he nodded in acknowledgment. Then he leaned down just a bit so he could look Iris full in the face, wanting to see every nuance of emotion there.

"I think you know something. Please tell us. If he did tamper with those brakes, he's got off easy. Nothing was much damaged but the car. Next time someone might actually die. If you know something and don't speak up—"

"Oh, I don't know." She clutched the spinning wheel with both hands. "Not really. Not for certain."

"But you think you do." He kept his voice as mild as he was able. "Just tell me about it. Maybe it truly is nothing. I'm not here to have your father taken away for poaching or petty theft, but if we're talking murder . . ."

"It was hardly anything," she said after a long silence. "There's a path that goes down to the stream and around the meadow and back again. It runs through some trees at the back of the house, and Da says nobody can see you come in or out that way unless you want. As you might imagine, he likes it that way. Anyway, I know the path very well, and unless the weather's bad, I like to take a walk when I can. I'd been out walking the other day, I believe it was last Wednesday or Thursday, and when I got back, I heard him talking to someone, that same man with the gentleman's voice I told you about before, Mr. Farthering. I didn't want him to be cross with me for idling out on the moor instead of having his supper on the table, so I was going to slip inside as quietly as I could. But then I heard some of what he was saying and stayed just where I was."

She hesitated again, and he waited.

"I'm not sure I remember it just right," she said finally. "He said something like 'Got it. First chance I get.' And the man with him said 'Her first. Make sure.' And then Da said something I couldn't hear, and the other man said, 'I know. Don't you worry about that. Just do your job.' It wasn't much at all, but I felt, I don't know, all quivery when he said that about 'her first.' There was just something . . . wrong about how he said it. And now you tell me about Mrs. Bloodworth's car."

"Anything else?" Madeline asked.

Iris shook her head. "It's a bit silly, isn't it? What's it mean anyway? 'Her first'? Maybe Da's going to do some horseshoeing for the man. Or, I don't know, deliver some kind of goods." She caught an unsteady breath. "No, that can't be it. Whatever that man wanted, for my father to do it had to be worth more than that. If Da is buying drinks down at the pub, it's not because he's come into an extra half crown all of a sudden."

"No. That isn't very likely." Drew took a slip of paper and a pencil out of his coat pocket. "Would you mind if I wrote down what you said? I don't want to get it all muddled up remembering it wrong."

"Go ahead."

He scribbled down what she'd told him, reading it aloud so she could hear it.

"Yes, that's it," she said. "It may not be what they said word for word, but it's very close."

"Good. Anything else you remember? Was he in a car?"

"No, I would have heard. Once they finished talking, he slipped off, and Da came in the front way, looking for his supper that wasn't even started yet."

"And was he cross with you over it?"

"Not at all. I suppose coming into a bit of coin as he did, he was feeling rather generous that day."

"Perhaps." Drew thought for a moment. "You don't suppose this gentleman who spoke with your father could have been from Westings, do you?"

"No!" She gave a nervous laugh half under her breath. "Not that I have much to do with that sort of folk, no more than with those up at the Lodge, but I've heard them speak more than once. I wouldn't say it was any of them."

"Might I ask a favor of you?"

Her brow furrowed once again. "I suppose."

"If you should happen to hear this man's voice again, will you get word to me at the Lodge?" He looked around the tiny cottage. "I don't suppose you have a telephone. No, no, that's quite all right. But do get word to me, eh?"

"I'll do that. Meanwhile, I'll be keeping an ear open for anything that could be of help. No one's been here but Da this past week or more, and him not all the time."

"It's all right," Drew said. "Though I might come round sometime in a day or two, just to check. You just be careful and don't put yourself in danger. If your father's involved in murder, I daresay he's not safe himself."

She nodded, her pale face grim. Then she thanked them again, and they made their farewells.

"What did you think of her?" Drew asked once he and Madeline were tracking back over the moor and back to the Lodge.

"The earrings are interesting," she said.

"Yes, I was wondering why Midgley would have bothered giving them to her. Even if he has come into money of late."

She looked up at him. "You think those were from her father?"

He stopped abruptly. The Lodge was still far in the distance, and they were surrounded by nothing but the blustery, empty moor. "What do you mean? Who else would have given them to her? Surely you don't think she would have bought them for herself. On what little she makes with her spinning?"

"No. I'm sure she makes barely enough to keep body and soul together. I'm just saying those look like something that would come from an admirer, not a father. Especially not one like Mr. Midgley."

He frowned and started them walking again. Little Iris with a beau? It just didn't seem quite the thing. "Perhaps they were something passed down to her. From her mother or something."

Madeline's laugh was light and clear in the cold air. "I suppose that could be. Does Mr. Midgley seem like the kind of man who wouldn't have sold anything he could lay his hands on to keep himself in drink?" There was sudden concern in her periwinkle eyes. "I don't like the sound of whatever plot it was that Iris overheard."

"Nor I. If it was about Sabrina, then the trick with her car was unsuccessful and there's sure to be another attempt. I think I shall have to consult with Mr. Selden on the matter. Midgley may have made some remark or other to him that would be illuminating."

"You haven't heard from Nick, have you? About the man in the asylum?"

"Not yet, but I expect to by this evening. I'll have to arrange another meeting for him with Mr. Stapleton."

As it happened, Mr. Selden returned to his lodgings in Partridge Row just after lunchtime that day. By late afternoon, he and Mr. Stapleton had convened a meeting at their usual place outside the village.

"Nick, old man." Drew shook his hand, eager for news. "How did you find this Faber fellow?"

Nick snorted. "I'm sorry to say I didn't find him at all."

"What?"

"I drove down to Norfolk, to this St. Anthony's, and called on this Grant chappie you told me about. He went a bit green when I told him I'd come from Beaky about Faber. He was ever so apologetic, about the letter and all."

Drew knit his brows. "Apologetic? Whatever for?"

"Well, for asking for Beaky's money for Faber when Faber hadn't been there for almost a year." Nick ran a hand through his tousled sandy hair. "I couldn't blame the fellow, you know, not really. It was rather a wretched place, and he seemed devoted to it, to the men who were patients there. I could tell he wanted to help them all and just didn't have the means to do more than the absolute necessity."

"But what happened to Faber? He hasn't died or anything, has he?"

"This Grant says he escaped. Got through a door that was always kept locked, that was still locked, and just walked away. He said they just don't have the staff to properly look after everyone there and no money to pay for more."

"But Faber, man. Wherever did he go? Didn't they go to the police?"

"They did," Nick assured him. "Grant said that Faber would often talk about living in a grand house, but said he wasn't wanted there anymore, that he'd been cast off. Naturally, hearing that, and knowing he'd served at the Lodge, the police made discreet inquiries. Up here, in Bunting's Nest, Harrogate, York.

Nobody'd seen the man, according to Grant. One of the nurses said Faber had sometimes mentioned wanting to go to Bath, so they made inquiries there, as well. A man fitting his description had been there, it was found, but he left not too long after, and that was months ago. Evidently he's not there now."

"Hmm . . . now I'm not quite sure what to think. Madeline will be disappointed to hear me say so, but perhaps the old kiln is a madman's hiding place after all, and not a den of adulterous iniquity."

"That or the stone church," Nick said. "Or both, eh?"

"Could be. Could be. He'd have to have someone helping him, though. Food and supplies and such. I don't know that he could make out alone."

"Midgley?" Nick asked. "Possibly, but I don't know why. What would he be in it for? Besides money, of course, but how would this Faber possibly pay him off? He's been in that asylum for ages and never had two beans to begin with."

Drew looked out over the moor. "And why would he want to kill the vicar and Miss Patterson in the first place? I'm not sure he's part of this at all. We have no proof he's been back to Yorkshire since he left to go to war. The old boy could have taken himself off a bridge the first day he left Norfolk after all."

"Very true. Well, what now?"

"For now," Drew said, "we put Faber in as a possible but not very likely suspect, with motive, means, and opportunity unknown. Midgley hasn't mentioned meeting with anyone or having a visitor, has he?"

Nick shook his head.

"Does he talk about Iris much?"

Nick blinked. "His daughter? Hardly ever. Why?"

"I was just wondering if he's ever said she has a beau."

"I thought she was blind."

"My good man," Drew said, crossing his arms over his chest, "just because the girl's blind doesn't mean someone might not be interested in her."

"I suppose not. I just hadn't thought of it. Anyway, he hasn't said anything of the sort to me. Why?"

"Oh, just a thought of Madeline's. Not important. But I'm wondering now about this Faber and Midgley and, possibly, whoever's been meeting Sabrina out on the moor."

"I thought you said it was Delwyn."

Drew glared at him. "I said I didn't know. You were the one who said there was talk."

"About Delwyn, yes, and about him seeing someone at the Lodge. Not about Mrs. Bloodworth per se." There was sudden mischief in Nick's hazel eyes. "I know. She goes out to the kiln to meet Faber!"

Drew's expression was severe. "Desperately amusing, I'm sure."

"All right. All right. Probably not Faber. But you haven't made much sense out of any of this yet, you know."

"No," Drew admitted, shoulders sagging, but then he stood straight and lifted his chin. "Nothing for it but to keep on. What haven't we done yet?"

Nick considered the question. "Might not be a bad thing to give the kiln and the church another look. Knowing about Faber now, we might notice something in either place that would prove or disprove he's been there."

"Possibly," Drew mused. "I want to look in that tower at any rate. It's been opened recently, I'm sure. It may be that whoever opened it has left some clue behind him."

They made their way out to the stone church once more,

discussing various theories about the case and swiftly discarding them.

"It's a devil of a puzzle," Drew said at last. "We have someone
living out in the kiln."

"Or the church," Nick observed.

"Possibly both. But why is he there? To meet with Sabrina,
or to hide while he murders people?"

"Possibly both," Nick said.

"Possibly both, yes, but what has that to do with the vicar
and Miss Patterson? If Sabrina wanted to dispose of Beaky so
she could have her lover and keep the estate as well, why kill
anyone else? And what, if anything, has that to do with Faber?"

The stone church was not far up ahead now, the late-after-
noon shadows accentuating the strange angles of broken stone
that had once made up its walls and the barren hillside it had
been set into. Drew walked toward it, looking over it but not
really seeing it.

"And what," he said half to himself, "has that to do with
the hound?"

"The hound," Nick breathed, coming to a dead stop beside
him.

"Yes, the hound. Don't try to be spooky. It's annoying. I said
the hound and I meant . . ." Following Nick's wide-eyed stare,
Drew caught a half-choked breath and froze.

There in the open doorway of the tower, huge and black,
gleaming teeth bared in a heaving snarl, eyes smoldering with
malevolence, stood the hound.

"What do we do?" Nick asked. "Run?"

"We'd never outrun him if he comes after us." Drew scanned
the ground for a stick or a rock or anything that might ward
the beast off. Moving nothing but his eyes, he looked over the

remains of the wall nearest to them. It was a long shot, but better than trying to escape a mad dog across the open moor. "What do you say, old man? Climb?"

There was a low command from inside the tower, and the dog lunged forward.

"Climb!"

Drew shoved Nick toward the hillside, toward the stones that jutted out, rough and uneven. They both leapt up just as the beast reached them, still snarling, drool hanging from its gaping jaws.

"Climb, man!" Drew urged again, feeling the hound's hot breath at his heels. "Climb!"

Nick clambered higher up, almost at the top of the wall, and the dog made a final, frantic leap. He caught the cuff of Drew's trouser leg, just enough to drag him off-balance. But Nick seized Drew by his coat collar and held him where he was until he could kick free and scramble up beside him.

"What now?" Nick panted, keeping a wary eye on the dog that still snapped and barked as it sprang up again and again, black legs flailing for purchase on the stones above its head.

"Someone's in there," Drew said, forcing his breathing back to normal. "In the tower. And I'd bally well like to know who."

Nick didn't look away from the dog. "I don't think he's of a mind to let us go find out."

The slanting shadows were darker now against the plunging hillside, the afternoon sun fading fast. Drew had to squint to make out the beast's still-leaping shape. He couldn't tell much, but it was clear this was no spectral hound from hell's fiery maw. It was also clear that, ordinary or not, the dog would likely tear them to pieces if they moved from where they were.

Before he could say as much to Nick, there was a low whistle from the open tower door, and with a yip the dog turned and trotted to it. A figure cloaked in black emerged and, after tilting its hooded head to look up at Drew and Nick, motioned to the animal and then vanished with it into the crevice between the hillside and the mound next to it.

Drew stood silent, watching to see if the figure or the dog would reappear, but there was now once again only the wind-whipped emptiness of the moor. He swung himself down to the ground, inspecting the paw marks left behind there.

"Not the same dog."

"No?" Nick looked where he was pointing. "I do believe you're right. Those aren't nearly the size of the ones we saw before."

Drew spread out his hand and shook his head. "Not by any means. I shouldn't be surprised if what we just saw was the elusive mastiff once owned by old Mr. Bloodworth. Come on." He strode over to the still-open tower door. "If nothing else, I'm going to see what's in there."

He leaned into the door and then struck a match. That was enough to show him there was a lantern hanging from an ancient hook on the nearby wall. The lantern itself was rather new and well-stocked with oil. He tossed away the spent match, struck another and lit the lamp. It gave enough light to show the tower was now unoccupied by man or beast.

Nick followed him inside. "Disappointing. Clearly no one has been living here." With the toe of his boot he nudged an empty bowl that sat on the floor next to a bowl of water. "Except perhaps that dog."

"No wonder Delwyn could never catch it. I'm surprised it didn't bark when we were here before. If it was in here then."

Nick made a face. "Clearly whoever has the dog here has

him well-trained. Did you hear him, when he called the dog off us?"

Drew nodded. Laughing. The villain had been laughing at them.

He blew out the lantern and hung it where he had found it. Then he stalked back out onto the moor. The wretch wasn't going to get away so easily. Not now.

"He can't have just disappeared, Nick."

"You wouldn't think so." Nick looked in the direction their adversary had gone. "You'd think as little cover as there is out here, we'd see him miles away."

"True. Come on. Hurry."

He followed the path the cloaked man and the dog had taken, around the side of the hill and then up the back.

"We can see a good distance from here." He scanned the moor again. "Look there."

Two dark shapes, one on four legs, one on two, loped across the moor toward Midgley's cottage and the abandoned kiln with the cot and other things in it.

"Come on," Drew urged. "We can at least see where they go."

They hurried along the top of the hill, looking down into the dale where the man and the dog were, and Drew glanced back at Nick with a grin.

"He hasn't seen us yet. He doesn't know we see him. We should be able to—"

There was all of a sudden no ground under his foot, only an open hole beneath him, and he fell headlong, landing on his stomach at the overgrown edge of the hole and then sliding down into it, clutching frantically at grass and rock and earth to keep from falling into the dark emptiness beneath.

"Drew!"

Nick flung himself down on the ground, catching him by the coat sleeve and one wrist. Drew hung for a moment in the blackness and then flailed his free hand, trying to find something to grasp. All he felt was a tunnel of old brick just big enough for him to fall through.

"What is it?" Nick called, his voice strained with effort. "Can you get out?"

"Must be part of one of the old chimneys. A big one."

Drew's head spun as he thought of the drop from where he was at the top of the hill all the way down to where the grim mouths of the kilns opened below. He tried to brace himself with his feet.

"Don't!" Nick tightened his grip, and Drew felt his arm slip down further inside his sleeve. "I can't hold on!"

Drew reached up with his free hand to get a better hold, yet he was at an awkward angle and caught only air. "Nick."

Nick was breathing in labored gasps now. "I. Can't. Hold—"

"Nick." Drew felt the wool of his coat sliding against the linen of his shirt, slipping away from him, pulling against his arm and shoulder. "Nick!"

Then he felt something grab the back of his shirt and coat collars both together. An instant later a strong hand grasped his free wrist and then his upper arm. And with Nick tugging at his other side, he was hauled back onto the grass.

He lay there squinting into the dim sunlight, trying to make out the face above him. "Delwyn?"

Before Drew could say another word, the gamekeeper grabbed Nick by the front of his shirt, shoving him back.

"What do you think you're doing, Selden? Trying to keep him from finding out what you and your mate have been about? Trying to kill him?" Dark eyes fiery, Delwyn shoved again, the palms of both hands slapping against Nick's chest, making him stagger. "I ought to toss you down that stack myself. You and that devil Midgley along with you."

"Steady on," Nick protested.

Drew struggled up to one elbow, breathless, not with panic but with laughter, for the moment too relieved to be out of that hole to worry about the man in the hooded cloak. "Selden, you cad."

Nick scowled at him, obviously not knowing whether to stay in character. Delwyn merely looked puzzled.

"No, no," Drew managed, sitting up. "I think at this point proper introductions are in order. Delwyn, this is Nick Dennison, a friend of mine. He's here to help me with the investigation."

Nick gave a wary little wave.

Delwyn looked him over, his dark brows coming together, and then he looked at Drew. "A friend of yours, sir? I thought he and Midgley—"

"It's what you were meant to think," Drew said, accepting a hand up from both men. "And so is Midgley. I trust we can rely on your discretion."

"You mean will I tell anyone? No, sir, I will not. You can be sure of that. I'd be more than happy to see Midgley get what he deserves, alongside whoever else he's in with." He turned again to Nick. "Beg your pardon, sir. I didn't know the way of it."

"No harm done," Nick said with a grin. "Though I'd rather have a Welshman on my side than set against me."

"Either way, I'd prove you right."

"I daresay," Drew said, and then he sobered as he peered across the moor once again. "Did you see him? Did you see where he went?"

Delwyn shrugged. "All I saw was Selden, as I thought, chasing you and then you going down the shaft." He looked at Nick with a shake of his head. "I'd never have taken you for a toff, and that's pure truth. You ought to be in the cinema, you had me that fooled."

"How did you happen to be out this way?" Nick asked. "We'd have had a rum go without you."

"Oh, uh, one of the cows got loose, and I told Johnson I'd have a look for her. I'm glad I wasn't too late to save the gentleman a tumble."

"Believe me, so am I." Drew hadn't taken time to be thankful that he was not now lying broken at the bottom of the kiln, though he knew very well it wasn't mere luck that had prevented it. "You are a godsend. Literally."

There was a touch of a sneer in Delwyn's mouth. "Doesn't seem very likely, if you'll pardon me, Mr. Farthering. As I told you before, God and I have an agreement. I'm fairly much the last man on earth He would send on His errands. And it's odds that, if He did send me, I wouldn't go."

"I fancy you just have."

The gamekeeper's sneer turned up into an almost pixyish grin. "Now what would He want with a reprobate like me?"

Drew scooped up the hat he had lost when he first missed his footing and put it back on his head. "You might ask Him one day."

Delwyn scoffed.

"For now," Drew continued, "I want to go talk to Midgley. He's had time to get back to his own place by now, worse luck, but I'd like to talk to him all the same. There's definitely a hound, Delwyn. I nearly had his teeth in my leg."

"What was he like?" Delwyn asked, eyes narrowed, and then

he nodded as Drew told him. "Old Baxter, from up the house, I don't in the least doubt. I wouldn't be surprised if it was Midgley with him, as well."

Nick frowned. "If we've driven him out of here, then he's likely, whether it's Midgley or someone else, to duck back into his lair in the kiln out near the cottage."

"No!"

Drew looked at Delwyn, surprised by the force in his objection. "Why not?"

"I, uh . . . I mean, I don't think Midgley would be out that way now, come to think of it. He's already gone into the village, like as not. For the send-off."

"Send-off? What send-off?"

"Oh, it's not much of anything really. One of the men is leaving the village, and the lads thought we'd all give him one last drink before he goes. Nothing fancy, mind, but I expect most everyone'll be there. Any excuse, eh? Midgley will certainly be there. He was never one to miss a round on someone else. Why would you want to go out to that old kiln anyway?"

"Because," Drew said evenly, "I've been there before. Someone's clearly been living there, at least temporarily. We've spoilt one hidey-hole for our man. Why wouldn't he dash back to his other?"

"I think you're wrong there, sir." Delwyn gave a shake of his head. "You might check the cottage if you think you ought. It's a bit early for the pub, even for Midgley. But that old kiln's nothing. Some tramp taking shelter, like as not. Nothing that need trouble you."

Drew's jaw tightened as he studied the man's face. Clearly he didn't want anyone near that old kiln. Had he really been out looking for a stray cow just now? Or was someone there at the kiln waiting for him? A partner in crime? A lover? Or both?

"Any reason you wouldn't like us going out there, Delwyn?"

"Me, sir? No. It makes no odds with me, but if Midgley or whoever he's in with is who you want, it would be a waste of your time—"

"It's mine to waste after all, though yours isn't."

"Sir—"

Drew looked pointedly toward the Lodge. "I expect Mr. Bloodworth would rather you got back to your job. Anything you need to be doing out at the kiln just now?"

Delwyn ducked his head, more baleful than sullen. "No, sir."

"Then you might do well to be off."

"Yes, sir," the gamekeeper muttered, tugging the brim of his cap. "Thank you, sir."

Drew didn't move, watching to make sure he went back to the Lodge and not some roundabout way to the kiln. Just a few yards away, Delwyn stopped and turned again.

"Mind where you step, sir," he called with a sardonic smile, and then he loped down the hill toward the Lodge.

Nick's eyes widened. "You don't think it's Sabrina after all, do you? And Delwyn?"

"I'm not quite sure what to think," Drew admitted. "I want to like the fellow, I really do. He just saved me from a reasonably grisly death after all. But just when I think I can count on him, I realize I haven't a clue what he's really about." Drew watched for a moment more, but though Delwyn was making good time along the footpath, he seemed to be headed straight for the Lodge. "How do you think things are between him and Midgley?"

"Bad as can be. No love lost, to be certain."

"You mean rather the way it is between that ruffian Selden and the toffy detective Bloodworth brought in?"

Nick's forehead wrinkled. "I don't—wait. You don't think theirs is all put on as well, do you?"

"Might be."

"But why did he help you just now? Why not let Selden finish you off when the opportunity was there? Neither of us had seen him. He could have just strolled off and left us to it."

"The only thing I know to do is to get out to the kiln as quickly as we're able. If he was meeting someone there, whoever it is can't know he's not coming. He—or she—will still be there."

"This should be fun," Nick said. "And Delwyn? If anyone knows a back route to anywhere on the moor, it's our gamekeeper."

"True. Even so, he still can't reach there before we do. Unless we dawdle here all day." Drew gave Nick's arm a tug. "Come on."

They made a swift trek across to the kiln. When they were atop the grassy mound that covered it, Drew put a cautioning finger to his lips.

"Let's just bide here a while and see if anyone comes out. If Delwyn was coming here, he's late by now. His companion may want to look out to see if he's on his way."

"Should I let myself be seen with you?" Nick asked, voice low. "There's nothing to be done about Delwyn at this point, but if he does keep quiet about me as he promised, we wouldn't want to spoil our little masquerade for everyone else, eh?"

"No. Not at all. Good thinking. If need be, I'll go down alone and talk to whomever is down there. You stay up here. Keep out of sight behind that old wall. That way you'll be close if anything happens."

"Right." There was something mischievous in Nick's solicitous expression as he concealed himself. "And mind where you step."

Drew didn't have to wait long before someone did come out. Coat over his arm and collar undone, hat perched hastily on his head, the man peered out of the kiln's gaping mouth, took a furtive look right and left, and then, with a touch of a self-satisfied grin, he began doing up his tie.

It was Morris Gray.

— Sixteen —

Watching from above the opening to the kiln, Drew was too stunned to do anything but stare. Morris Gray? What did it mean? Were he and Delwyn confederates in murder? If so, why? Or was Gray meeting someone here after all, and for whatever reason Delwyn didn't want the lovers found out? Could he possibly be protecting Sabrina? Or was it the master of Bloodworth Park Lodge he wanted to shield from scandal?

"Morris?"

The voice came from inside the kiln. A woman's voice, too soft and too distorted by the surrounding brick dome to be recognized. Sabrina's perhaps? Drew couldn't tell.

His expression tightening with annoyance, Gray turned back to the kiln. "I promise it won't always be this way. Think of Paris and Venice and the Mediterranean, maybe even the South Seas, but you must be patient. These things take time."

Drew waited. *Come out, come out, whoever you are.*

The woman said something more, and with a sigh Morris

shrugged into his coat. "Please, my dear, don't let's start all that again. I told you I do. Of course I do. How could you ever think otherwise?"

"You always say that." The woman's voice grew louder, closer. She was coming out. "You say that, but you never do anything about it." She stepped into the waning light, slender, girlish, dark hair down around her shoulders, with the glimmer of pearl at her ears. Drew nearly fell from his perch.

"Miss Midgley."

She turned her frightened face up to the sound of his voice, her cheeks flushed with red. Gray gaped at him, and Drew could almost hear the thoughts whirring through the man's head. *How much did this infernal meddler hear? What did he know? How could it all be made to look like something other than what it was?*

"F-Farthering. You— We—"

"I was just looking for Mr. Midgley." Drew made his way down the side of the mound to where they were, his manner as mild as if they had just met at a garden party. "He's not in there as well, is he?"

Iris's face turned even redder.

"I . . ." Gray cleared his throat and began again in a lower register. "I believe he's gone down to the Hound and Hart for the evening. At least that's what Miss Midgley told me when I came to inquire after him. I'd talked to my father, you see, and we wanted to let Midgley know in no uncertain terms—"

"He came to see me, Mr. Farthering." Her unseeing eyes were defiant, and she took hold of Gray's arm. "It will come out before long anyway, but it won't matter. We're going away from here, out of the cold and the wet and the wind. To someplace sunny where we can be together. Tell him, Morris."

"Now, Iris, dear, ah, well . . ." Gray glanced at Drew, nearly cringing, almost as if he thought Drew might strike him.

Drew wanted to. Instead he challenged Gray with a look, daring him to make answer to her.

"He's going to leave Mrs. Gray," Iris said when he did not, her lips trembling. "We're going to be married."

Gray seemed to shrivel a bit. "I merely said if there were any way. You know there's my father to be thought of and Frances herself, of course, and you know how people would talk, and . . ."

Again he glanced at Drew, but Drew gave him no quarter. Instead he waited for the man to falter into inevitable silence.

Iris stood perfectly still, and then she wiped the back of one hand across her eyes. It was a gesture of resignation, not of shock or even pain. She seemed to realize that her romantic dreams were nothing more than that. Just dreams, false and fleeting. Here, with Drew as witness, she could deceive herself no longer. Without a word, she stripped off the pearl earrings and pressed them into Gray's hand.

He took her arm. "Iris, darling—"

"Don't." She freed herself in one savage motion, tapped her cane on the ground to get her bearings, and then, head held high, strode back toward her cottage.

Gray shifted on his feet, unable to meet Drew's steady gaze. "I, uh, I suppose I ought to see her home, eh?"

"Was that what you usually did?" Drew asked. "Afterwards, I mean."

"Well, there was always the chance her father would be there, you know. I really couldn't risk . . ." Gray halted in his struggle to explain himself. "Look here, Farthering, you're a man of the world. You understand these things, surely. One must have these

little escapes now and again. Good heavens, mired up at Westings day in and day out with Frances and her sheep and Father
every bit as plodding, what was I to do? It's not as if the girl
came out badly from it. She was just as keen as I to hear about
those places, to hear me read grand novels and poetry, to talk
about art and music. Do you think her father would have given
her that? And I did what I could to make things better for her.
Money when I thought it wouldn't be too much missed. A gift
now and again, discreetly, of course. Do you think some shop
boy or shepherd would do that for her? If he'd take her at all,
blind as she is. And if he would, I know she wouldn't have him.
She's too fine for all that. She's turned down Bloodworth's man
time and again, I happen to know. So don't imagine—"

"Delwyn?"

Drew was startled out of his cold fury. Delwyn? If he wanted
the girl, why in the world would he not want this affair to be
exposed? This had to feel like betrayal, even if Iris didn't return
his interest.

"Yes, Delwyn. The gamekeeper. The glowering brute, he probably reads nothing but penny dreadfuls. That's if he can read
at all."

Drew recalled his brief glance at Delwyn's bookcase. There
were depths to the man. Puzzling, but there all the same. Morris
Gray, on the other hand, was as shallow as a reflecting pool.

"I'll send her along some money when I can," Gray went on,
suddenly very businesslike. "It's awkward, yet we both knew it
couldn't go on forever."

The cold fury came back. Drew's fists tightened. "Did you
both know that?"

Gray had no answer. At least he had the decency to look
ashamed.

Drew waited until the man was well on his way back to Westings before he went back up to where Nick was waiting.

"I suppose you heard everything."

Nick whistled low. "Gray and Iris? They're the last ones I thought would be trysting out here." He glared toward the now-distant figure that scurried up a hill in the fast-fading light and then vanished over it. "I wish you'd biffed him one. Just on principle."

"I'd be brought up on charges if I'd done what I'd like to do." Drew thought for a moment. "Do you suppose Delwyn really did want to pay court to her?"

Nick shrugged.

"And she turned him down?"

"Maybe she does think herself too good for a working man," Nick said. "Wouldn't be the first girl in the world to hold that opinion. Do you suppose she'll be all right on her own now?"

"I can't imagine there's anything I could say or do at this point that would help, and my presence would only bring her embarrassment on top of everything else." Drew exhaled heavily. "Well, at least we know who's been using this place and why, but it doesn't tell us anything about our cloaked visitor from earlier. I still think a few words with Mr. Midgley are in order."

"That would point us in the direction of the Hound and Hart, eh?"

"Precisely." Drew brushed off the front of his coat and smoothed back his hair with both hands. "Am I presentable enough? Or do I look as if I'd just fallen down a hole?"

Nick peered at him in the fading light. "You'll do, Beau Brummell. Dust off the knees of your trousers and straighten your tie, and you'll do."

"Don't look so smug," Drew said. "You could use a bit of tidying yourself."

"All part of the costume," Nick replied. "We ruffians needn't be so particular about our sartorial details as you proper gentlemen."

"You ought to go back to your room anyway. It wouldn't be wise for us to enter the pub together."

"Right." Nick gave a salute. "Be there in a bit. Maybe I can get Midgley to tell me where he was this afternoon."

Drew lowered his brows, not having considered this before now. "You know, if that really was Midgley out there today, he already knows we're conspiring against him. He might give you a warmer welcome than you're expecting."

"Or he might pretend ignorance and seem the same as always. It's hard to say, but I'll keep my eyes open."

By the time Drew made his way into Bunting's Nest, night had fallen. It was only the presence of a full moon in an unclouded sky that had made his path across the moor clear and easy. It was early yet, but the Hound and Hart was already busier than usual, filled with men just coming from their work, eager for some cheery companionship and a respite from laboring.

Delwyn hunched over the table in the far corner, looking balefully into the mug he clutched in both hands, everything about him a warning for others to steer clear. Drew sat down across from him.

"Good evening, Delwyn. Been here long?"

Delwyn didn't look up. "Long enough."

Long enough to get drunk, Drew judged by the slur in the

man's words. "There seems to have been a good turnout for this send-off, eh?"

"Doesn't take much to bring everyone in."

"And the guest of honor?" Drew asked, scanning the dimly lit room. He didn't see Midgley.

"Blackstock there." Delwyn gestured with his mug toward the bar, where the milkman stood looking embarrassed and delighted to be surrounded by well-wishers.

Drew smiled and nodded, and the milkman excused himself and came to their table.

"Good of you to come, sir. Very good, I'm sure." His bearded face was flushed, perhaps with excitement, perhaps with drink, but his eyes sparkled behind his thick spectacles. "I didn't expect we'd have any of the gentry turn up."

"And I didn't expect you'd be the one leaving Bunting's Nest. This is sudden."

"I wish it was a happier cause, sir, believe me. Better yet, I wish there was no cause at all and I was staying right here." He glanced at Delwyn and dropped his voice. "I'm sorry there's no more I can do to help you. You know, in the particular *matter* we've been discussing."

"I hope nothing serious takes you away," Drew replied, cringing inwardly at the man's weak attempt to be subtle. He hoped the general rumble of conversation would make his words difficult to overhear.

"It's hard to say yet, sir. My brother, well, he's never been very strong. His heart, you know. He wrote me to see if we might not all get on better if I came to help him and his family on the farm. Not that he can pay me anything, just my keep, but how could I tell him no?"

"No, of course not. Family ought to stand together, eh?"

246

"Just as I always say, sir. I can't imagine these folk who leave their own kin to fend for themselves when they've had a knock of one kind or another. Ought not to be done, I say. Not in a Christian land."

"It's not at all the thing, is it? When do you leave? Soon?"

"Oh, tonight, sir. The last train to York. From there to London and then Southampton and on to America. Who'd have thought it? And at my age?"

"Can I get you something, sir?" the barmaid asked, her plain face lit with a smile.

"Cider," Drew told her. "Thank you."

He gave her half a crown, making her smile even brighter, and she quickly brought him back a mug. He lifted it in a toast to Blackstock. "I wish you all the best. Safe journey and Godspeed."

"Thank you, sir." With another glance round the room and a tap to the side of his nose, he leaned closer to Drew. "And good luck solving your little mystery."

Drew managed not to scowl. The fellow meant well, and he was leaving the village. It wouldn't matter who knew he was in on the game at this point.

"Mum's the word, eh? And you've been very helpful."

"Clearing out, are we, Blackstock?"

Blackstock shrank back as Midgley loomed over him with "Selden" at his elbow.

"You little worm," the poacher spat. "I ought to take my boot to you, that's what. What do you mean creeping about spying on folk and carrying tales? Good thing you're off, and good riddance, I say. We don't like your sort here."

Drew stood, putting himself between the two of them. "What about my sort? Or would you rather your dog saw to my sort?"

Midgley looked as if he wanted to spout off and then thought better of it. Drew might be a stranger in Bunting's Nest and an infernal nuisance, but he was friends with the master of the Park Lodge and with the police. And he was gentry. It wouldn't pay.

"Haven't got any dog," Midgley said.

"How about something to cut the brake lines on an Austin 10?"

The poacher's eyes narrowed to malevolent slits. "Trenton had me in over that, thanks to you."

"Did he now?"

"Go on." The poacher waved a dismissive hand. "You got nothin' against me you can prove. Nor did he." He looked around Drew and Blackstock to where the gamekeeper sat sullenly in the corner. "Nor do you, Rhys Delwyn, for all your pokin' and prowlin' about. I done nothin' but ply my trade to provide for me and mine."

"And a poor job you've done of it," Delwyn muttered.

"Come over here and tell me that, ye dirty-nosed pup, and I'll fetch you a clout like last time."

"Don't tempt me, old man."

The poacher's gimlet eyes flashed. "And don't think you can come sniffin' around my girl either as if she were some scullery wench. Blind or no, she has finer fish to fry than the likes of you."

With a screech of chair legs, Delwyn was on his feet, shoving his way past Drew and the others gathered there. "You shut your mouth, Jack Midgley. You got no business talking about Iris like that!"

"Iris?" Midgley gave a bark of a laugh. "Iris? What should you care what I say about her? Devil take the girl, she's no better than she should be."

This time Drew didn't consider getting between the two of them. Apart from a few looks of disgust turned Midgley's way and a few low protests about the unseemliness of the man's comments, no one else seemed to object either. They merely backed off.

"You've been warned once now," the barman said, hurrying over. "You take your differences outside. Go on."

Delwyn took a sudden step toward Midgley, and the barman caught his shoulder. "I mean it, Mr. Delwyn. Not saying you don't have cause, but this is neither the time nor place."

"He wants you to hold him back," Midgley taunted. "He's yellow and he knows it."

He gave the gamekeeper a ringing slap across the face, and with a roar Delwyn threw the barman off and caught Midgley by the front of his coat. There was a gasp from the crowd as Delwyn lifted him off the ground, looking as if he would hurl him through the window that overlooked the street, but then he shoved the poacher into a nearby chair, almost turning over man and chair both.

Midgley sat there frozen, his usually florid face bloodless, his eyes saucer wide and his breath coming in terrified hitches. Delwyn glowered at him and then turned away, wiping both palms on his coat as the barman once more hurried over to him.

"Mr. Delwyn—"

"Don't worry, Jenkins. I wouldn't soil my hands on the likes of him."

Midgley sat blinking for a moment. Then the color came back into his face, deep and angry, and he pushed himself to his feet. "You turn round, Rhys Delwyn. Just turn right round."

Delwyn turned, gave a smirking little laugh, and then went back to his pint.

"Come on," Nick said, taking Midgley's arm. "You've stood me to a drink or two before now. Let me return the favor."

"Let me go, Selden. I swear—"

"Ah, let him alone. The bully's not worth spending a night in chokey." By then Nick had the man over at the far end of the bar. "Come on, Jenkins. A little service, eh?"

The barman glared at the two of them. "Not tonight. Not for either of you. Now, Mr. Midgley, I've warned you time and again. Don't make me ring up the police. Another word and I will."

"Aw, I didn't do nothin'," Nick moaned. "Have a heart."

"I'm sorry, Mr. Selden, but I have nothing more to say on the matter. If you're his friend, you'll take Mr. Midgley on home without any more trouble. Otherwise you leave me no choice."

Midgley pushed himself away from the bar. "Never you mind, Jenkins. I can do better than that watered-down excuse for ale you overcharge for. Come on, Selden. I have a bottle of something at home we can have a taste of, eh?"

Nick grinned. "Now that's the best news I've had all day." He turned Midgley toward the door, grabbing his arm when he stumbled a little and then urging him forward. The poacher made his way like a monarch sweeping through a throng of peasants. When he reached the door, he fixed Delwyn with a baleful eye.

"Don't think this ends it, Welshman. You haven't seen the back of me yet."

Delwyn said nothing, his dark eyes fixed on Midgley until, with a disdainful sniff, the poacher pushed open the door. With Nick at his heels, he lurched out of the room.

The men went back to their drinks, murmuring among themselves as they did. Drew turned to go back to Delwyn's table and found himself face-to-face with the milkman. "Mr. Blackstock, I beg your pardon. I didn't see you there."

Blackstock laughed. "Ought to be a bit quieter now. At least I can tell my brother about my little adventure when I get to America."

"I'm sorry to lose your help."

The little fellow seemed shyly pleased and began talking about his brother and his family. As he spoke, Drew glanced over at Delwyn, still sitting in the corner, and wished he could talk to him privately, to find out what he knew about Iris and Morris and the hound from the church tower. There was definitely something that made those paw prints, something much bigger than old Mr. Bloodworth's mastiff.

"Mr. Farthering?"

Drew smiled at the milkman as if he'd been listening all along. "What part of America are you going to?"

"It's a place called Weston, in Missouri. Somewhere in the middle of the country."

"I'm sure your brother . . . what did you say his name was?"

"Oh, it's Mark—" Blackstock coughed and then took a sip of his drink, looking embarrassed. "I beg your pardon. It's Mark. He's married to Alma and they have—"

"Are you going to stand chatting there all day, Blackstock?" one of the men at the bar called. "Come and have a drink."

"Come on, lad," another said, taking him by the arm. "Last night and all, eh?"

Blackstock looked flattered and troubled all at once. "Mr. Farthering, I do apologize—"

"Oh, don't mind me. You're the guest of honor."

The milkman was soon engulfed with well-wishers, and Drew sat once again across from Delwyn. "Sounds like he's off on a grand adventure."

"Good on him," the gamekeeper said, still with the dour expression that hadn't left him all night. "Someone ought to be."

Drew studied him for a moment, remembering what he had said about his attachments here in Yorkshire, wondering where he would go if he felt free to leave. "I went to that abandoned kiln, the one over by Midgley's."

Delwyn huffed but said nothing.

"Why didn't you want me going there?"

"Never said that, sir," Delwyn said, his eyes on his ale.

"But it's true all the same."

The gamekeeper looked up, mouth taut, chin belligerent. "If you went, then I expect you know why."

"But if Gray and—"

"Why, sir," Delwyn said, that pixyish grin turning up his mouth, still leaving it hard and bitter, "you give yourself out to be a Christian man. Don't you know love covers a multitude of sins?"

Delwyn had been trying to protect the girl. Even knowing where she was and with whom, he'd tried to shield her. Anyone who looked at the situation rationally would know it couldn't last. Not for long. And then patient love would step in, not full of pretty words and dreams of what might be, but clear-eyed and steadfast, facing what was. Drew found himself hoping that somehow, soon, and despite her blindness, Iris would truly see.

"True," Drew said, then he drained his cider and stood. "Oh, I say, Delwyn."

The gamekeeper sniffed and blotted a fresh trickle of blood from his nose with the back of his hand. "Sir?"

"I thought you might like to know that there were . . . developments out by Midgley's today. Mr. Gray will not be going out to the kilns anymore."

Delwyn looked wary. "No? Why's that?"

"He's got no reason to. I have it on very good authority that if he does, he'll find nothing waiting for him but an empty hole in the ground."

For a long moment, the gamekeeper's expression did not change. Then the tiniest smile flickered across his lips, only to be sternly banished. "What's that to do with me?"

"Whatever you care to make of it," Drew told him, and with a wink he walked out into the October night.

Drew strode down the high street as if he were headed back to the Lodge, but as he passed a narrow alleyway between the tobacconist's and the post office, he turned aside and made his way along an unpaved path, through another alley and around the side of a mechanic's garage that was closed for the night. Nick was slouched against the garage wall, waiting for him.

"Selden," Drew said quietly, joining him next to the seven-foot-high letter A in the name of the petrol company painted there.

"Stapleton," Nick replied. "Glad to see you've arrived in one piece."

"Your mate Midgley is a fine fellow. You must be proud of the acquaintance."

Nick made a face. "I'll be glad when this is done and I can

toss these rags into the fire. You think it's bad having him as your enemy. Try having him as your friend."

"You're a brave man, Selden," Drew said, clapping his shoulder. "Now, did he happen to say anything about where he was this afternoon?"

"Sadly, no. We went back to his cottage and he got well soused on some vile sort of rum he had there." Nick shuddered. "I left him snoring in his armchair, and his daughter practically ordered me out."

"Poor girl. She's had quite a day. But Midgley didn't tell you anything new?"

"He did mention he's about to come into some money. Wouldn't say how much or from where, but it couldn't be a small matter. Not the way he was chortling over it."

"Or perhaps he was just chortling over us," Drew said. "His didn't happen to be a chortle you recognized, did it?"

"You mean from earlier today? I'm sorry to say I didn't in particular. It could have been the same, but I was too busy dealing with the barghest to really notice much else."

"Droll, Mr. Selden, very droll. But you do remind me of a very important fact. That dog we saw today was definitely not the maker of the enormous paw prints we've seen."

"True. Which means that something else is making them, and we haven't the slightest notion what that something else might be."

"Leave that to me, old man. I have a job for you, if you will."

Nick saluted. "So long as it doesn't involve great black hounds or fathomless black pits, I'm your man."

"I've been thinking about Sabrina rather a lot since Beaky's accident. Suppose she is involved with someone—"

Nick opened his mouth to protest, but Drew held up one hand.

"I merely say *suppose*. If she has nothing to gain by Beaky's death save her freedom to go to someone else, then I can't see her resorting to murder. She'd simply divorce him. For mental cruelty or something of the like."

"From what you've told me about her, that seems a reasonable assumption."

"But if his will or his life insurance names her to get everything, I'd say she's firmly in the running still."

"So you want me to go find out how Beaky's set up for insurance and all that. Shall I go down to London and start asking gents on street corners if they happen to know the names of his solicitors?"

"Of course not." Drew reached into his coat pocket and pulled out a slip of paper. "I happen to have the names written down for you."

Nick's eyes widened. "You didn't go through Beaky's desk, did you?"

"No. Just his mail."

Nick raised an eyebrow. "Isn't that an actionable offense?"

"Only the envelopes. Just to get the names and addresses. They weren't new letters, but he had them there in the tray on his desk, and I took just a quick look. I can't imagine he's changed solicitors or anything lately."

"All right." Nick took the paper from him, glanced at the London addresses, and then put it into his waistcoat pocket. "And if they want to know what business I have asking?"

"That's where you must employ the Dennison charm, my lad. Surely some file clerk or girl from the secretarial pool can be persuaded to give you just that morsel of information."

Nick didn't look entirely convinced, but he made no more objections. "And after that?"

"Well, with Mr. Midgley being such a shy, retiring creature, unwilling to speak of his own excellences, I think we should spend an evening watching his cottage and seeing what arises."

"You mean sit out in the cold for hours so we can catch him bringing in a few of Beaky's grouse."

"Or see our killer come to plot with his chief henchman." Drew narrowed his eyes. "Whether he was aiming for Beaky or Sabrina, he missed with the brakes on the Austin. I can't imagine it will be long before he has another go at it. But if Sabrina's mixed up in this in any way whatsoever, I want to know. Or count her out of it."

"Fair enough. I'll head to London in the morning and be back as quickly as I'm able. You are going to tell Madeline what you're about, aren't you?"

"She might otherwise wonder why I didn't come home that night."

"Just don't start out without me," Nick warned. "I don't want you falling down any more holes, am I understood?"

Drew ducked his head as if he were spending his first night away at school. "Yes, Matron."

"Off you go then. No running in the corridors."

Drew chuckled. "See you tomorrow night. Say after sundown? I'll bring sandwiches."

"Not those nasty things with fish paste."

"No fish paste. On my honor."

"Right you are," Nick said. "At the kiln?"

"That'll do nicely. From there we'll set up near Midgley's and see what's what."

"Tomorrow it is," Nick said, and then he sprinted off toward Partridge Row.

Drew returned to the Lodge just before time to dress for dinner.

"Drew!" Madeline leapt up from the drawing room sofa and hurried to him as he stood there in the open doorway.

He gave her a lazy smile. "Hullo, darling. Miss me?"

"You could have told me you'd be this late." She frowned, looking him over. "What have you been doing? Are those grass stains on your waistcoat? And on your knees?"

He was mortified, but whether it was from the stains themselves or her notice of them or the smirk on Sabrina's face as she looked up from her magazine, he wasn't certain. "They're not so bad, are they?"

But the light was brighter here than it was in the Hound and Hart or along the path from the village. The stains were, in fact, just so bad.

Madeline smoothed his hair at the side. "Maybe we should go upstairs and change, and you can tell me all about it."

The mantel clock whirred and then struck. The dressing gong sounded half a moment later.

"Time anyway," Sabrina said, standing and putting her open magazine facedown on the sofa. "I'd better get Beaky. He doesn't notice the bell half the time, not when he's busy with something, but he'll want to know what you've found out. Come along, Raffie. Din-dins." She disappeared into the corridor with the dog yipping at her heels.

Madeline took Drew's arm. "I know you don't want to say anything in front of anyone. You've got that look."

He kissed her cheek. "You know me too well."

"Just tell me you're all right."

"Darling." He kissed her lips. "Of course I am."

"And that you'll be more careful."

"I will. I promise."

She pressed close to his side. "Well, come get all tidy and beautiful again and you can tell me everything."

He laughed as he followed her up the stairs. While he changed for dinner, he told her what had happened at the stone church, at the kiln, and later at the pub.

"I told you those earrings didn't come from Iris's father."

He nodded as he struggled with his cuff links. "That would be the first thing you commented on. You're perceptive as always."

"Though it would have been better for her if she hadn't had them at all." Her mouth tightened. "Oooh, that Morris Gray. If I ever see him again, I may not be able to keep from slapping him."

"Now, now, I am beginning to suspect your heart is not so filled with Christian charity as one might wish."

"What I wish is that this would all be over so we could go back home. Nick, too. Carrie has enough to handle without anything happening to him."

"True. But try not to worry, love. We'll have her come visit the minute her father doesn't need her. How would that be?"

She flounced one shoulder at him. "I've already invited her. I can't think of any time that wouldn't be good for her to come for a visit."

"Excellent." He looked her over and then tapped his finger against her powdered nose. "You are as kind as you are beautiful, my darling. And Carrie is always welcome."

"I'm glad. Now, what are we going to do about Beaky and Sabrina?"

He sighed. "I don't know, but I'm still betting that Midgley is in with whomever is behind everything. I've decided there's nothing for it but to spend the evening watching his cottage."

"Oh, Drew, must you? I don't like the idea of you being by yourself out there. You were nearly killed just today."

"I won't be by myself. Nick's coming along. And so is the Webley."

Now she looked annoyed rather than apprehensive. "I'm glad Nick's coming, but I don't like the idea of the gun. I know. You need some kind of protection. I just wish you didn't have to go into places where you do. Couldn't the police watch him? It is their job after all."

"Trenton thinks Midgley's harmless. I expect he'd rather be home by his fire than huddled out on the moor waiting for something that may never happen."

She pouted but made no other objections.

"Don't be cross, darling, and don't wait up for me when I go. I'm likely to be very late, if not all night."

"Yes, yes, I know."

A sudden thought came to him. "I want you to be careful, too. Something or someone has definitely been in the north wing. If Sabrina is involved somehow—"

"Drew—"

"I mean it. I can't say whether she is or isn't. Nick's going to London tomorrow to find out about Beaky's will and insurance. It's possible what he learns can more or less rule her out. But for now I want you to be extra careful. Don't stay in the room with her unless someone else is there. Preferably Beaky, but at least one of the servants. Ring for coffee or tear your hem or something so one of the maids will have to help you. And when you go to bed, keep the door locked."

"I think it's ridiculous, but if it will make you feel better . . ."

"It will."

"Silly boy." She leaned up to kiss his cheek and then took his arm so he could escort her down to the dining room.

After dinner, as Madeline and Sabrina were looking at pictures of furniture that might go in the refurbished north wing, Beaky pulled Drew aside.

"A word, if you don't mind."

"Of course. How's the leg tonight?"

"Oh, tolerable, I'd say. Aches something fierce from time to time, but I suppose that'll go away before long. I'm more concerned about the car. Trenton phoned me up to let me know they'd had the remains looked at."

"And?"

"The brakes on Sabrina's Austin were definitely tampered with. The man at the garage says there can be no doubt of it."

"And the Bentley?" Drew asked.

Beaky winced, leaning against the mantelpiece and briefly rubbing his injured leg. "There's nothing very certain there, but Basset thinks something could have been put into her petrol tank. Just enough to make her hiccup a bit and put her out of commission for a day or so." He glanced over at Sabrina. "Don't tell her just yet, eh? She's jittery enough thinking someone might have wanted to kill her."

"Or you."

Beaky blinked behind his thick spectacles, then licked his

suddenly dry lips. "I—I just don't know why anyone would want to kill either of us. What have we done?"

"It's not always what you've done, old man." Just then Sabrina laughed over something Madeline had said, and Drew didn't dare look back at her. "Sometimes it's merely because you're in the way."

— Seventeen —

The next day, not long after sundown, Drew made his way out to the abandoned kiln. By now it was truly abandoned. The lantern was gone, the books nowhere to be seen. Only the empty crate, the cot, and the battered woolen blanket were left. Drew sat down on the crate.

"Start at the beginning," he told himself aloud. "Start with the vicar."

He went over everything he knew about the case, bit by minuscule bit, from when Beaky had turned up at Farthering Place up until Midgley and Delwyn had had their last squabble at the Hound and Hart. Motive . . . motive. Who would want to kill the vicar or the nursery maid or Beaky himself?

The time crawled by. The kiln was no more than a black pit now, but he didn't turn on the electric torch in his pack. It was better this way. His eyes had adjusted to the darkness, and he could see almost clearly where the moonlight shone over the moor outside the bricked opening. His stomach growled, surprisingly loud in the night silence, but he didn't take out one of the sandwiches he had brought. Nick would likely be hungry too when he arrived.

"Where are you?" Drew growled, peering out of the kiln but seeing not the slightest movement.

It wasn't like Nick to be late. Perhaps he'd run into difficulties in London. Anything could have delayed him. Drew paced in the darkness. He didn't want to have to come back here tomorrow night and do this all again.

"Come on, old man."

He paced a while longer. The vicar and the nursery maid, they had to have seen something they shouldn't have. They had to have been silenced. But over what? Sabrina wasn't seeing Gray. Delwyn had it bad for Iris, so that ought to let Sabrina out, as well. If whoever sabotaged the Austin meant for Sabrina to be driving it, what would he gain from her death? If it was meant for Beaky after all, then who would benefit from his death? Sabrina. It seemed there was no other alternative, but Drew wouldn't know. Not until Nick told him what he'd found out in London.

Again his stomach grumbled. He took out his watch and held it so the moonlight fell over it. It was nearly eight. Nick should have been here well before now. Drew rummaged in his pack and took out a sandwich, the eating of which cheered him immensely, but that cheer was short-lived.

He waited until after nine and then slung his pack over his shoulder. Feeling the comforting presence of the Webley in his pocket, he stole out of the kiln and out toward the cottage. Nick would just have to come find him.

There was a stone wall running along the edge of the path that went down to the cottage. It wasn't very high. In several spots it had tumbled down altogether, but here in the dark, if he was quiet and kept low, Drew thought it would give him a decent view of the front of the cottage and just the cover he needed. He crept over to it and, in a few quick strides, settled himself behind it. There weren't many places to hide anywhere else, so he didn't doubt that Nick would find him quickly.

Drew wasn't sure if he was angry or worried or both, but he wasn't going to waste the time he'd already spent by giving up now. He waited a long while more, ate another sandwich, and wondered what Iris was doing inside the cottage. Spinning, most likely. Or maybe cleaning up after her supper. Had Midgley eaten there too, or was he off somewhere as he was most nights? How was she feeling now that she had broken off with Morris Gray? Sad? Betrayed? Or perhaps she was relieved to be free of someone she knew in her heart of hearts was not the man she had imagined him to be. Perhaps now she—

Drew froze when he heard a door open on the other side of the cottage.

"You there?"

That was Midgley, Drew was sure. A man's voice came in reply, but Drew didn't recognize the speaker and could make out none of the words. Midgley's voice was equally muffled, and Drew dared to peer around the wall that concealed him. There was a candle in the window, but the poacher was nowhere in sight.

His muscles and bones protesting his long inactivity, Drew crept nearer, but the two voices were still only a low muddle of sound, nothing of any use. He was about to move closer still when he heard a piercing cry and then a gurgling gasp. Then came the thud of something heavy hitting the ground.

"Midgley?" Drew slipped his hand into his coat pocket, around the solid little Webley concealed there. "Midgley?" There was a scrabbling noise, and Drew stole up to the cottage. "Come out where I can see you!"

No response, only silence.

Drew peeked around the corner of the cottage. There was no one there but Midgley. The poor rotter was huddled on the ground, something darkly red soaking into the mud beneath him. Already dead.

"Da?" The door flew open, rattling against the back wall as the girl flew into the yard, using her distaff, still wrapped with wool, as a makeshift guide. "What happened? Da?"

"Stay where you are. Please."

She turned, her grip tightening on the distaff. "Who's there? What do you want?"

"It's Drew Farthering, Miss Midgley. You remember me. Please don't come any farther."

She frowned, looking more angry than frightened. "What are you doing here? Where's my father? I heard him. Da?"

Drew took her arm, startling her. There was just no easy way to do this. "I'm sorry. He's dead."

"Da?" She tried to shake him off. "You're wrong. I just heard him. What did you do to him? Da!"

"Please, Miss Midgley—"

"Where is he?"

She wrenched away from him and, tapping the ground with the distaff, strode toward the shed behind the cottage. Almost at once the distaff came into contact with something she wasn't expecting, something still and heavy and unyielding.

"Da," she whispered, sinking to her knees beside the body, patting his hands and then his still face. "Da, what have you done?"

Drew crouched down beside her. A touch at the fallen man's

wrist was enough to assure him her father was beyond help, and he couldn't help but remember what Beaky had said about the two lambs that had been left out on the moor. A threat or a warning? Perhaps it was practice.

The girl grasped Drew's sleeve, her face turned to him. "What happened? I heard him. I heard you arguing with him and then I heard him cry out. What happened?"

"I wasn't the one he was arguing with." Drew looked around. "Someone else was here, but I didn't see who it was."

"I heard—"

"We haven't any time to waste." He pulled her to her feet and put the distaff back into her hands. "We've got to get him inside."

She found her way back to the door and went inside, leading Drew with his still-warm burden to a little closet of a bedroom. She pulled off the bed a patchwork coverlet that looked older than the girl herself, and Drew lay the body down.

She spread the coverlet over her father, patting it with both hands, smoothing it when it was already smooth, shaking her head all the while. He hated to leave her.

"I've got to go for the police," he said. "Will you be all right here? Would you rather come with me?"

"No," she breathed. "Wouldn't be right to leave him here alone."

"I'll come back as quick as I'm able," he assured her. "You latch the door and keep that blunderbuss at hand."

She nodded, and he hurried back outside. Feeling once more for the Webley in his pocket, he took a quick look around, but the killer had been wily, even in his escape. Though there were footmarks in the mud, he had taken care to blot them out, turning his foot this way and that, sometimes on his heels and sometimes on his toes, stepping into the same print two or three times so the type and size of his shoe would be obliterated.

It wasn't far to the stream, and the fugitive had taken advantage of it, stepping from rock to water-slicked rock so that trailing him was impossible. Drew blew out a hard breath and turned toward Bunting's Nest. He hadn't gone far when he realized he was not alone. This time he drew the gun.

"Who's there?"

A tall figure stepped out of the darkness.

"Beg pardon, sir." Delwyn tugged the brim of his cap. "I thought I'd heard something up near Midgley's. Thought I'd best see what it was."

Drew slipped the Webley back into his pocket and looked him over. The gamekeeper was rather disheveled and out of breath, but that could be because he had hurried from where he'd been. There didn't seem to be any blood on him, but he did have one hand in his coat pocket. The right one.

"He's dead."

Drew watched the other man's face as he said it, the involuntary widening of the eyes, the startled intake of breath, the instinctive lurch toward the cottage, and then caught his arm, managing to pull his hand out of his pocket as he did. It was bare and empty, innocent of blood.

"You can't just leave his daughter up there alone, sir. Not if he's dead. Does she know?"

"She does." Drew released his arm. "I had no choice but to leave her. I have to go for the police."

Drew considered for a moment. There were no footprints here save the ones the gamekeeper had made just now, but that didn't mean he mightn't have come the opposite way from the cottage and around through the kilns and down in the dales and then back through here. If Midgley knew too much, mayn't his killer wonder what Iris could have heard, as well?

"I think it would be best if you get the police, Delwyn. I'll stay with the girl until you get back."

"But Iris—she knows me. We've known each other for years. She wouldn't want no one else."

"All the same." Drew nodded toward the village.

Frowning, the man tugged his cap once more. "As you say, sir. I'll be back soon as I'm able."

Drew rushed back to the cottage and found Iris sitting beside her father's body, perfectly still except for her fingers stroking his gnarled hand.

"I wish I could say he wasn't always this way, Mr. Farthering. Mum, well, she loved him anyway, whether or not he deserved it."

"I expect that's the way of real love," he said gently. "It's rarely, if ever, deserved."

She made no reply to that, and he wondered if she was thinking now of her father or of someone else.

"I'm very sorry." He pulled up a chair next to her. "I've sent Delwyn for the police."

She caught a quick breath. "Rhys? Why would you send him? How did you get to him?"

"He was coming towards the cottage when I was heading for the village. I thought I'd best send him on and come back to be with you."

"Did they fight?" she asked. "That Selden Da's been bringing round, he said Da and Rhys been fighting round at the pub. Did they, sir?"

"Not fight. Not really."

The girl bit her lip. "Da said he'd beaten Rhys till he couldn't stand."

"No, nothing like that. Just a bit of squabbling and shoving. It was nothing." He didn't like to tell her the reason for it. "Delwyn wasn't here earlier, was he?"

"Here?" Her voice trembled just the slightest bit. "Not here, sir. He don't generally come here. Not anymore."

"Anymore?"

She shrugged. "He used to . . . when we were children."

"But he doesn't anymore."

"No, sir. Not now."

"Was that his idea or yours?"

She lifted her chin. "He didn't need the likes of me slowing him down."

"Not because you think a working man's beneath you?"

"Who told you that?" Her words were fierce and hot. She caught a hard breath, and the sudden anger was gone. "I never said nor thought such a thing. It's just a working man, or any man, needs a woman who can help him, not one who will be nothing but a burden to him all his life. He deserves better than that."

"And you deserve better than Morris Gray."

She ducked her head. "I'm a fool who deserves everything she got and more. And now look what's happened. God forgive me."

"He will. Just ask. I have a feeling He'd tell you to go in peace and don't go back to what you were doing. That's not so hard, is it?"

"The not going back?" She drew a shaky breath, somewhere between a laugh and a sob. "Not hard at all. If he were free and came to me now on his knees begging to make an honest woman of me, I wouldn't take him." A tear slipped down her cheek. "I think I always knew, deep down, that he was only trifling, but in those moments, when he'd tell me all the things we'd do, the glorious places we'd go, when he'd read me poems that said I was everything to him and more precious than all the world, it . . . well, sir, it was something for me. For once in my life just for me, even if it wasn't no more than a dream."

"Just be glad you woke up before there were more complications."

For a moment she looked puzzled, and then she colored. "No, sir. Nothing like that, I don't think . . ." She hugged herself and started to cry in earnest.

He wasn't sure what he ought to do, but all this at once was more than those slender shoulders ought to have to bear. He put his arm around her and, feeling her tremble, pulled her close. "It's all right now," he murmured. "It's all right. I know things couldn't be much worse, but I daresay that just means you're due something better to come."

She sniffled and then pulled away.

He hesitated for a moment, not wanting to be indelicate. "If you do find yourself . . . in difficulty, I hope you will let me know. My wife and I would be happy to give you whatever assistance we can."

She swallowed hard and licked her lips but said nothing. Again he hesitated. She'd already been through so much, he hated to press her, but it had to be done.

"Forgive me, Miss Midgley, but I must ask you what you heard just now. When your father was killed."

She patted the bed beside her until she found Midgley's hand again. "I don't know. There was a knock at the back door. Just a tap really. Secret-like. Da told me to stay here and went out. So I went over by the sink there, just to try to hear something of what he was about."

"And what did you hear? As exactly as you can remember."

JULIANNA DEERING

Her fine brows came together. "It was hardly anything, I'm afraid. Da said, 'Are you there?' and the other man said, 'It went well. Now there's just a few loose ends to see to.' And then . . ." She tried to go on but was too choked with tears. She had heard the same scuffle, the same terrible cry Drew had heard. He hadn't heard the killer's voice, not distinctly.

"What sort of voice did he have?"

"I couldn't hear very much. A gentleman's voice."

"The one you've heard before?"

"Might have been." She fished a handkerchief from the pocket of her dress and blotted her eyes and nose. "It wasn't much at all. It was all too fast. Why did he do it? Da thought he was going to get payment. I could tell by the way he was acting before he went out there. He thought he was going to be set for a long while after. Now I suppose he is, God forgive him."

"God forgive him," Drew whispered. A bad end to a bad life. It was a pity and a waste, no doubt a life that God meant for better.

The two of them sat in silence for a while, waiting for Delwyn's return. Delwyn was as good as his word, and they weren't obliged to wait very long. Unfortunately it was young Teddy Watts and not his uncle the gamekeeper brought back.

"Mr. Delwyn says there's been a murder done," Watts said, peering around the front room of the cottage the moment Drew admitted him and looking as if he thought the murderer might pop out of the cupboard at any moment.

"The body's in there with the girl," Drew said quietly, "and I'd appreciate it if you'd remember she's his daughter."

"I do know that, sir, begging your pardon, as I've been a resident of this area all my life."

He blundered into the tiny bedroom, startling the girl, but

even he didn't need more than a look to know the poacher was dead. He came back into the main room, took out his note-book and pencil, and looked expectantly at Drew. "As we have established, there has in fact been a murder. I'd like to know exactly what happened. From the beginning, if you please."

Drew frowned. "Where's Trenton? Oughtn't he be handling something as serious as this?"

"He's with Aunt Mae on account of the baby coming. But he said I can see to things for one night, and don't think I won't. I am a constable, duly sworn, sir, as I'll thank you to remember."

"I've already told you the little I know," Delwyn growled. "Let me go see to Iris."

Watts gave him a hard look but evidently could think of no objection. "Mind you stay put, Rhys Delwyn."

The gamekeeper didn't deign to make any answer. Instead he pushed past the constable to the bedroom doorway. "Iris?"

For a moment there was no answer. Then she said something too low to hear, and he stepped into the room and pulled the door closed.

Watts merely stood there until Drew indicated the two chairs near the fire. "Shall we sit?"

Evidently knowing of nothing in the regulations that pro-hibited it, Watts sat. Drew took the chair at the spinning wheel.

"What would you like to know?"

"From the beginning, sir," the constable repeated, so Drew told him everything he had seen and heard.

"Precious little, if you'll pardon me, sir. Precious little."

"Believe me, I wish I could tell you exactly who it was. Better yet, I wish I'd caught him before he could kill the man, if only for the girl's sake."

"Didn't like Midgley, did you, sir?"

Drew pressed his lips together. "Couldn't recommend him, no."

"And you say you didn't see the supposed murderer in the doing of the deed?"

"No. He was on the other side of the cottage from me. In the back."

Watts stood and said, "I think you'd better just show me, sir. Where you were hiding, and where you were when you saw the body."

Drew took him to the stone wall and then to the front corner of the cottage and then out to the back. Even in the dimness, there was evidence of a struggle, and a dark pool glistened in the moonlight. Watts took copious notes and afterward gestured for Drew to go back inside.

"That's all I know. I took the body inside and laid it out on the bed as decently as possible. Then I went to fetch you. Ran into Delwyn along the way and sent him instead. I didn't like to leave Miss Midgley alone."

"I see," Watts said, his face professionally suspicious. "You didn't see who killed the man?"

"No, I just told you where I was. I couldn't see anyone."

"And you didn't do for him yourself? Just in a temper perhaps?"

"Of course not. Why should you think that?"

"It's only that you've got blood on you, sir."

He pointed with his pencil, and Drew looked down to see his coat and one formerly pristine shirt cuff were smeared with blood. Good heavens, the man couldn't really think he—

"I carried the body inside, Constable, and I must have gotten blood on me then. That hardly means I murdered the man."

"You've admitted you didn't get along, sir. Tempers flare and next thing we know a man lies dead. It's been known to happen. In my experience—"

"Just how many murder investigations have you conducted?"

"That's well beside the point, sir."

Drew managed not to say anything unseemly. "Delwyn in there had not one but two actual fights with the man in the past few days. I don't see you questioning him."

"Mr. Delwyn don't have blood on him, sir. You see my difficulty."

This wasn't going well, not in the least. And where in the world was Nick just now? Drew could use an ally. "Perhaps you should interview Miss Midgley. She can tell you I had nothing to do with it."

"You want me to ask the blind girl to tell me what she saw, sir?"

"You could ask her what she heard and also what she noticed before she came out of the house and after. It might be quite useful in a murder investigation to question *all* the witnesses."

"And we will be interviewing Miss Midgley, all in good time. For now I'll have to ask you to come along with me."

Drew blinked at him. "What?"

"To the station, sir, if you would. On account of Mr. Midgley being dead and you being the only one caught red-handed, as it were, I'm obliged to have you in for questioning. Are you armed, sir?"

"Don't be ridiculous, man. I didn't kill him."

"I must ask you to be civil while we are attempting to investigate a serious offense. Now, are you in possession of a firearm?"

Drew took the Webley from his pocket with two fingers and handed it over. "Do bear in mind that Midgley was stabbed, not shot."

"That's as may be, sir."

"I still didn't kill him."

"I understand your position," Watts said. "I do hope you'll

understand mine and come along quietly." He moved to take Drew's arm, but Drew was already on his feet.

"Look here, you have no reason to arrest me. Just talk to the girl. She knows I'm innocent. She heard what happened."

"The young woman has had a shock, sir. I'll have to send the doctor by to look at her, and when he says she's ready to be interviewed, I will see to it. For now—"

"Talk to her. She has had a shock, I grant you, but she's not hysterical. There's no reason you cannot ask her whether or not I killed her father. Just that."

Watts looked dubious. Obviously this was not recommended procedure.

"Good heavens, man, I came here to solve a murder, not commit one."

The constable still looked reluctant, but he finally nodded. "I'll just ask her about what happened. Just a question or two, mind you, until the doctor's come to say she's fit."

"Fair enough. Shall I fetch her?"

Watts shook a thick finger at him. "You just stay where you are, sir, and don't be getting too close to the door. I'll get Miss Midgley."

She was already at the bedroom door with Delwyn at her elbow.

"I heard you talking," she said thinly. "I'm ready to answer any questions you have, Teddy."

"You ought to sit down," Delwyn urged, guiding her to a chair and then standing behind it.

"Do you know who killed your father, miss?" Watts asked once she was seated.

"No. I didn't hear very much. Just a voice from out in the yard."

Watts took down what she said. "Did you know this voice?"

"I—I'm not sure. I might have heard it before, but I really couldn't tell much about it. It was an educated voice. Not a country fellow. I'm sure of that."

The constable looked at Drew as if he'd scored one off him. "You know Mr. Farthering here, do you, miss?"

She looked puzzled. "Yes."

"And has it been a long acquaintance?"

"No. Just the past few days. Why?"

"I see." Watts made another note in his book. "Would you know his voice if you weren't expecting to hear it?"

"I don't know. I suppose."

"But you're not certain."

"No. I don't think I could say for certain." She bit her lip. "I just don't know."

A concentrated gravity came into Watts's expression. "I want you to think very carefully now, miss. Is it possible that the voice you heard talking to your father before he was killed could have been Mr. Farthering's?"

Delwyn's mouth dropped open, but he kept quiet.

"No," Iris protested. "It couldn't have been. I mean, I don't think so. Why would he kill my father?"

"That's still to be seen, miss," Watts said. "He says he was outside listening when your father was killed. Do you know that he was?"

"No. I don't *know*, I suppose. But I don't think—"

"I just want to know what you heard, miss. Now, Mr. Farthering says he came upon Mr. Delwyn on his way to fetch help after the murder. You are better acquainted with Mr. Delwyn than Mr. Farthering I gather?"

Iris looked as annoyed as Drew felt. "Of course I am. You know that, Teddy."

"Just by way of proper evidence taking, Iris. Now do be agreeable."

She huffed. "Yes, Constable. I have known Mr. Delwyn a great many years."

"Mr. Farthering here says Mr. Delwyn and your father have had recent altercations. Could you have heard Mr. Delwyn's voice outside when your father was killed?"

"No!" Iris pressed her lips together. "It wasn't Rhys. I told you it was a gentleman's voice. An Englishman. Not a Welshman."

"And was there anyone else you were aware of out in the yard, miss?"

"No."

"Did you see anyone, Mr. Delwyn?" Watts asked. "Apart from Mr. Farthering?"

Delwyn shook his head, his dark eyes wary as he gripped the back of Iris's chair. "Not a soul."

"Right." The constable made a note of that, then fixed a grave eye on Drew. "And you, sir? Did you see anyone else out by the house when you were observing?"

"No," Drew admitted. "I didn't see anyone except Midgley after he had been killed and then Delwyn on my way to the village."

"Exactly, sir. Now I'll thank you to come along quietly."

"I did *not* kill Midgley."

"That's more than I know, sir. Not just yet."

"This is ludicrous. I didn't—"

"It is just for further questioning. No charges will be filed as yet."

Drew huffed. "If this isn't a waste of your time, Watts, it certainly is of mine. Meanwhile the actual murderer is out on the moor, free to kill again."

"It will all be sorted in due time, sir. Just come along."

"I'll see to Iris," Delwyn told Drew.

Drew stared at him, wondering if Iris truly hadn't recognized the killer's voice or if she didn't want to admit she had. If Delwyn had done for Midgley, surely Iris wouldn't lie to protect him. Or would she? And if she had been foolish enough to do so, would he repay her by silencing her when they were alone?

"You will send the doctor right back, Constable?" Drew asked.

"He has been notified, sir. I expect he'll be here soon. If you'll just come this way, please."

Surely if Delwyn had killed Midgley, he wouldn't be so daft as to do Iris harm when he was known to be alone with her at the cottage. And the doctor was coming. It would have to do.

— Eighteen —

They made the brief trip back to Bunting's Nest without a word, Watts leaning over the steering wheel, concentrating on the dim road ahead, and Drew sitting in silence beside him. Clearly the man meant to do his duty to the letter, and Drew couldn't fault his intentions, but this was beyond absurd. Trenton would be much more reasonable to deal with.

"Constable Trenton will not be available until the morning at least, sir," Watts announced once they'd reached the police station and Drew made his request. "I do apologize, but the circumstances are unavoidable. Now, if you'll just turn out your pockets here on the desk, I'll give you a receipt. For the pistol, as well."

Drew eyed the little metal tray Watts pushed over to him. "I realize he has a baby on the way, but couldn't you just telephone him, tell him the situation and ask his advice?"

"I don't know that that's possible, sir. Seeing as Dr. Pine has been called over to see to Mr. Midgley, I don't think Uncle, er, Constable Trenton will appreciate being troubled by me just now, even if Mrs. Newgate is over to help." He tapped the side of the tray, making a dull thump. "Your pockets, sir, if you please."

Drew complied. Wallet, handkerchief, keys, coins. He pulled his watch out of his waistcoat pocket and put it with the rest. The little sixpence Madeline had put in her shoe for luck at their wedding hung from the chain, gleaming in the green-shaded light from the desk lamp. She'd be snickering at him just now, he was certain of it. And Nick would be braying like a donkey. Blast the man, where was he?

"Couldn't you just telephone Trenton?" Drew took a deep breath and forced a smile. "I realize you have certain protocols that must be followed, but in this particular instance we would all benefit from a moment of reflection."

Watts observed him with a jaundiced eye but said nothing.

"I can tell you are a scrupulously fair man, Constable, and I fully appreciate that these matters often take time to clarify. All I ask is that you make one inconsequential telephone call to Constable Trenton and ask his opinion on the matter. I am certain that he will commend your diligence and consideration."

Watts stuck out his cleft chin. "I have been left in charge, Mr. Farthering, sir, and have full authority to make whatever decisions need to be made until Constable Trenton returns."

"Oh, have a heart, man!" Drew stopped himself and managed to make his expression pleasant once more. "Just a telephone call. That's all I ask."

"But Aunt Mae—"

"You know babies take forever to come. Trenton's probably sitting there wishing for something to take his mind off things for a bit. At least try. I promise to be a model prisoner, if you'll just oblige me in this one little thing."

Watts was wavering.

"Please."

Watts put his hand on the telephone. "Only because Cousin Jimmy says you've helped him a time or two."

Drew made a mental note to send Chief Inspector Birdsong an enormous box of bonbons the minute he was back at Farthering Place. The constable asked the operator for two-seven-three, and soon he had Trenton on the line.

"Uncle Bilby?"

Drew could hear the tinny hum of the other man's voice over the line, but only a few of the words. ". . . doing, Teddy? . . . waiting . . . Dr. Pine . . . call . . . Get off the line!"

That last was clear as a bell.

Watts gulped. "I will. I just wanted to know—I mean, about the Midgley case—"

Trenton's voice hummed again, rising and falling in volume. ". . . handle things till then, right?" There was more Drew couldn't make out until Trenton was running out of patience. ". . . sort it all out in the morning."

"Yes, sir, I will. It's just that Mr. Farthering wanted me to ask you—"

A woman's piercing scream came from the telephone, and Teddy nearly dropped the receiver. "Uncle Bilby?"

"Where is that doctor?" Trenton shouted to someone on his end of the line, the words as clear as if he'd been standing in the station beside them.

"Uncle Bilby?"

"Get off the line, Teddy!"

"But Mr. Farthering—"

"Handle it, man!"

Watts cringed at the abrupt and final sound of the receiver on the other end of the line being slammed down.

Drew smiled thinly. "I take it that's a no."

Watts pursed his lips and gestured toward the small holding cell visible through the door on the other side of the desk. "If you'll be so good, sir."

Drew gritted his teeth, remembering his promise. "Fair enough. At least you made the attempt. I'd like to telephone my wife and let her know where I am."

He didn't tell the constable that Madeline wasn't expecting him till morning anyway. If he could get word to her, she would no doubt tell Beaky what the situation was, and Beaky would use his influence to get Drew out right away.

"I'm sorry, sir, but prisoners are not allowed telephone privileges."

Drew looked heavenward. "Surely I am to be allowed a telephone call. Isn't that the usual thing when one has been arrested?"

"But you're not under arrest, sir. You're only here for questioning."

Drew beamed at him. "Excellent. Question me and let me go."

"I'm sorry, sir, but that'll have to wait till morning."

"Then I am a prisoner."

Watts thought for a moment. "Well, yes and no, sir. You're not under arrest, but I can't release you either. I'd say you are a party of interest."

"And I take it parties of interest also may not use the telephone?"

"I'm not sure, sir. I don't recall a specific regulation about that. But I'll find out."

"Good, because—"

"In the morning."

Drew squeezed his eyes shut and then smiled again. "Constable Watts, I take it you are not a married man."

The constable blushed, looking every bit of nineteen. "No, sir."

"My wife, you remember her, don't you?"

Watts nodded. "Very lovely lady, sir, if you'll pardon my saying."

"No pardon necessary, Constable. She is that. She is also a very loving wife, and she would find it distressing if anything were to happen to me. Now, I don't like my wife to be distressed any more than I can possibly help. It seems the slightest of courtesies to at least let her know where I am, don't you think?"

"Of course, sir. I'm sure that won't be any trouble at all. In the morning."

Drew scowled, thinking again. "What if you were to make the call for me? Just to let her know why I'm delayed?"

"I'm sorry, sir, but officers are not allowed to make calls for detainees."

"Oh, come on, Watts. Teddy. You're a fine officer, I'm sure, but you're also a human being. How can you let my poor wife suffer all night long?"

To his credit, Watts did look genuinely distressed. "It's not regulation, sir."

"Couldn't you make the call in your capacity as a private citizen and not an officer of the law?"

The constable's distress congealed into disdain. "Private citizens are not allowed to use the station telephone."

With that he took firm hold of Drew's upper arm and removed him to the holding cell. Drew sat on the narrow cot, his chin propped up on one hand. Marvelous. The whole deuced evening had turned out just marvelous. Nick hadn't turned up at Midgley's, and Drew had made a hash out of the matter on his own. Not only had he not caught the killer, he'd allowed him to kill again. And now he would be spending the night in jail to think it over.

He sighed, looking longingly through the bars, able to see little more than Watts hunched over the desk, his tongue protruding slightly as he wrote out a receipt for the things in the metal tray. There had to be a way out before Trenton returned. There was no guarantee it would be in the morning. There was no guarantee it would be tomorrow at all.

"God," he breathed, "I need a way out. Please."

He got up and tried the barred door, not quite knowing what he would do if he found it unlocked, but the question was moot. The door didn't budge.

He sat on the cot once again. It was going to be a long night. He might as well try to sleep. He stretched out on his back, one arm over his eyes in an attempt to block out the light from the bare bulb overhead.

The next thing he knew, there was a pounding on the door that led to the street. "Open up! Open up!"

Drew sat up, looking blankly at P.C. Watts, who glared back at him.

"We don't have anything happen for months on end round here, and now there's not a minute's rest." He thumped into the front of the station and threw open the door. "Keep it quiet out there or I'll have you in for causing a disturbance!"

"I wanna know who is in charge here," someone demanded in a low growl. "Lemme see the manager."

"This isn't a hotel and this isn't a pub and I haven't time for tosspots this hour of the night. Quiet down and clear off."

"Lemme see the manager." The voice was thick and unsteady. "Someone's took my bed. It was just there not ten minutes ago."

"Go on," Watts warned, "or I'll find you a bed right here."

"You've found it? About time. Saved me going to the police about it."

Drew clenched his jaw in annoyance.

"Yes, we found it all right," said the constable. "Come in and identify it."

He stepped out the door and returned a moment later with the supposed drifter Tom Selden in tow. With his free hand he unlocked the cell and then pushed the new prisoner inside.

Nick stumbled over to the cot along the far wall and then started as if he had only just seen it. His whole face scrunched up as if he were struggling to make a decision and then he staggered back to the bars where Watts was just locking the door.

"That isn't it at all," Nick protested. "Mine was blue with sort of a stripe on it."

"Well, you give it another look," Watts soothed, dropping the key into his uniform pocket, "and we'll talk about it in the morning."

"You're a good bloke," Nick said, reaching through the bars to drape himself from Watts's shoulder. "But I tell you, mate, that's not mine. It ain't blue and it don't have no stripe. 'Sides, if it was mine, what would it be doing in this post office?" He patted the constable's chest with his free hand. "You see what I mean?"

Watts removed the prisoner's hand from his shoulder, causing him to slide down against the bars until the constable pulled him upright again.

"I tell you what you should do about your little dilemma," Watts said. "That gentleman over there is in charge of our lost-

and-found department, and he would be very happy to help you find your missing property."

The prisoner's face lit. "Right! Right! Just the ticket. Who's your governor, eh? Tell him you ought to have a rise in your pay. Better yet, I'll tell him. You have him look me up proper early, eh?"

"I'll do that." Watts took hold of Nick's shoulder and turned him to face Drew. "Now off you go, and remember this is a post office and we want to keep it quiet."

"Right," the prisoner said, putting a finger to his lips. "Quiet as mice, to be sure."

Watts watched him stagger over to Drew's bunk and then, with a chuckle, went back to his desk.

"A three-penny stamp if you please, guv."

Drew scowled at Nick and made his voice low. "That was laid on with a trowel."

"It got me in, didn't it?"

"What do you think you're doing?" Drew demanded. "Where have you been? I thought you were coming just after sundown."

"I've been stuck in the middle of the empty countryside, waiting for a track to be mended or connected or switched or some nonsense of that ilk," Nick whispered. "I was coming just after sundown, but evidently the engine driver hadn't been given prior notice of the plan and rather took his time getting us up here from York. Nonetheless, I've come to get you out."

Drew glanced toward the other room. Watts had pulled the intervening door nearly closed, and all he could see was the constable's heavy boots propped up on Trenton's overburdened desk. He lifted an eyebrow, uncertain how Nick could possibly make good on that statement.

"I didn't get to look at Beaky's will or his insurance policy."

Drew frowned. "I thought you were going to charm some file clerk or girl from the typing pool into helping you."

"At the insurance company the only one who'd see me was a Miss Ellis. She wanted to see a letter from Beaky's solicitors or from Beaky himself granting me permission to see his policy."

"And at the solicitors'?"

Nick looked positively distressed. "It turned out that the girl from the typing pool was an elderly gentleman of between sixty and seventy years called Roussel. He arrived at the front office in ill humor and was not about to be charmed. Barring written permission from Mr. Bloodworth or a properly executed court order, I was not going to be seeing his will this day or any other."

"I don't guess any of that matters now, old man. Midgley, he—"

"I know all about that. I was coming up to the cottage when the police arrived to take you away. I saw reason wasn't going to move young Teddy over there, so I thought I'd best come get you out."

Drew gaped at him. Nick produced an unconcerned smile in return.

"You realize we're both in here now."

"I do," Nick said cheerfully.

"That means neither of us is out there."

"It means precisely that."

Drew pursed his lips. "And this helps because . . . ?"

"Because contrary to popular belief, our beloved constable there does not possess the key to this cell."

"No? And why would you think that?"

"Because," Nick said, producing the object in question, "I do."

Drew couldn't keep back a grin. "I'm sure you've just broken a number of local ordinances."

"Not as many as the two of us will have in just a few minutes more."

Drew glanced toward the feet on Trenton's desk. "Please don't tell me that bit will include assaulting a police officer."

"All right," Nick said sunnily, "if you'd rather I kept it to myself."

"Nick—"

"Look here, we've got to get out. That Blackstock is up to something."

"The milkman? I thought he'd gone."

Nick's mouth turned down in disdain. "He made a great show of it, that's sure, but I swear I saw him not half an hour ago."

"What?"

"I saw what happened when you were arrested."

"You saw Midgley get killed?"

"No. I wasn't there till Constable Watts was taking you off. I thought I'd better go get Trenton, but he wouldn't listen. Said to talk to Watts about it. But I heard what Watts told you, and I know that would be a bust all the way round. So I thought I'd better get you out myself. I don't know what Blackstock's up to now. At first I didn't quite think it was him. It was hard to see in the dark, and he didn't look the same, but I'm certain now it was him."

"What would he have been doing out there? Especially this time of night? The only place he could have been was Midgley's or . . ." Drew sprang to his feet. "We've got to get out. Nick, we've got to get out now."

Nick nodded. "Right."

"The key, man. Give me the key."

Drew snatched it from Nick's hand, almost sending it flying across the cell and then fumbling with it as he reached through the bars and fitted it into the lock.

"Quiet now," Nick whispered. "You'll have Teddy in here before you can say jailbreak."

"We've no time. God help me, Nick, why didn't I see it before?"

There was a loud clank and then a metallic shriek as he shoved the cell door open.

"Here now!" Watts was on his feet, standing between Drew and Nick and the door to the street. "You just give me that key and get back where you were. It's a violation of Ordinance 126—"

Drew stepped right in front of him, putting his face not a foot from the constable's. "Shut up and listen to me."

The constable blinked.

"Mr. and Mrs. Bloodworth and my wife and who knows who else might very well be being murdered at this instant. Now either my friend here and I can shove you into that cell and leave you locked up until we've stopped those murders from happening, or you can come along with us and do your job."

"Murders? Just hold steady there, sir. We've been through this about Midgley already. Now you claim Mr. Bloodworth—"

"Blackstock's headed towards the Lodge right now. He killed Midgley. I daresay he did for the vicar and Miss Patterson, as well."

"That nice Mr. Blackstock? But he's gone to America."

Drew and Nick seized the constable each by an arm, hurrying him toward the door.

"Here!" Watts protested. "You can't—"

"I'll tell you everything on the way." It was all Drew could do to keep his voice low and even. "So help me, if anything happens to my wife because you stood here dithering—"

The constable swallowed hard. "We'll take the car."

Madeline sighed and put down her book. It was a new one by Sayers, *The Nine Tailors*, and whether it was the author's long, technical passages on parish bell ringing or her own restlessness, she couldn't seem to truly engross herself in the story. Perhaps the problem was that for the first time in nearly two years, Drew was not lying beside her in bed, reading over her shoulder or listening to her read aloud or reading aloud himself.

They had fallen into the habit of not just reading mystery stories, but solving them along with whatever sleuth happened to be in the starring role. They discussed the clues and the suspects, forming and discarding theories as the story progressed and then judging their success not by whether they found the same answer the book presented, but by whether, with the clues they had been given, their solution had been superior. And woe betide the author who did not play fairly with his reader. Reading mysteries on her own was never as engaging as it had been when she was single.

She removed the two pillows she had behind her, bunched them into rather square packet-looking shapes, and put them behind her once more. She didn't like Drew being out there on the moor all night. Surely that wasn't really necessary anyway. If Midgley was going to have a clandestine meeting with whomever was paying him, there was no actual need to have that meeting at the stroke of midnight under a full moon or any other such Gothic nonsense. The whole thing would probably, as Drew liked to say, be a bust.

She picked up the book again, determined not to worry, and felt a wave of grogginess roll over her. It was ten past twelve now, not so very late. She had spent the time after dinner playing cards with Sabrina while Beaky saw to some business matters, and their conversation had been illuminating. It had nothing to do with the case, though it said much about Sabrina herself, yet it wasn't something Madeline felt she could share with Drew. Sabrina deserved to have her confidences kept.

The book slipped into Madeline's lap, and she blinked, sitting up straight again. There was a sudden throbbing in her head. She couldn't seem to draw a steady breath. Something was wrong. Wrong with the air. Something nasty in the smell of it. She knew it was wrong, although she couldn't seem to remember why, and yet she was vaguely aware that she should get out. Get out. Still, she was so tired, her head was heavy, and her eyes would hardly stay open. That was all right. It was getting a little dim anyway.

Get out. Get out.

There was something urgent in the words. Her words? She didn't know. She wanted to just lie down and sleep, but she couldn't. She had to get out.

She pulled herself up against the bedpost and managed to put her feet on the floor. She wouldn't say anything to Drew about Sabrina . . .

Sabrina? Sabrina and Beaky.

The door seemed a mile away. She staggered to it, somehow remembering to turn the knob, somehow remembering that smell. That rotten, sulfurous smell. It was still faint, but it was growing stronger.

She flung open the door and stumbled down the hallway, coughing now, her head pounding. Pounding. She pounded on the door to Beaky and Sabrina's bedroom, trying to call to them but unable to manage more than a breathless wheeze. She had to get out. *They* had to get out. She pounded again, barely able to hold herself upright, and then she pushed the door open.

Beaky was lying in bed in his pajamas, mouth open, looking

strange without his glasses. His face was oddly pink, his lips unnaturally red, hair flaming against the pillows. He had been pulled to one side. The upper half of his body looked as if it might slide off the bed. Across him at an odd angle, one hand twisted into the front of his pajamas, lay Sabrina, as pink and red as he. She must have known, too. She must have been awake and smelled the choking foulness. Must have been overcome with dizziness.

Madeline grabbed her arm. "Sabrina, get out. Have to get out. Sabrina."

She tried to shout, to shake her, to wake her, but nothing seemed to work. Not her voice, not her limbs, not her eyes. It was getting dimmer, the throbbing in her head was almost unbearable, and her stomach heaved as if she would be sick.

"Get out," she sobbed.

She gave Sabrina's arm another useless tug. Then the room spun, and a rushing blackness swallowed her.

— Nineteen —

Bloodworth Park Lodge was dark and still.

"Stop here," Drew said when they'd reached the bend that turned toward the house. "Turn out the lights. We'd better walk from here. I'd rather see what's going on before we make our presence known."

The constable complied, and the three of them started toward the house. There was just enough moonlight to keep them from stumbling, just enough to illuminate the dark figure hurrying across the moor toward the north wing. Drew caught Nick's arm and pointed at it. Nick nodded, motioned for Watts to come with him, and disappeared around the far side of the house.

Drew moved into the shadows near the house, waited until the figure drew closer, and then stepped forward. "I think you ought to stop right there."

"Mr. Farthering." Rhys Delwyn glared at him and lowered his shotgun. "I thought you were locked up."

"Obviously. Leaving you and your mate the perfect opportunity to—"

"Don't be foolish. He's gone inside already, into the north wing. The Bloodworths and your wife—"

"I'll have that if you don't mind," Watts said, taking the gun from Delwyn as he and Nick emerged from the other side of the house. "We've been watching you for some time, lad."

"Give it a rest, Teddy," Delwyn said. "Keep the gun if you like, but don't waste time out here. He's already inside."

"Odd your being here just now," Drew said.

"It was Iris. She told me what her father said to the man who killed him. She didn't tell the police. She wasn't sure what it all meant and, him having just been killed, she didn't like to speak ill of her father. But she said they were going to finish things off tonight. Evidently, Midgley said he wanted more money or he'd go to the police with what he knew, and that's why he was murdered. I tell you, Mr. Farthering, we haven't time for this. She didn't hear any details, but it's supposed to look like an accident. Something to do with the furnace."

"We've got to get them out of there." Drew sprinted toward the house. "God help us. Come on!"

"What about Blackstock?" Nick asked, running after him. "He might well blow the whole place to kingdom come if he knows we're onto him."

"We've got to get them out," Drew repeated, calling back as he ran, "Watts, go round to the servants' wing and see they all get out. Away from the house!"

He didn't wait for an answer. He rushed to the front door, opened it with the latch key, and dashed into the hallway.

"Madeline!" He took the stairs two at a time with Nick and Delwyn just behind him. "Madeline!"

The door to the room he and she shared stood open. The bedcovers were thrown back, one of the pillows lay on the floor, but she was nowhere in sight.

"Over here!" Delwyn shouted from down the corridor. "They're here!"

Drew ran to him and skidded to a stop in the doorway of Beaky's room. He was sprawled on the bed with Sabrina collapsed over him. And there on the floor—

"Madeline."

She lay there in her white nightgown, curled up on the thick carpeting, her skin too pink, her lips too red. He stumbled to her side, half choked on the noxious air.

"Madeline." He patted her cheek. "Madeline. Darling."

"Quick, let's get them out," Delwyn said, feeling the pulse at Sabrina's throat and then at Beaky's. "It may already be too late."

"No," Drew breathed. "Nick, get that window open. Hurry."

Nick glanced back at him, eyes wide, wheezing with effort. "It's not budging."

"Get it open!" A prayer for help shrieking inside his head, Drew gathered Madeline into his arms as Delwyn picked up Sabrina.

Nick seized the chair from in front of the dressing table and smashed it through the glass. There was a sudden rush of cold air, and Drew's head cleared just the slightest bit.

He stood, swayed for an instant, then started for the door. Delwyn was already in the corridor. Nick had Beaky heaved across his shoulder. The three of them staggered to the stairs, down to the entryway, and out onto the front lawn. Watts and all the servants were coming from the other end of the house, frightened and confused, dismayed to see their master and mistress and the American lady laid out on the dead grass and not moving.

Sabrina coughed first, wheezing and choking, soon joined by her husband in that. Nestled against Drew's chest, Madeline was still.

"Darling," he murmured against her cheek as he chafed her wrist. "Please, darling."

Please, God, please . . .

She drew a little gasping breath and then began to cough, struggling for breath, struggling to free herself from whatever was holding her.

"Shh, Madeline. I've got you, love. You're all right. Just breathe."

She clung to him, coughing and shaking as he stroked her hair. He laughed softly, his face turned heavenward as he too gulped down the sweet cold air of the October night, his eyes stinging with tears. *Thank God.*

"It's all right, darling."

Sabrina was struggling to sit up, to breathe, to talk. Delwyn gave her into the capable hands of her maid and went over to Nick and Beaky.

"How is he?" the gamekeeper asked. "Sit him up a little."

Nick did so. "Come on, Beaky, old man, rise and shine now."

Beaky wheezed and choked as if he would be sick, but then his eyes snapped open. "Sabrina? Where's—?"

"She's all right. She's right here."

Beaky squinted into Nick's face.

"That's more like it," Nick said with a grin.

"That's not Nicky Dennison, is it?"

"The very same," Nick said. "Getting you out of a fix as always."

Beaky tried to laugh and wheezed instead. "Sabrina—"

Sabrina pushed her maid away and managed to wriggle closer to him, her expression severe. "Beaky, you idiot," she rasped, but she twined her fingers into his, and his hand tightened around them.

Drew frowned and then noticed that Madeline's eyes were on him. Drat the girl, she was smirking. Not caring, he hugged her closer and felt her shiver. At once he had his coat off and around her shoulders.

"We've got to get them inside somewhere," he said, "until the house is safe." He looked around, trying to see into the darkness. "We've got to find Blackstock, or Faber rather. Before he gets away."

Madeline's forehead wrinkled. "What?"

"I'll tell you everything later, darling. Are you all right for now?"

She nodded, still looking perplexed.

"I'll see to her, sir." The cook, Mrs. Norris, came to Madeline's side and put her own slippers, worn and a world too wide, on Madeline's bare feet. "Come on, dear. We'd better get you out of the cold."

"The garage, if you think it best, sir," Halford said, helping Nick get Beaky to his feet.

Beaky kept hold of Sabrina's hand, and she stood with him.

"You'll see to things here, Halford?" Drew said, still scanning the area.

"Certainly, sir."

Beaky's valet, Anderson, had already taken charge of his master, clucking over his thin pajamas and unshod feet there in the wet.

Drew kissed Madeline. "You rest and catch your breath,

darling. Nick and I are going to see to our mysterious Mr. Faber."

She was too dazed still to make much protest. Halford began helping everyone toward the relative warmth of the garage.

Drew motioned to Nick and Delwyn. "Come on."

Watts fell in with them. "I am a constable," he said when Drew gave him a hard look.

"You'd better keep that gun at the ready then," Drew said. "Or give it back to Delwyn."

Watts kept stubborn hold of the weapon. The gamekeeper only huffed and strode toward the house.

"He can't be long gone," Drew said. "They'd all be dead if we hadn't come fairly soon after he'd done his tampering. I don't know where—"

He froze at the sound of a low growl, and then a large black shape stalked out of the darkness of the north wing, snarling and showing white fangs. Behind it, another figure, barely visible, laughed low.

"Come out, Faber," Drew said. "The game's up. We know who you are."

That elicited another low laugh. "You say there's no hound. Maybe. Maybe not. But I can promise you this one will tear you to bits unless you stand aside and let us go."

The man's voice must have been the one Iris had heard when her father was murdered. It was a gentleman's voice. Not Blackstock's.

Watts leveled the gun at the dog. "Step back, Mr. Farthering, sir."

Swearing under his breath, Delwyn snatched the weapon from him, still keeping it trained on the dog. "You think again, Blackstock, or Faber, or whatever you go by. Don't make the poor beast suffer for what you've done. Just call him off and come out quietly."

For a moment there was absolute silence. No one dared move. Then with a sob the man threw himself to his knees beside the dog, pulling its head against his heart, shielding it with his body.

"Poor old Kedgeree. They turned us both out, didn't they?"

The animal whined and wriggled, its heavy tail thumping the ground.

"Come on, Baxter," Delwyn coaxed. "You remember me, boy, eh?"

The dog looked at him, old eyes wary, puzzled. Not forgetting their last encounter, Drew took a careful step forward. The dog immediately lowered its head, growling low in its throat.

"Never mind now," the man kneeling there soothed, and the dog thumped its tail again. "Never mind."

It was Blackstock all right, the man they had known as Blackstock at any rate, even if his voice was different now and his beard and spectacles were gone. Gone too was the bland, eager-to-please expression. In its place was something craftier, watchful, defensive.

"He hasn't done anything," he said, eyes narrowed. "Don't hurt him."

"I'll see he's looked after," Delwyn said, holding out his hand but keeping the gun at the ready just the same.

"You'll have to come with me, sir," Watts said, looking uncertain of whom he was arresting and on how many charges. "Better let him be seen to now."

The other man glared back and then took his arms from around the dog. "Go on."

"Come on, Baxter. Come on." The gamekeeper patted his leg

encouragingly, and the dog padded over to him and sat down at his heel. Delwyn put his hand on its head. "There's a boy."

The other man stood. "What now? I suppose you'll put me away again. Wouldn't want to upset things now. Wouldn't want to make the family uncomfortable. Not after fifteen years, would we?"

"You've been busy since you left Norfolk," Drew said. "We'll have a nice talk about that once everything here is cleared up, wouldn't you say, Faber?"

"Faber? I'd say you're as much a fool as Dr. Grant at the asylum. Faber's dead. Killed at Amiens with all the rest. I'm not Faber. I'm—"

"Uncle Vester."

Drew turned to see Beaky standing just behind him. He was wrapped in a flannel dressing gown, likely Anderson's, far too short for his gangly frame and large enough to go twice around him. Someone had given him slippers, as well. He squinted, still without his spectacles, and moved closer.

The moonlight shone silver on them all, and looking at the man with the color leeched out of him, Drew saw it too. It was the photograph all over again. The firm chin, the pale eyes, the hawklike nose that was nothing like his brothers' or his nephew's. The hair could be either blond or gray, it was all the same in this light. The lines of age and care softened in the dimness, but there was Sylvester Armstrong Bloodworth, captain in His Majesty's armed forces in the late war. Presumed dead.

Beaky coughed and sputtered and then shook his head. "I—I don't understand. Why in the world would you do it? What had we ever done to you? What had any of us ever done to you?"

Drew took the erstwhile milkman by the arm. "Do you want to tell him or shall I?"

300

"Tell him what you like," the older man said, pulling free of Drew's grip.

"What happened to you?" Bewildered, Beaky gaped at him, his brows starkly red against his still-purplish face. "We thought you were dead."

"Dead?" his uncle spat. "Maybe so. Maybe so. There's no doubt I've been in hell nearly twenty years."

Beaky reached out a hand to him. "Why didn't you come home? Grandmother never stopped waiting to hear."

Sylvester Bloodworth started away from him and then sneered. "Touching. My brothers weren't so sentimental, it seems. And you were happy enough to come into the estate, I warrant."

"It would have been his even if everyone had known you were alive," Drew said. "But then I expect you're well aware of that."

"Oh, yes." Sylvester's eyes narrowed. "Lovely laws of England, leaving the younger brother out in the cold. The Lodge should be mine. It should have always been mine."

"You could have come back home," Beaky said. "You know you would have always had a place with us."

"A place?" Sylvester muttered, and then his voice rose and cracked. "A place? I've been in *a place*. A place with smells and sounds and sights that would turn that red hair of yours white as mine. Shall I tell you about it?"

"Uncle," Beaky breathed.

"I was there for an eternity, not knowing where I was, *who* I was. Hubert and Marcus, it must have pleased them to have me out of the way. A gibbering idiot caged up and neatly taken care of. Never mind how, so long as it was hushed up."

"No," Beaky protested. "It wasn't like that. I remember when we found out you were dead, at least when we were told so.

We all mourned, your brothers most of all. How could we have known we had been told wrong?"

"Don't lie to me!" Sylvester roared. "Don't you dare lie to me now! I saw the letter. Oh, yes. I've been in and out of the house, *my* house, often enough. I saw it there on your desk. Your uncle Hubert had been paying them off, making sure I was kept out of the way, and you carried on for him."

"You didn't know who you were," Drew reminded him, "and I understand you had Faber's identification on you. How could the army have known you were someone else? All of your men were dead."

Sylvester wrinkled his forehead, straining to remember. "He'd landed on a mine, Faber had. He was so torn and bloodied I don't think his mother would have known him then. I pulled him into my arms as he died. 'So cold,' he said. 'So cold, Mr. Sylvester.' I put my jacket round him, and when he was gone, I took his papers. I wanted his people to know what had happened to him. I stuck the papers inside my shirt and then . . ." His whole body trembled. "I don't know. That was all. Then I was suddenly a gray old man locked away in Norfolk."

"But your family didn't know."

"They could have checked. They could have come to see for themselves instead of having me locked away. They knew. They always knew."

Beaky blinked at him. "It wasn't like that. It was never like that. They thought you were Faber. We thought you were Faber and tried to do what we could. We—"

"You left me there." Sylvester's voice was barely a sob now. "I knew there was someplace I belonged. I told them so, but they never believed me. For the longest time I couldn't remember. I couldn't tell them where or who to ask, but then it started coming back to me. And I knew. I knew what you had done. What all of you had done."

"So you found a way out and disappeared," Drew said quietly. "Then you set yourself up as Blackstock, someone who had a reason to be up and around everywhere in the early morning when no one was about, meaning to dispose of your nephew and his wife."

"I'd known about the old gas lighting in this wing since I was a boy. It wouldn't take much to make use of it. Once my way was clear, I could go back to Bath where I'd made sure to be seen wandering a time or two. Nobody notices a vagabond on the road, not so long as he doesn't trouble anyone. Who could say I hadn't been round there ever since I left Norfolk? And if I should somehow come upon an item in the news that brought back my lost memory, who could deny that for truth?"

Drew nodded, looking away from the horror in Beaky's eyes. "Your nephew and his wife lost due to an unfortunate fault in the heating system, you could suddenly remember you're the last Bloodworth of Bloodworth Park Lodge and take possession of the money and the estate."

"It was only fair," Sylvester muttered.

"And the vicar? Miss Patterson? I expect they recognized you."

Sylvester snorted. "I saw the look on the vicar's face. I tried to stay clear of anyone I'd known before, just a wave and a nod as I went about my business, but I could tell he recognized me when he stepped in front of my wagon one morning. I was startled and shouted for him to mind where he was. And I had been so careful to make myself sound like a country man up till then. I telephoned him that night, asked if I could meet him at the church. I told him where I'd been and that I was confused and asked if he could advise me."

Beaky looked grieved. "And of course he was willing to help."

"I didn't expect I'd have to deal with Miss Patterson too, I must admit." Sylvester went on as if he hadn't heard. "I bumped into her when she was coming out of the post office. I don't know which of us was more surprised."

"Of course," Drew said. "She was your old governess."

"She didn't say anything at the time. I think she wasn't quite sure at first, but then I saw her peering at me the next morning as I drove by. That was after the vicar, you know, and I could see the fear there in her eyes. When I went to see her, I told her I didn't want her to be afraid. I said I only wanted to talk to her, to explain. She was always rather easy to get round, even when I was in the nursery."

No one said anything at that. There was a general chill at the matter-of-factness in his tone.

"And the hound?" Drew asked finally. "That dog never made those prints."

"Did you never read Doyle?" Sylvester asked, looking disdainfully at all of them. "'The Adventure of the Priory School'?"

"Good heavens," Delwyn said. "The horseshoes."

Beaky squinted at everyone. "Wait. What?"

"Horseshoes," Nick said as P.C. Watts gaped at him. "They used horseshoes that left tracks like cows' hooves so the horses couldn't be traced."

Drew looked at Sylvester. "You used shoes that leave paw prints so you could walk about in the north wing and have it look as if no man had been there. An animal large enough to leave those prints would be unnatural indeed."

"Unnatural, true," Sylvester said. "As unnatural as two brothers keeping a third locked away, wouldn't you say?"

"I was at the asylum," Nick said, his face grim. "Not exactly a palace, but they do as best they can with what they have. The sister I spoke to—"

"Liars," Sylvester spat. "All of them. What do they know? They can't know. They haven't been there. They haven't seen. They don't carry it inside." He pounded his head with both fists, punctuating each word. "Inside. Always there. Every minute. Every. Single. Day."

Watts and Delwyn took hold of his arms, pulling his fists away from his head, pinning him until he was still once more. He half crouched in between them, some wild thing in its lair, and watched them, the whites of his eyes gleaming in the moonlight.

"Just calm yourself, sir," Watts said, looking as if he feared the prisoner might bite. "Everything will be seen to. You'll be looked after."

"Looked after. Looked after."

With a low moan, Sylvester shrank more deeply into himself. For a moment he was perfectly still, and then with a shriek he threw off his keepers and bolted back into the north wing.

"After him!" Watts shouted. "Don't let him get away!"

"Stay where you are!" Sylvester Bloodworth stood wild-eyed in the black opening to the old wing. "Don't move, the lot of you. I know this place. Follow me inside, and I promise you no one comes out."

"Uncle Vester," Beaky pled.

"I mean it," Sylvester said. "Stay where you are." He whistled, high and piercing, and with a startled yip the dog darted away from Delwyn and ran to him. The two of them vanished into the darkness.

"I'd best be after him," Watts said, looking uncertain but duty-bound.

Drew stopped him. "We don't know what he has in there. We'd do better to have a couple of us go round to the other side and wait to see if he—"

There was a terrific boom as the north wing went up in an explosion of heat and fire and shattered glass. Drew shielded his face with one arm and watched with the others as the flames shot up into the night sky.

"Uncle," Beaky breathed. "Merciful God, Uncle!"

Drew grabbed his arm before he could rush into the inferno. "You can't help him now."

Beaky turned his face away. "Uncle Vester."

"No, wait!" Nick said, and he pointed out behind the house. "Look there!"

Lit by the flames, hardly more than shadows against the dark, sloping hillside, Sylvester and the hound ran out onto the moor and disappeared into one of the dales.

"He's got to be stopped," Beaky said, taking a futile stride toward him.

Watts shook his head. "Unless you want to lose your entire house, sir, we'd best get this fire out right away."

Beaky breathed out an almost-silent "Oh" and then stood a bit straighter.

The servants were peering out of the garage door, and most of the men were heading out to give whatever help they could.

"All right. Watts," Beaky said, "drive into the village and round up whatever men and buckets you can. Get ahold of Mr. Tims and the fire brigade, if they didn't already hear that blast."

"Right you are, sir."

Watts jumped into his car and, bell jingling, raced back toward the village.

Beaky turned to Delwyn. "Go and get Johnson, if you would, please, and the rest of the men."

The gamekeeper squinted into the darkness toward the south side of the house. "Beg pardon, sir, but they're just coming. I didn't think they'd sleep through that blast."

There were five or six of them, sturdy-looking workhands carrying buckets.

"Excellent," Beaky said. "But all of you stay back. I don't know if there's anything else liable to blow."

"I don't think so," Drew said. "There was just that one tank, and it was mostly empty. I'm rather surprised it hadn't gone long before now."

Beaky nodded, and then he laughed unsteadily. "Sabrina wanted to remodel anyway."

Drew gave him a hearty swat on the back. "Stout fellow."

Beaky moved a step closer, his expression troubled. "My uncle . . ."

Drew could hear the faint sound of the fire bell from the village and knew help was coming. He glanced toward Nick and then Delwyn. "What do you say? Shall we give it a go?"

"There's a good moon," the gamekeeper said, looking up. "But I don't like to leave Iris. I know she has her shotgun and won't let anyone in she doesn't know, but I don't like the idea of him going back there."

Drew nodded. "You get her and bring her here. The ladies will look after her. I'm sure you can catch up to us after that."

Delwyn looked to Beaky.

"Yes, go," Beaky told him. "Hurry now."

The gamekeeper ducked his head and loped into the darkness. The house servants and farmhands were already carrying water to douse the flames, and Drew and Nick headed toward the slope where they had last seen Sylvester Bloodworth.

Delwyn caught up with them not very much later, bringing a pair of lanterns to light their way. They searched for a full hour, around the stone church and in the kilns, anywhere that might conceal a man. Then Delwyn said it was just no use searching any longer in the dark, that they'd do best to start again at dawn.

The fire was burning itself out by the time they returned to the Lodge. Miss Windham was seeing that everyone had blankets, and Mrs. Norris had made sandwiches for the exhausted firefighters. Fortunately, the explosion had been confined to the far end of the north wing, and it seemed, once Johnson and his boy cleared the furnace, the only real damage to the main part of the house was that some of the windows had been shattered in the blast.

Drew was glad when Madeline hurried to him and pressed herself into his arms. There wasn't much to be said.

No one slept that night, and when the sun came up again, Beaky, Drew, Nick, and P.C. Watts tracked the fugitive over the moor to Merlin Hill, the craggy precipice overlooking all the Bloodworth lands. There they found Sylvester Bloodworth spread-eagled on the bare rock, glittering in the morning light and early frost, eyes turned up to the open sky but seeing nothing. The black hound lay at his feet, whining softly.

"Exposure?" Nick asked.

Beaky looked up from where he knelt, his hand pressed over the still chest. "It wasn't as cold as that last night."

"He'd have been uncomfortable, sir," Delwyn said. He hadn't

bothered to button his own coat that morning. He patted the head of the dog that had slunk over to him, leaning against his leg, still with his mournful eyes on the dead man. "But it shouldn't have killed him. Not in just the few hours he was gone."

"No." Beaky removed his wool scarf and draped it over his uncle's face. "No, it wasn't that cold."

Delwyn and Watts carried the body back to the Lodge and laid it out in the room that had once belonged to Sylvester Bloodworth, and Beaky set beside him the fading photograph of a young man with clear eyes and a firm chin and a surprisingly gentle mouth. The Victoria Cross was still draped over one corner of the frame.

— Twenty —

Drew and Madeline stood at the graveside with Delwyn and Iris as the body of Jack Midgley, poacher, thief, accessory to murder, and God knew what else was lowered into a humble grave near his cottage, the place hallowed only by his daughter's tears.

"I'm sorry, Da," she whispered as she tossed a handful of earth onto the plain pine box. She hid her face against Delwyn's chest while two of the hands from the Lodge began covering the box with dirt.

"He chose his own way, love," he said when it was all done. "You couldn't make him do anything but what he wanted."

"I know."

"I don't like to think of you out here alone," Drew told her. "I'm sure Mr. Bloodworth could find you a position at the Lodge, and then—"

"I don't want his charity, Mr. Farthering," she said, lifting her pale face to the sound of his voice. "Nor yours, I thank you very much. But you needn't worry. I won't be alone." She squeezed Delwyn's hand. "Not for long."

He looked somber, but there was a glimmer of light in his dark eyes. "We've had time to talk, Iris and me, since I brought her back to the Lodge that night. Or I should say, she's finally listened to me."

"Rhys," she said, coloring faintly.

"It's true, Iris, and you know it, but never mind that. We're burying the past right here along with your father. Starting fresh and not looking back, right?"

Her color deepened, but she smiled. "Right."

"We're having the banns read come Sunday," Delwyn told Drew.

"Really?" Drew glanced at Madeline, startled but somehow not completely surprised. "Best wishes to you both."

"I'm so happy for you." Madeline squeezed the girl's hand. "You'll be a lovely bride."

"Thank you, ma'am," Iris said, suddenly shy.

"I'm a lucky man, Mrs. Farthering," Delwyn said, pulling the girl to his side.

Madeline's eyes twinkled. "I'd say you were blessed."

"That may be, ma'am," Delwyn agreed. "That may well be." He looked at Drew with a hint of a grin. "Maybe those errands might not be so bad after all, eh?"

"Mine have always been quite an adventure," Drew said, "and you seem the adventurous type. You might just give them a try."

"I might," the gamekeeper said, and then he gazed fondly at Iris. "We might."

The funeral held the next day was just as quiet. Just as sparse. But there was something sadder about it. This time Drew and Madeline stood with Beaky and Sabrina and Nick as the October wind blustered through the family plot out behind Bloodworth Park Lodge, there among the marble monuments to Bloodworths long past and surrounded by all the staff. This coffin was not a cheap pine box, but a finely crafted casket with an engraved plaque. *Sylvester Armstrong Bloodworth.* The vicar from a neighboring parish read the service, asking God's mercy on a soul who had borne much and sinned much and suffered much.

"It was his heart, according to the doctor," Beaky said as they walked back to the house. "I thought it might be that. He likely shouldn't have gone to war at all."

"I'm curious," Drew said. "Why did he call the dog Kedgeree? I thought his name was Baxter?"

"That dog, yes," Beaky said. "But Kedgeree was Uncle Vester's dog. Before the war. He was old even then. Grandmother said he died of a broken heart when Uncle Vester didn't come back. Baxter was, oh, I don't know, some multiple of great-grandson to the dog Uncle Vester remembered. Uncle Hubert always kept one of them about. I suppose in his brother's memory." He winced as if something had suddenly pained him. "I don't know how Uncle Vester could have imagined the family didn't want him. If my father and my uncle had known he was alive, they'd have had him home that very hour. Poor Uncle Vester, believing he'd been purposefully shut away all those years when nothing could have been further from the truth."

Madeline gave him a sympathetic smile. "I'm so sorry. About all of this. It's such a tragedy."

"Yes," Beaky said. "I just have to believe he's found peace at last."

"I pray he has," Drew said. "God knows what he's been through and how ill he must have been. He will give him both justice and mercy. It's His way."

312

Madeline leaned closer to kiss his cheek and then put her arm through Beaky's. "I'd love to hear about him," she said gently, "from before the war."

As they walked on ahead, Nick fell back to talk with Johnson about the sheep, and Drew found himself next to Sabrina. He knew he had to say something, but it was deuced hard to know where to start. They were quiet for a long while.

"I've come to realize what a very perceptive woman my wife is," he said at last.

Sabrina looked arch. "You're just now noticing? I thought you were supposed to be a detective and all that."

His face turned hot, but he managed a smile. "I've been more wrong than right this time out, I'm afraid. And I owe you an apology."

"Me? Whatever for?"

"I rather thought you were in on this whole thing. Trying to kill Beaky for his money or, uh, at least trying to cover up the affair you were having."

That startled a laugh out of her, making several of the others who had been at the funeral glance her way. "I had no idea you thought so highly of me."

His face turned hotter. "Madeline kept telling me I had it all wrong and that I had nothing but my own prejudices to go on, but I'm afraid I didn't give her advice the consideration it deserved."

She struggled to make her expression more appropriate for the occasion, but she wasn't very successful. "I ought to be cross with you, you know. Whatever did I do to make you think so highly of me?"

"I'm sure you're aware that you are a very attractive woman."

She rolled her eyes. "So I've been told."

"Well, Beaky's a capital fellow and I think the world of him, but he's never going to come in anything but dead last in a beauty contest."

"I see." She still looked as if she wanted to laugh. "So naturally I am only in it for the money and, as it must follow, I have a lover on the side. Who was it? Delwyn?"

"Mr. Delwyn is a rather fine-looking man, I suppose, and near at hand. But, as you may have noticed, he's rather attached to Iris Midgley. I had to rule him out."

She arched one pencil-thin eyebrow. "In favor of?"

Lord help him, this was painful. "Well, it seemed rather obvious that Mr. and Mrs. Gray weren't as devoted as one might wish, and you were paying him a great deal of attention when we were at dinner, and naturally I—"

"Morris Gray? You've got to be joking. Morris Gray? Oh, I really should be angry now. That little weasel? Why in the world would anyone go from Beaky to a toad like Morris?"

"I know." Drew gave her his most apologetic look. "I can't tell you how embarrassed I am to tell you all this. But it just seemed that you and Beaky, well, I just didn't see you were very affectionate toward him."

She pressed her lips into a tight line. "I'm not a romantic, Mr. Farthering. I never have been, not even when I was a girl. I've never been the dewy-eyed type. That doesn't mean I don't love." He caught a flash of emotion in her dark eyes before she looked away. "Beaky knows how I feel, and it's not anyone else's business."

He bowed his head briefly. "You're quite right. I just couldn't help remembering how it was when you were out with Bunny."

She exhaled heavily. "I like Bunny. Enormous nitwit that he is, he's a lot of fun. How could I help liking him? And I could have married him. You know that as well as I do. But I didn't love Bunny." She looked at Drew as if he were a great fool not to have seen it. "After a month or two of being his wife, I would have had nothing but contempt for him. He would have let me do anything, given me anything, put up with anything. How could I respect a man like that? How could I love a man who has nothing to talk about but the theater and clothes and his motor car?"

"But Beaky—"

"Beaky loves me. Not the idea of having me on his arm for fashionable occasions or to show his mates he got the prize they all wanted, but me. Myself. Whatever looks I have will be gone one day, and far sooner than I'd like to think, and then what would I have had with a man who didn't care about anything else?"

"I was wrong about you, I know. I just thought—"

"Beaky's not much to look at. He's not stylish or clever or particularly entertaining." She lifted her chin. "But he's kind and gentle and thoughtful. Not all men are, you know, and—" Her voice caught, and there were sudden tears in her eyes. "And I know he would never hurt me."

She said nothing more. She didn't have to.

"I'm sorry," Drew said with a bow of his head. "I'm a perfectly beastly detective. I told Beaky straight off I was, and he still insisted I come up. I ask you, what could I do?"

Her lower lip quivered but then she laughed. "I think you'll do nicely, when you stick to the facts and not your assumptions. Do you know why I broke things off with Bunny?"

"You just said—"

"That was only part of it." They were almost at the house now, and she slowed to a stop, clearly wanting to finish their talk. "I met a man, handsome as that Errol Flynn from the cinema, funny, clever, romantic. No family and no money, of course, but what did I care? I had money enough for both of us, or at least my father did. But then I found out that was all he wanted, he and the waitress he was keeping on the side. Right after that, I met Beaky. I thought he was ridiculous at first, but then I saw him for who he really was. And I saw true and lasting love. How could I ask for anything better?"

"You make me ashamed," Drew said softly. "And you've taught me a great deal. Thank you."

"Coming, my dear?" Beaky called from the doorway.

Sabrina gave Drew a cheeky grin and took his arm. "Come out of the cold, Detective. It ought to be very cozy inside."

"You took your time," Drew said when Nick hopped onto the train as it was pulling out of the little station at Bunting's Nest the next day.

"Sorry about that." Nick dropped into the seat across from Drew and Madeline. "I went to post a letter to Carrie and ran into a couple of chaps from the Hound and Hart. I was afraid they might be a bit vexed with me for my part in our little charade, but turns out they thought it rather admirable. It seems we're local heroes. Oh, and I could have bought myself a rather natty red Alfa Romeo."

"Really?" Drew asked. "You can't mean Morris Gray's."

"I do. There's a notice at the post office that it's for sale. Very reasonable."

No one said anything else. Gray had preyed on Iris's youth and inexperience, her wistful desire for romance, to be cherished and loved, and her fear that no one ever would. But he had deceived himself, as well. Drew seriously doubted Gray would or could find what he was looking for with his own wife. He didn't seem the type to risk asking her to start over with him, and Frances certainly didn't seem the type to agree to such a scheme. There would be no recaptured youth or adventure or adulation. He'd given up.

"Now that Iris has figured out what a sham he is and found an honest man, I can't help feeling sorry for the poor blighter."

"I think someone should have hit him with a poker," Madeline said with a fierce frown.

"Now, now, darling," Drew said. "I'd say he's already well punished. Iris was able to leave him behind, but he'll always be stuck with himself. It's not something I envy him."

She huffed. "I suppose you're right. He and Frances and old Mr. Gray don't have a very happy home, do they?"

"No, but I think Iris and Delwyn will. And Baxter, too."

Her expression softened and she nestled against him. "I hope so. Delwyn loves her very much, doesn't he? To have waited for her and protected her even when she was hurting him."

"And 'love covers a multitude of sins.'"

"True," she said. "And whoever is forgiven much, loves much. Yes, they ought to be very happy together."

"I daresay God's not done with any of them yet," Drew said. "Them or the Grays. I'm just glad our part of it is over and done. I've eaten about as much crow as I can bear for at least the rest of the year."

"I thought Sabrina was remarkably gracious about it," Madeline said. "Of course, if you had listened to your wife in the first place, you would have not been so quick to jump to conclusions." She looked decidedly smug.

"I suppose you knew. About the man who betrayed her before she met Beaky."

Madeline shrugged. "We had a lot of nice talks, Sabrina and I."

"You might have told me."

"It wasn't mine to tell." She kissed his cheek. "But I'm glad she loves Beaky. I'm glad you don't have to worry about him anymore."

"Good old Beaky, I think he's well able to look after himself after all."

"I ran into Trenton when I was posting my letter to Carrie," Nick said, sitting up a bit straighter as the train chugged through the countryside. "He wanted me to tell you his little son was christened this morning."

"Lovely," Drew said, and he made a face. "I hope he and Watts have had a long heart-to-heart about taking initiative when necessary."

"They've worked that all out, but listen here, I'm supposed to make sure to tell you the baby's name."

"Oh, tell," Madeline said. "It couldn't be worse than Bilby."

"It *is* Bilby," Nick said. "Well, his second name is Bilby. His first is Andrew."

Drew leaned his head back against the seat, wincing. "Good heavens."

"No," Madeline said, giggling. "It's not really. Andrew Bilby Trenton? Oh my."

"Oh, yes." Nick leaned forward, his hands on his knees. "He told me he couldn't very well do anything less. Not after the famous amateur detective solved the most celebrated case in the history of Bunting's Nest, and on the very night his son was born."

"Ludicrous," Drew muttered, his eyes closed now. "Absolutely ludicrous."

"Why?" Madeline said. "Andrew's a very nice name."

"Here's the best part," Nick said. "Think how nice it will be for our dear Chief Inspector Birdsong to have little Drew about at every family gathering for the remainder of his life. That's got to put a smile on your face, old man."

Despite Drew's best efforts, it did.

ACKNOWLEDGMENTS

To the British Broadcasting Corporation for making delightful period television series like *Poirot*, *Campion*, and *Jeeves and Wooster*, to the actors who bring them wonderfully to life, and to the writers of their brilliant source material, for letting me see and hear England in the 1930s.

To Aidan Turner, who by some amazing coincidence just happens to look exactly like Rhys Delwyn, even if he is Irish and not Welsh.

And to my dad, who looks nothing like Aidan Turner, but that would be weird anyway . . .

Thank you for making this book possible.

Julianna Deering, author of the acclaimed *Dressed for Death* and *Murder at the Mikado* in the DREW FARTHERING MYSTERY series, is the pen name of novelist DeAnna Julie Dodson. DeAnna has always been an avid reader and a lover of storytelling, whether on the page, the screen, or the stage. This, together with her keen interest in history and her Christian faith, shows in her tales of love, forgiveness, and triumph over adversity. A fifth-generation Texan, she makes her home north of Dallas, along with three spoiled cats. When not writing, DeAnna spends her free time quilting, cross-stitching, and watching NHL hockey. Learn more at JuliannaDeering.com.

Sign up for Julianna's Newsletter!

Keep up to date with Julianna's news on book releases, signings, and other events by signing up for her email list at juliannadeering.com.

If you enjoyed *Murder on the Moor*, you may also enjoy . . .

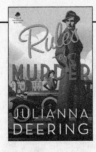

Drew Farthering loves a good mystery. So when a body is discovered on his country estate, he decides to do his own investigation. Trying hard to remain one step ahead of the killer, Drew must decide how far to take this dangerous game.

Rules of Murder
A DREW FARTHERING MYSTERY

◈ BETHANYHOUSE

More from Julianna Deering

Visit juliannadeering.com for a full list of her books.

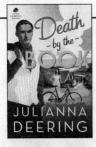

Drew Farthering has always loved mysteries, but he's only recently started taking on cases outside the pages of his books. When the family lawyer is murdered and found with an unusual clue, can he and Madeline Parker solve the case before the hatpin murderer strikes again?

Death by the Book
A DREW FARTHERING MYSTERY

Answering a plea for help from a retired actress—and an old flame—Drew and Madeline, now his fiancée, dive into investigating the murder of the lead actor in a stage production of *The Mikado*. But they discover more going on behind the scenes of this theater than they could ever have imagined.

Murder at the Mikado
A DREW FARTHERING MYSTERY

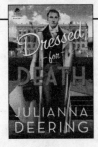

While attending a Regency costume party, Drew and Madeline Farthering are immersed in a new case when the fiancée of a friend dies mysteriously at the event. Drew's friend insists she was murdered. In the face of a shocking revelation and arrest, Drew begins to doubt his own abilities and finds he is unprepared for the dangerous secrets he uncovers.

Dressed for Death by Julianna Deering
A DREW FARTHERING MYSTERY

◊BETHANYHOUSE

Stay up to date on your favorite books and authors with our free e-newsletters. Sign up today at bethanyhouse.com.

Find us on Facebook. facebook.com/bethanyhousepublishers

Free exclusive resources for your book group! bethanyhouse.com/anopenbook

You May Also Enjoy . . .

After a night trapped together in an old stone keep, Lady Adelaide Bell and Lord Trent Hawthorne have no choice but to marry. Dismayed, Adelaide finds herself bound to a man who ignores her, as Trent has no desire to connect with the one who dashed his plans to marry for love. Can they set aside their first impressions before any chance of love is lost?

An Uncommon Courtship by Kristi Ann Hunter
HAWTHORNE HOUSE
kristiannhunter.com

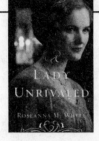

Lady Ella Myerston is determined to put an end to the danger that haunts her brother. While visiting her friend Brook, the owner of the Fire Eyes jewels, Ella gets entangled in an attempt to blackmail the newly reformed Lord Cayton. Will she become the next casualty of the "curse"?

A Lady Unrivaled by Roseanna M. White
LADIES OF THE MANOR
roseannamwhite.com

The lifeblood of the village of Ivy Hill is its coaching inn, The Bell. When the innkeeper dies suddenly, his genteel wife, Jane, becomes the reluctant owner. With a large loan due, can Jane and her resentful mother-in-law, Thora, find a way to save the inn—and discover fresh hope for the future?

The Innkeeper of Ivy Hill by Julie Klassen
TALES FROM IVY HILL #1
julieklassen.com

BETHANY HOUSE

Gloucester Library
P.O. Box 2380
Gloucester, VA 23061